The Esau Swindle

A Thriller

By

Gerald Rothberg

1663 Liberty Drive, Suite 200
Bloomington, Indiana 47403
(800) 839-8640
www.AuthorHouse.com

This book is a work of fiction. Places, events, and situations in this story are purely fictional and any resemblance to actual persons, living or dead, is coincidental.

First published by AuthorHouse 10/19/04

ISBN: 1-4184-8661-2 (sc)
ISBN: 1-4208-0761-7 (dj)

Printed in the United States of America
Bloomington, Indiana

This book is printed on acid-free paper.

CHAPTER ONE

At half past ten, on a morning budding with the promise of joy, Esau Rose hurried to a FedEx office on Columbus Avenue, filled out the international shipping form, and sent a package containing a rolled-up canvas to former general De Solis in Argentina. It was a late spring day, and a light wind followed him. Crossing over to West 81st Street, he reached inside his jacket pocket, pulled out a note he'd written to his twin brother, checked the address on the envelope, and dropped it in the dark blue mailbox on the corner.

Returning to his apartment, Esau smiled: *This is a good day for singing a song*. Truth be told, he felt like jumping up and kicking his feet in mid-air. He settled for singing a Doors' tune:

Love me two times, baby.

Love me two times girl ...

He mixed up words and stanzas and he didn't care. This was unquestionably the moment to phone the general in Argentina.

The general picked up the phone immediately. "Your mission is accomplished?"

Esau paused a moment to hum the tune he'd been singing. "Yeah, all squared away. Dotted the i's and crossed all the t's. The package will arrive tomorrow in the a.m."

"And we'll drink a toast with champagne when you get to Buenos Aires tomorrow."

"Yeah, we'll toast with the most expensive bottle of bubbly from your collection," he lied. For Esau, double-dealing and lying had been part of his adult life as a covert operative for the U.S. military for twenty-five years, and as a key aide to De Solis for the last six.

He glanced at his watch. Six hours and thirty-two minutes before he'd lock the door to the apartment for the final time, hail a cab to drive across Central Park, then down to the Midtown Tunnel, and on his way to JFK to board his flight. He'd leave yet again, this time for good, arriving the following dawn for the Fiji Islands to meet up with his lover and live secretly, thousands of miles from New York or Buenos Aires with funds from a numbered bank account stuffed with eighty million dollars.

Esau was a brutish man of fifty-one years, with an abundance of red hair on his head and body. For the past four days, he'd been closing deals with Saudi bankers as a liaison for the general. Yesterday, he transferred money electronically into two nameless, numbered bank accounts—one in the Cayman Islands and one in Switzerland. The plan was to avoid any paper or disk trails. Once the weaponry that General De Solis was selling arrived at its destination, Esau would encrypt account numbers representing the $88 million on the back of the painting. Instead, Esau set aside a generous portion of that money—some $80 million—for himself. He could have kept all the cash, but took pleasure in picturing the general's face when he realized he'd been duped.

But at 2:25 p.m., after putting away three tumblers filled with bourbon over ice, he stumbled through the living room of his West Side apartment and made it to the sofa. When he got there he hollered, "The attaché case." He staggered back into the kitchen to check on the rolled-up painting—an identical canvas to the one that he'd sent off this morning to De Solis. "That's eighty mil in the bank!" Attempting to refill his glass, his hand shook and he spilled the contents on the kitchen floor. Esau groaned. He edged his way back to the sofa and finally collapsed in a stupor.

In the bedroom, a broad-shouldered figure emerged from behind the thick, brown draperies that remained drawn to keep out the mid-afternoon sun. As this man with one arm and a pinned-up sleeve that hung to his left side stepped into the living room to look down at Esau's body, which had tumbled to the floor, he cracked a broad smile. The tablet of Flunitrazepam that he'd dropped in the bourbon decanter worked.

With a latex glove on his right hand, the man placed the glass and decanter in a plastic bag, pushed an old .38-caliber pistol in Esau's mouth, placed Esau's anesthetized hand on the gun, checked the silencer, pulled the trigger, and left the apartment as quietly as he had entered.

CHAPTER TWO

At 8:40 the following morning, Special Agent Alfred Sullivan entered the flat with his key. The high-rise served as a retreat for the Committee to Reelect the President—a place where the team could relax and strategize on the campaign away from pressures and demands of the White House. Lately, Esau had been using it as his place.

Calm shrouded the apartment—no running water, no coffee dripping into a carafe, no refrigerator door opening and slamming shut. "Hey, hotshot!" Sullivan called out, as he stepped into the living room. A rotten stench almost overwhelmed him as he looked down at Esau, clutching a pistol—his brains splattered across the burgundy red rug in a puddle of vomit. Turning his back to the body, he stumbled for an instant then hit two keys on his cellular telephone.

"The retreat! The whole team! Now!" Sullivan set the air conditioner on high, hoping to diminish the odor, but it was no use. The stinking smell of vomit had sunk into the room.

Within minutes, agents rushed in.

"Look for a note. Anything he might have written." Sullivan savagely stuffed a bagel in his mouth. "Check his clothing. Check the bedrooms. The kitchen. The bathroom. Check all drawers and his desk."

One officer brought him an attaché case found on a kitchen chair. Sullivan snapped the case open. "What the hell is this?" He pulled the rolled-up painting from it. The agent shrugged. "Make sure I take it back to headquarters for inspection."

Twenty minutes later, Sullivan heard an earsplitting noise as an emergency medical team arrived by helicopter on the rooftop above. Two men in green scrubs sprinted down to the twenty-first floor.

"Easy with the body," Sullivan yelled. He looked down at Esau and shook his head several times. "You stupid son of a bitch!"

Medics placed Esau in a black body bag and zippered and tagged it.

Sullivan watched the emergency team roll the body onto a stretcher and carry Esau up the two flights.

Agent Sullivan was a compact man with a smile of unmistakable cynicism and a pinned-up sleeve that hugged his left side when he wasn't wearing his artificial arm, the result of an encounter with a Bolivian coca sharecropper who'd attacked him with a machete about eight years ago. The man had mistaken Sullivan, then a top-ranking official working at the U.S. Embassy in La Paz, for a drug trafficker seeking control of his business.

On the roof, the chopper whipped up gusts of warmed air against a muted blue sky as it lifted away from the building. The aircraft crossed Central Park and navigated down the East River to Bellevue Hospital, where the chief medical examiner and federal agents were already waiting at a side entrance to the morgue.

CHAPTER THREE

Jacob Rose had never met Agent Sullivan, who called to notify him that he was Esau's colleague and needed to talk with him

"I'll be at your store in half an hour."

"My store? This is an art gallery. And talk about what?"

"I've got to see you in person."

"I'll be here," said Jacob, hanging up the phone, only to pick it up seconds later after a momentary reflection. He pressed the speaker button on to call Lester Hughes at Sotheby's.

"I want a guarantee on your bid for the Trumball painting."

The octogenarian Laban Trumball had startled the art word earlier this year when he switched his affiliation from his longtime New York art dealer Leopold Katz to the Jacob Rose Gallery. And Jacob quickly bought at auction a couple of the artist's early works that were painted in the 1950s.

Hughes' baritone voice echoed through the room. "Trumball is a *has-been*. You understand where I'm coming from?"

"Hughes. Listen. The man's about to die. Prices will go up. Okay? That punches holes in your theory that he's a *has-been*."

"We ought to keep the opening bid low," Hughes replied.

"Yeah?"

"Yes, Mr. Rose."

"So your private clients can steal this one? You do that, and I'll have your balls on a platter."

Hughes was silent. "I'll call you back."

"Yes, of course." Jacob hung up the phone. "I'll call you back," he mimicked. "Arrogant faggot. Trying to rip me off."

"Mr. R!" Sandra Mellon, his assistant for the last five years, stood shaking her head. "That's no way to speak." Jacob shuffled through papers that Sandra had placed on his desk earlier, signing a few sheets and then handing her the folder.

He was one of New York's more prominent art dealers. Accustomed to making swift decisions, Jacob enjoyed a reputation as a sharp art dealer, always at the forefront of the *Next Big Thing* and discovering and establishing new artists. He could hardly complain about his good fortune. He rarely lost an artist to the blue-chip galleries and maintained a stable of prominent artists, among them Laban Trumball.

Jacob's double-breasted blue blazer and spread-collar shirt with French cuffs were testaments to his business acumen, wealth, and good taste. He liked to joke that his clientele were mostly first-time art buyers, Wall Street brokers, and yuppie lawyers whom he had persuaded to buy art as real estate for their walls.

Jacob stood six feet tall in his stocking feet, and at fifty-one was as physically fit as a man half his age. He wore his hair slicked back and had an angular face with classic good looks and a squared jaw enhanced only slightly by a surgeon's knife, just to appear "refreshed," as he put it. His gallery on Ninth Avenue and West Twenty-second Street in the Chelsea section of Manhattan was in a red-brick, five-story building with a black cast-iron fire escape. Jacob lived in the top-floor loft with views of the Hudson River, and a roof garden landscaped with large Norway spruce and rhododendron in wooden half-barrel containers. He had green views all year long.

An hour later, Sullivan walked up the ramp leading to Jacob's office on the mezzanine level of his gallery, with Sandra trailing behind.

"Sorry I'm late."

The two shook hands vigorously.

"Please have a seat."

"I needed time to get an official report."

"Some coffee or a drink? I'm ready for a martini. And you?"

"I'm on duty. Coffee would be good."

"Sandra, coffee, cakes, and a martini for me."

The two men sat in the middle of the office in a little conference area with Brno chairs surrounded a Mies coffee table. Behind Jacob on a stark white wall, a silkscreen of a huge Trumball hung, "Nude on Le Corbusier Lounge Chair."

"How do you keep from spilling your drink, with that hanging above you? Damn ... that body and those tits...," Sullivan asked noticing the large canvas. When Jacob didn't react, Sullivan quickly added, "I suppose I'm not a connoisseur of modern art."

"Taste varies, when it comes to art," Jacob said.

Sandra carried in a tray and handed Sullivan his coffee. He stared at her for a moment as she sat down.

"Is it okay? This is a private matter."

The art dealer nodded yes.

"Mr. Rose, I'll get right to the point. Forgive me for being blunt." Sullivan hesitated. "Your brother Esau is dead. He took his own life. It was a suicide."

Jacob's hand shook visibly and he knocked his drink on the table. "When did he do this? Where? I don't understand this. How could this be?" Sandra moved to Jacob's side, placing her hand on his arm.

"Yesterday, Mr. Rose."

"It's Jacob, please."

"I'm sorry. I'm sure this is difficult."

"Yes. It is. How did he kill himself?"

"Do you really want to know?"

Jacob nodded. "Don't hold back any details."

"Shot himself. In the mouth. A .38 caliber." Sullivan looked at Jacob. "Are you all right?"

"Yes. No. I don't know what to say. Is there anything more you can tell me?"

"No, nothing more."

"Where is Esau, now?"

"At the morgue at Bellevue."

"I see."

"Oh, there was something. We found a painting in his apartment. The canvas had the insignia of your gallery. We'll return it, of course, as soon as we document his belongings."

Jacob closed his eyes for the moment, shaking his head. "Esau was supposed to take that painting to Buenos Aires. Was there a note?"

"No."

Staring vacantly at Sullivan, Jacob moved around the room in pain as if punched in the gut. He lowered his voice to a level slightly above a whisper. "Hadn't seen Esau for thirty years, and didn't hear much from him either."

"I'm sorry, Mr. Rose."

"The son-of-a-bitch brother came back into our lives less than a year ago. Now this?"

"Here's my card," the FBI agent said. "Call me anytime, when you need me. I mean any time."

"Don't inform other members of my family. I'll need to tell my parents."

"Sure. I'm sorry to bring this news. I'll see that the body is returned quickly for burial."

Sullivan was gone.

"Sandra, please close up for me. Thank you."

"Mr. R? Is there anything I could do for you now?"

"Be strong Sandra, that's all."

He walked along Tenth Avenue and then up to Twenty-Third Street, certain that Esau's suicide had something to do with forgeries. *Why would an FBI agent contact him and not the NYPD?*

About ten months ago, when Esau had resurfaced in their lives, he showed Jacob copies of lithographs by Dalí and Miro that he'd reproduced. Jacob made it clear to him to stop. "You'd kill my gallery if this dirty little secret got out." Esau's response then had been a hearty laugh, which angered Jacob even more.

Wrapped in thoughts of their years growing up together, he walked to Park Avenue before hailing a cab to his parents' apartment. He searched in vain for clues, any quirky behavior that would shine a light on this act. He found none. He considered that now he was the lone carrier of their destiny. And it was left to him to tell their parents that their son had killed himself.

A few minutes later, his cell phone rang.

"Sullivan here. Your assistant gave me this number."

"Yes, of course."

"Look, I hate to ask you, but you'll need to identify the body."

"I'll be there. Tell me where."

"The morgue at Bellevue. First Avenue and—"

"I know where it is."

"And you'll be able to make funeral arrangements immediately."

"Thank you."

"You understand that because of his connection to the White House, investigations had to be conducted."

"Yes, I understand."

"I will personally see that the painting is returned to your gallery as soon as possible."

"Agent Sullivan, will you do me a favor? Have the painting authenticated by the National Stolen Arts File Division.

"That's necessary for you as an art dealer, isn't it?"

"Yeah, it is."

"It will be done."

CHAPTER FOUR

The following day at noon, the limousine with Jacob and his grief-stricken parents arrived at an above-ground cemetery in northern Westchester, some twenty-five miles from Manhattan. Interment for Esau was private. A few attendants stood behind, joining a handful of relatives. The body rested in a closed, simple pine box. Jacob and his father stood respectfully in dark suits and black felt hats; his mother between them, wearing a black dress adorned with the triple-strand set of pearls that Esau had given her when he landed his official job with the president's re-election team one year ago. The rabbi intoned the mournful sounds of El Maleh Rachamim, first in Hebrew and then in English translation, ending in, "May he lay in his resting place in peace." The Rose family recited Kaddish in deliberately slow and stately tones. They took the three traditional steps back and pronounced, "Oseh shalom bimromav, hu ya'aseh shalom alenu v'alkol yisrael v'imiru amen. That, which creates peace in the spheres above, grant peace to us, and to all Israel and we will say, amen."

Isaac Rose paused a moment, then eulogized his son. "Esau was bold. He was brave. He followed his sense of right and wrong, and fought for his convictions. He was a decorated soldier in Vietnam, a patriot, a valiant man." Rebecca, his mother, added her remembrances: "Esau explored South America, advocating programs for the poor and programs to protect human rights. He was my son and I loved him."

The word "love" weighed heavily on Jacob's heart for so long that it felt like loathing, something well past a sibling rivalry. In Jacob's mind, the cost of his twin's career as a veteran and patriot came at a cost to the family Esau had essentially abandoned. It had been years since their parents had seen Esau, tethered to them only through his occasional cards and letters and rare phone calls—never in the flesh. It was Jacob, left behind as the sole custodian of their parents' needs, who understood what his parents wanted to see and what the truth really was. They may have forgiven Esau, but Jacob had not. He remained unrelieved and hurt. Even in these last months, Esau paid only scant attention to his brother's success in the art world and he seemed wholly unaware of his brother's celebrity in a town where fame was the name of the game.

For Jacob, his twin brother's return stirred mixed emotions. Were the few postcards they had received over the span of years filled with truth or deceptions? It seemed to Jacob that he had spent his whole life seeking his brother's admiration and approval, the very sentiments their parents had reserved only for Esau.

Soon the attendants placed the casket in a middle vault. Jacob and his parents wept openly. After embracing relatives and shaking hands, the three left the cemetery for the ride back to New York City.

Later, at home on Sutton Place, his mother asked, "Why?" She recalled how happy she was when Esau returned after decades of absence, though she continued to ask him if there'd been something they had done or said to him that made him leave the family for decades. Isaac told his wife months ago to forget the past. "Be happy he's back. Open up to him. How many years do we have left?"

That afternoon, their father sat glumly, at times trembling, when he recalled, "He phoned me. It was maybe five years ago. He was crying bitterly. A big man like Esau. A *bullvan*," Isaac Rose said, using the Yiddish term for a strong man, an adventurer. "I told him, 'You'll die by the sword, because you live by the sword."

Eight hours later that night, when Jacob left his parents' home, he locked his eyes for a moment on the midnight black sky. A conversation with his brother a few days before intruded on his thoughts. Esau had arranged a dinner date for Jacob with an Argentine actress. "Raquel will change your life. You're married to your art gallery. That's not healthy," he said.

Why try and make nice by arranging a dinner date and then blow your goddamn brains out? Jacob asked himself. He never mentioned to his parents that Esau set this dinner with Raquel for tonight, a date Jacob had canceled.

What also baffled Jacob was the letter that he received earlier today.

"Where the Obelisk meets the sky. 9 1970 July. These are key words. You used to remember mine, I remembered yours. Meet up with Raquel." Then more elliptical prose. So much of it nonsensical, thought Jacob, as he stepped into a cab. He hadn't shown the yellow sheet of notepaper to anybody, not even his parents.

Out of respect for the Rose family, neither those who attended the funeral nor visitors to their home referred to Esau's death as a suicide.

CHAPTER FIVE

The clap of thunder that accompanied Jacob's arrival with the celebrated film actress Raquel Gingold at Ezeiza International Airport was altogether fitting, he thought. After all, she was a well-known Argentine actress, escorting him to a gala at the prestigious Buenos Aires Art Museum of the Moderns to honor Laban Trumball. And so, on this ordinary Thursday morning in late July—a month after Esau's funeral—Jacob felt a sudden surge of pleasure as he thought about romancing Raquel in her native city. General De Solis had everything planned, and paid for a four-day weekend and a retrospective for Trumball.

Outside the Arrivals Terminal in Buenos Aires at 9:00 a.m., the temperature was seventy-five degrees Fahrenheit. A smiling, thickset chauffeur in a black gabardine suit, white shirt, and black tie hobbled toward the two of them. He grabbed the luggage from an airline attendant, placing three valises and two garment bags carefully in the trunk of the limousine. Jacob told the driver that he preferred to hang his bags in the car. He wasn't about to reveal that he kept the well-known Trumball painting *Lea with Two Love-Apples* rolled up in his garment bag inside a jacket sleeve for safekeeping. He had learned that attracting little or no attention to himself was the safest way of handling a painting; of course, the insurance company encouraged this technique.

Raquel interrupted in Spanish, "Señor Rose is fussy with his dinner jackets."

The weekend in Buenos Aires held another element of interest for Jacob: to reconcile troubling feelings for Esau, the man he'd been eternally compared to. Perhaps he could arrive at some understanding of who his brother really was. Then, Jacob reasoned, it might explain their father's contentment with Esau's behavior over the years, an appreciation he could never show with Jacob—no matter what Jacob had accomplished. Did whatever Esau was involved with during his years in Buenos Aires cause him to blow his brains out back in New York? He had little to go on except for the letter, handwritten on a yellow sheet.

Ortiz, the driver, held the door to the limousine with an aloof courtesy. Jacob slid into the backseat of limousine, following Raquel. He forced himself to focus on their schedule of events. The first three days were set aside for sightseeing, and Ortiz was a private driver hired and paid for by General De Solis, Jacob's buyer, the man who was about to break the record for the highest price paid—$9 million—for a living artist in Jacob's stable. This was an auspicious moment fraught with tension and disbelief, romance and mourning. Jacob took a few deep breaths and smiled at Raquel.

In the limousine, a muscular man with a military-style buzz cut and aviator glasses grabbed Jacob's hand and shook it vigorously. The limousine began moving slowly. "Smith. My name is Smith. I represent your buyer and host for this weekend, General Juan Domingo De Solis."

For an art buyer's representative, Smith was extraordinarily physical, Jacob thought.

"You're more striking in person—than in your films," Smith added, turning to the actress.

Raquel blushed at his flattery, but after an all-night flight from New York to Buenos Aires in a linen pantsuit, she was eager to get to the hotel and change. "Thank you. You're very kind."

"Mr. Rose, has the painting cleared customs?" Smith asked.

"Not yet." Seized with habitual suspicion at Smith's somewhat superior demeanor, Jacob decided to remain cautious until he could be sure the man was who he said he was.

"I can speed up that process."

"Thanks. That's not necessary. The painting will be ready later today."

"I can cut through the red tape. These are my instructions."

"Everything will be in order as soon as my artist arrives," Jacob said. "Trumball decided to take a later flight to Buenos Aires."

"I see." A polite smile broke through Smith's thin lips.

Smith was born Archibald Smith, a Southie from Boston, fifty-four years ago. He stood five feet ten inches tall, with the sloping wide shoulders of a boxer. He'd traveled with Jacob's twin brother Esau in Vietnam, then Cambodia, Egypt, Saudi Arabia, and years later in Buenos Aires. When he spoke, he rarely cracked a smile, and his green eyes offered little insight into his personality.

The limousine picked up speed.

"My condolences to you and your family."

"Thank you, Mr. Smith, thank you very much."

"Esau and I saw a lot of combat. Did you know that?"

"No. I didn't know."

"Esau was a helluva guy. A terrible situation. Terrible way to go. He was my buddy."

"Maybe we'll have a chance to talk about him." The news that Smith had known Esau well put Jacob in a slightly more tranquil mood.

"You understand that I can't tell you much." Smith studied the similarities of face and gesture between Esau and Jacob.

"Why is that?"

"Much of our work together was covert."

"Yes, of course," said Jacob, who believed that with time he'd get Smith to talk. He wasn't going to press it now.

Smith poured a glass of whiskey and asked if his guests wanted a drink from the bar. "You are our guests. May I?"

"Please," Jacob replied, receiving Raquel's glass first.

The limousine moved along Argentina's grand boulevard, Avenida 9 de Julio, on the way to the Sheraton Buenos Aires Hotel in the center of the city.

Raquel leaned over to take Jacob's hand. "This is 9th of July Boulevard. Our Independence Day. Like yours is July 4th." She acted as a sort of tour guide. Her dark, vibrant eyes shone a deep brown color. Raquel sipped her whiskey. Jacob smelled her cool talcum smell, moved closer, and nuzzled her nose. They'd begun to enjoy each other more, which he had imagined and hoped would deepen their relationship on this trip to Buenos Aires; and in this moment he freeze-framed a picture of her in his mind, lying naked, face up on his bed, admiring him warmly, her flowing brown hair spread out on a silken white pillowcase.

At the avenue's center, an obelisk marked its intersection with Corrientes. "Slowly, Señor Ortiz," Jacob said, as they spun hard around the obelisk. *A monumental erection of a former dictator, to be sure,* Jacob thought. The truth was that the military government in 1936 had demolished old French-style mansions to make way for what portenos, the Buenos Aires locals, referred to as the Big Phallus.

"Darling, the Barrio Norte is on your right. It is like the Right Bank. I live in this area. In this barrio is Recoleta Cemetery. Evita Perón is buried here."

Just a glance at the cemetery left Jacob silent. He remembered the visit he'd received from Agent Sullivan at his gallery. "Your brother Esau is dead. He took his own life. It was a suicide," the FBI agent had said, matter-of-factly. All at once, Jacob had felt a small part of him die as well.

"The Teatro Colon, on the street behind us, is like La Scala," Raquel went on. "Are you listening? You must play the Colon Opera House to make it in the concert world."

"I hear you," Jacob said, but his thoughts were still hovering around the obelisk they had just passed.

"Darling, Buenos Aires is a late-night city, much like New York. I can't wait to show you my favorite night spots."

"You've met Mr. Smith before, haven't you?" Jacob asked Raquel.

"No. Mr. Smith must be new to General De Solis' team? Yes?"

Smith nodded. Then after a moment, "That's Smith, by the way, not Mr. Smith. I would appreciate that. I first met your brother in Cambodia. We worked together years later in Saudi Arabia. He must have told you that much."

"He told me very little."

"Well, it's not surprising. As I said, most of our operations were covert."

"He was estranged from the family—since college graduation. Esau popped back into my life—a year ago."

"You guys probably played catch-up after he contacted you."

"No, sorry to say. Esau was guarded, or at least he was with me." A family dinner at Montrachet's flashed through Jacob's mind, where Esau had explained that secrecy was in his past. "Now I'm an open book." Rebecca had hugged him, Isaac had raised his glass in a toast, and Jacob had pushed his hand in a high five across the table.

"He was a good man," Smith said.

"I feel you knew him better than I."

"I don't believe that he took his own life. That wasn't Esau. He was a true soldier."

"Thank you, Smith. But we were given assurances by the FBI that Esau's death was a suicide," Jacob said, skeptical himself that Esau would have sought death by his own hand. He finished his drink. "It's still painful for me to talk about him."

—"I'm sorry." Smith became tight-lipped and shook his head. "Very sorry."

The limousine continued moving along 9 de Julio. Jacob looked out at clusters of parking garages in the middle blocks. What alarmed him were armed soldiers posted at the intersections. Only when they arrived at the Sheraton Hotel, on the far end of Plaza San Martin, did he ask Smith about the soldiers.

"POTUS is visiting Argentina this Sunday. He'll take this route when he comes in from the airport. The hotel you're staying at was Esau's favorite. You knew that he was on the president's reelection team."

Jacob nodded. "Is the president staying at this hotel?"

"Yes. The locals call it the Buenos Aires White House." Both men chuckled.

"By the way, Mr. Rose."

"Jacob, please."

"My condolences, again."

"Thank you."

CHAPTER SIX

An excited crowd of journalists, photographers, and fans surrounded the limousine as they pulled up to the hotel. Ortiz leaped out to hold the door for Raquel. Reporters' voices filled the area outside the hotel as they jockeyed with photographers to get close to Raquel.

"This way, Raquel!"

"Over here, Señorita Gingold!"

"Just two questions, please!"

"Will you sign this napkin for me?"

Ortiz, the perfect servant, pushed the people aside with brisk authority before handing Jacob his card and offering his services day and night. "I'm my own boss. This weekend the general retains me. I am with you day and night. Señor, when you might again be in Buenos Aires, call me anytime for hire."

Jacob nodded.

"We'll see you at dinner. General De Solis wants to meet with you," Smith called out from the limousine, over the commotion of the crowd. "Let me know when the painting gets here."

After checking in at the hotel, the schedule called for lunch, just Jacob and Raquel, at the Café Tortoni; and then a stroll to the Plaza de Mayo to view the elaborate flower gardens and tall palm trees. Afterward, the director of Buenos Aires Museum of the Moderns, at a late afternoon tea for Jacob and Trumball, would outline the tribute and gala for that Sunday afternoon.

The general arranged a dinner this evening with Raquel, Trumball, and Jacob at the Vincente Lopez Restaurant in Recoleta barrio. Friday, after a tour of the Casa Rosada, Argentina's Pink House and seat of the executive branch of the government, they planned a walk along Avenida Corrientas, the Broadway of Buenos Aires. Saturday evening, Raquel's parents organized a cocktail reception for the artist at their San Isidro home.

When they entered the lobby, hotel security personnel swarmed around the couple, attempting to cordon them off from the onslaught of autograph seekers.

Eighteen floors above, in a pre-arranged suite, two inconspicuous looking men in gray suits, striped ties, and blue shirts strained to finish their work before Jacob and Raquel arrived. As they packed up their equipment, one of the men's cell phone rang. "They're in the lobby. Checking in," Smith said on the other end of the phone, "and you're still in the room?"

"Just finishing up."

"Move it."

"We have the place covered. Bedroom, bathroom, terrace, dining area. Even if he thinks any bad thoughts, you'll get it in surround sound," the man laughed.

"All right, good. Now get the hell out of there," Smith barked and hung up.

The two men worked without hesitation from carefully drawn plans. Tiny video cams and sound transmitters were set strategically between recessed ceiling lights. They pushed the on buttons, and green lights flashed immediately.

They finished the ceiling work and planted tiny microphones the thickness of a human hair in the six telephones placed throughout the suite and in the bathrooms. Sound and image data were transmitted wirelessly to a hallway linen closet and from there to receivers in General De Solis' bunker in Palermo. Surveying their work, they folded the floor plans, placed them in an attaché case, removed their disposable gloves, pushing them into their jacket pockets, and left. The job had taken fifteen minutes. They got on the elevator and soon walked nonchalantly through the lobby, catching a glimpse of the celebrity couple as they exited.

In the hotel lobby, Raquel slid her large, dark glasses down her nose after acknowledging several more admirers. She chatted in Spanish with the hotel manager, while the hotel people grinned. She informed the bellhop to take the suitcases to their suite.

Jacob enjoyed the fanfare with a famous actress at his side and perfected an ability to mug for the camera. He wore his vanity like his double-breasted blazers—with the casual arrogance of a businessman at the top of his game. He had no idea how big a star she was in Argentina. He first met Raquel through Esau at a special dinner this past April for the Friends of the Whitney Museum. Jacob had been the keynote speaker and had to leave his brother and Raquel for his seat on the dais.

He had taken the memory of this beautiful woman, with her lovely Latin accent, with him as he sat. Throughout the evening, they had glanced at one another. He looked forward to spending time with them afterward. After dessert, he had sought Raquel, only to discover she'd already gone.

Jacob had been married once, briefly, seven years ago. He had wed Amanda Schiff, a recent divorcée with two children. At the time, he thought he'd entered a wonderful stage of life; an instant family was suddenly his, and he could move his career forward. After a year of marriage, Amanda still pined for her first husband. The following year, Jacob divorced her and she remarried her former spouse. He had reacted to the situation indifferently and had remained philosophical about marrying on the rebound. "I'll never again marry a woman who's just getting out of a situation," he had warned himself, though he knew himself to be too insecure to heed it.

Jacob and Raquel connected a few weeks after the Whitney event when he had called her for dinner at 21. They had clicked immediately, and the following week he invited her to a showing at his gallery for his younger artists. Raquel was impressed with the commanding way he had handled himself. A few weeks after, she had said that she felt comfortable with him, that she liked his company and wanted more of it.

Two weeks ago, when they'd been walking hand in hand along Tenth Avenue in Chelsea following an opening at his gallery, he asked about her life in Argentina. She revealed that she was a political activist early on, a rebel with a very definite cause.

"Well, I'm overstating it, because in the early 1980s, I lived at home in my parents' elegant house. I've always been concerned with human-rights issues. I still am. At that time, I was close to Juan Domingo. I had hoped to persuade him to come out more publicly for the people."

"A weekend radical?" Her face was blank. "You're not laughing."

"It's not funny, Jacob."

"I wasn't trying to patronize you. Really. I respect your commitment to human rights."

She hesitated, but then decided that this response was sufficient. She went on to reveal that she had had an affair with the then-Lieutenant De Solis that lasted seven years. "I was an ingénue, barely twenty, and your twin brother and Juan Domingo were the best of friends."

Jacob remembered reading a large press packet on Raquel, amid travel brochures and books on Argentina that his assistant had prepared for him. He looked at pictures of the iceberg on Lago Argentino, a rainbow over the Pampas, the vast boulevard of 9 de Julio Avenue in Buenos Aires leading to the Rio de la Plata, and the Atlantic Ocean. In the first few days after they had met, he read a biography of the Argentine painter Quinquela. He skimmed through brief histories of Juan Perón, the junta period, and the "disappeared ones." He had pulled from his bookshelf Jacabo Timmerman's *Prisoner Without a Name, Cell Without a Number*. He so frantically needed to know about her surroundings.

From her press clippings, he learned that Raquel was eight years younger than he, the daughter of Holocaust survivors from the Dachau death camps. Liberated by American troops on April 29, 1945, they immigrated to Argentina, where they later married. How strange, he thought, that after the Second World War, tens of thousands of European Jews sought refuge in a country that gave sanctuary to fleeing Nazi war criminals. Here Raquel had been born, a beautiful woman aglow with an erotic energy that defied the horrors of the death camps and historical lunacy.

"I'm an artist," she'd told a reporter who asked if she preferred to be called an actress or actor. "I grew up in Buenos Aires, as a middle-class child, you might say." Her family had lived for a while in Villa Crespo in a residential neighborhood with a few small shops that sold Jewish pastries, bagels, Challah, smoked fish, and the like. Later, she admitted, "Father made money in the diamond business, and we moved to San Isidro." The story revealed that at eighteen she'd begun singing in the cafes of San Telmo. That was 1981, during the military dictatorship and the "dirty wars." She quickly became popular among her peers. In interviews, she claimed that she represented the values of people her age in what she sang, wearing the clothes the young people wore and expressing their beliefs. Her singing career was short-lived, however. Raquel was discovered by Luis Puenzo and screen-tested for her role in *Pride of the Pampas*. Her success was almost immediate, and the critics adored her.

Moments after settling in their suite, two waiters in white jackets arrived with a basket of fruit and a silver tray filled with white truffles and a bottle of Louis Roederer champagne. "Thank you," a surprised Jacob called. He returned to the window, looking out at the machine gunners on the surrounding rooftops. "So ... Smith was Esau's buddy. I'm glad we met him," he told Raquel.

"I'm sure he's just as glad to meet you."

"Maybe I'll get facts about my brother's life here."

Raquel smiled affectionately. "Promise me you'll think about enjoying yourself."

"I promise."

"Then why such a sad face?"

"I don't have a sad face."

"You're not worried about the sale, are you?" she asked.

"No. But all the machine guns around this place don't exactly put me at ease!"

Raquel moved toward the window and put her arms around him. Armed soldiers peered down from the rooftops of every building. The president of the United States was scheduled to arrive in seventy-two hours. Security seemed intense.

"We'll have an exciting weekend, I assure you," Raquel said, kissing him on his lips.

"Look down at the tugboats, the ships with machine guns. This is crazy," Jacob said.

"I've seen worse in that river."

"Worse?"

"Bodies floated in these waters at the end of *la guerra sucia*, the 'dirty wars,' almost two decades ago." She paused. "I'm being morbid. Enough." In her characteristic way of swiftly shifting her moods, she tasted a truffle and offered him a bite, but he swallowed it whole. She feigned a grimace, when the doorbell rang.

It was room service with coffee and a note for Raquel. She recognized the handwriting at once. "It's from JD." She seemed mildly curious but not surprised.

"JD who?"

"We're friends, after all. Listen to what he says.

"My dearest Raquel:

I look forward to seeing you tonight with your friends, Señor Rose and the artist Señor Trumball. Bertha Lavazzo, Señor Rose's representative here in Buenos Aires, will be joining us along with my chief aide, Smith. Please inform the art dealer that Smith is a shy person and that he was familiar with his brother Esau. Señor Rose will most likely enjoy talking with him. I've arranged for a private table for us to enjoy ourselves. My driver will pick you up promptly at 9:00 this evening.

Your loving friend,

JD

"Juan Domingo still has a crush on me."

Jacob shook his head. The question of former lovers suddenly weighed in. "Were you in love with him?"

"Why do you ask that?"

"He was a fascist. Wasn't he?" He seemed angered by her liaisons with the military in the former dictatorship, an experience so removed from his own that he questioned his sense of self with the usual *what am I, who am I,* knowing that led him only to the dead end of gloominess and inaction. He'd learned years ago that abstract thoughts created morbid feelings. Jacob quickly recalled once, during their freshman year at Cornell, catching Esau in a moment of sadness. "What's up, buddy? This is not you," he'd asked. Esau just shook his head. He could swear now that he'd seen tears in his brother's eyes. "Nothing, man. Let's party. I got to keep busy," Esau had said. "Hey, do me a favor. No more reflection like this. It doesn't serve us. We've got to move and move on,"

Raquel remained silent for the moment as if giving Jacob time with his reflections. "What are you talking about?"

"De Solis. Wasn't he part of the junta?"

"Are you jealous?"

"I'm not jealous. I'm not the jealous type."

"Oh, if you could just see your face. So dejected."

"Hardly."

"Jacob, you want the honest truth?"

"From you, always. Even if it hurts."

"I was young, he was attractive. I wanted to sleep with him. Politics was power to me. It was not until later that I had become aware of what he stood for. Don't blame me for being young."

Jacob pulled her close and kissed her hard.

"Men," she said pulling away. "You use sex to hide your feelings."

"Raquel, kissing and hugging isn't sex. It's called affection." He retorted, as if he needed to set the record straight.

"I'm sorry darling. I like giving you a hard time. I really shouldn't do that."

"You can do whatever you want." Jacob stretched out on the bed.

"We're going to have a wonderful time. You'll love Buenos Aires. Trumball will love the city, too. He is a bit conceited, though, isn't he?"

"Not conceited. Pompous."

"Why is that?"

"Well, he claims that he took to drinking because history shortchanged him, giving DeKooning more praise."

"That's why he is so hungry for compliments?"

"I think so. Trumball is a better artist. He believes it. And so do I."

"Then why are you restless, darling?"

"Because this is the biggest sale I've ever had."

"Juan Domingo is very honorable," Raquel assured. "So, darling, relax. You're supposed to forget troubles on a vacation."

"Okay, I will."

"This is a time to bask in the sunshine of Señor Trumball's glorious moment."

"I know, and I will."

"Well, start enjoying right now. Try to relax."

Jacob picked up a cup from the tray and poured himself some coffee. He returned to the window.

"I can't relax."

"You promised, Jacob."

"How can this buzz-cut leatherneck Smith know more about Esau than I do—or my parents? I keep seeing them in my head the moment I told them Esau's dead. The suicide of a child."

"He was a grown man, not a child."

"Not from my parents' point of view. To them Esau is still the overachieving sophomore at Dalton."

"Jacob, you are right to mourn your brother. I'm sure Smith will be a great help in learning more about him. Maybe then you'll get closure. Right now, I want you to rest. Remember why you're here. Think about tonight. We have a big celebration. JD likes to do things in a grand manner."

"You're right," Jacob sighed.

"You'll like him. He's your kind of man."

"Why do you say that?"

"Well, Esau liked Juan Domingo."

"What would that have to do with me?"

"Because you're twins. Don't twins think alike?"

He'd heard that argument during Esau's long absence. "Wouldn't you have a gut feeling of what he's doing now, son?" Jacob recalled his father asking. Word from Esau had been scant in 1975. "Is he in danger? I worry so much," his mother added. His answer then bordered on the hysterical. "Look, I'm not a psychic. I don't know."

These thoughts ceased suddenly and Jacob lifted his head. "I'm not sure twins know the other's mind, Raquel. You're a political person. I guess Esau might have been one too." He hesitated for a moment. "I remember when the letters stopped coming, sometime in '75. After he'd arrived in Cambodia in the early '70s, he sent the occasional letter home with picture postcards from Phnom Penh, before their the civil war. Never mentioned Pol Pot. Esau wrote one stinking letter. About Cambodia's tropical climate and tobacco farming and a peasant family he befriended. That was it. One million Cambodians are killed by the Khmer Rouge and not a word about this from him. He never even told us why he went there. Damn."

"I guess your parents were anxious for his safety."

"Yes, with concerns for a son who deserted them. First, he went to Vietnam. Esau had volunteered."

"And you, darling, what did you do?"

"I went to graduate school at NYU for a master's in Art History. Enough of my life story. To answer your question ... no, I don't think I knew him then. And why are you asking these questions about me and about Esau?"

"You know much about my life," she said. "I told you parts of my story, and you said that you read all about me from press clippings. Yes?

Well, there is no press packet about you. So you're going to have to tell me."

He'd never gone to this point with her—asking details about her days with Esau. Would he truly want to know? His whole life had been a struggle with Esau, and he yearned for that harmony with himself, which he'd concluded years ago would be his blessing. But the impulse to understand his brother assaulted his consciousness with a strength equal to his desire for her. Quietly he asked, "How do you remember him?"

"Esau was—as I remember him—how do you say, an impressive individual and quite a ladies' man." She suppressed a giggle, kissed him quickly, and left for the bathroom to fill the tub.

Alone for the moment, Jacob pulled the yellow sheet from his jacket pocket the handwritten note he'd received two days after his brother had killed himself. Stirring his coffee, he got up from the bed and nestled himself into a plump, velvet chair and proceeded to read Esau's letter for the umpteenth time, a letter dealing with memories but which made no mention of an intended suicide. All it said on the top of the page was, "Read in case something should happen to me."

Among his remembrances, Esau wrote about their soccer days in high school at the Dalton School in Manhattan. He reminded Jacob, "Though you were calculating and wily, I pleaded with our coach to take you on. You wouldn't have made the team on your own." Not so, Jacob thought, shaking his head. Why invoke such a memory, anyway?

According to Jacob's recollection, the coach had concluded that he couldn't pick one brother over the other and therefore decided on both. The letter then segued to their college years at Cornell where the boys had roomed together. What brought a hint of a chuckle as he read further was the picture that Esau had drawn on the margins of the sheet—a sketch of their dad, who had suffered a heart attack when the two were sophomores.

At the time, scared and disoriented because they had never dealt with their parents' mortality, they had rushed into the room at New York Hospital only to find their father sitting at the edge of his bed with a cigar in his mouth. Their mother, cool as a cucumber, embraced them and assured, "Don't worry, he's not trying to make me a widow. The cigar isn't lit." They were getting on in years, but remained in good health. Both Isaac and Rebecca played tennis at the bubble underneath the East 59th Street Bridge and swam at least three times a week at the Excelsior Gym. Though they lived on fashionable Sutton Place, Rebecca Rose often strolled outside in her tennis shoes. She felt no obligation to dress up in designer clothes, and Isaac was adamant about keeping a cigar dangling from his lips, a cigar that he hadn't lit for more than twenty years.

Jacob looked intently at the note once more. "Where the Obelisk meets the sky. 9 1970 July. You used to remember mine, I remembered yours. Meet up with Raquel."

"What is he saying?" He rarely told you what he honestly was up to, Jacob concluded. He folded the letter and placed it back in his pocket, beginning to feel more tormented about the secret life of his twin brother.

Still, he wondered if it was risky to look into Esau's life, the unreality of it all. Would he, in this quest for larger truths of Esau's doomed existence—after all he had killed himself—uncover a reality about himself, like the big bubble that sometimes his dad had said he lived in? Had he barricaded himself from a larger genuineness because of his fears?

Half an hour later, Raquel emerged from her bath, wrapped in a large white bath towel folded barely above her breasts. He must have dozed. Jacob's uneasy dreams of shooting in the streets and soldiers throwing bodies into the water now faded. He pulled Raquel toward him and flipped open the fold of her towel.

"Let's do it," she said.

Jacob took only seconds to throw off his clothes and to divert his attention away from Esau's death and imagined shootings in the street below. Her quick brown eyes excited him, and not for one more moment would he allow himself to think about his twin. Above all, he told himself, there was the third reason for making this trip: to advance a loving relationship with this quixotic woman. Jacob kissed her passionately, and she responded with equal ardor. They groped each other until suddenly she shuddered and rolled into an embrace with him. He felt strong and secure as he satisfied his desire and hers with several deep thrusts. They laughed as they groped each other again. He felt stronger and more secure as he satisfied his longing with several pelvic thrusts with his still-chiseled torso, and they both moaned with breathy sighs, until Raquel cried out suddenly in uncontrolled excitement, which aroused Jacob to his own climax. "Yes, yes," he shouted, as they remained joined together until his erection faded and they smiled tenderly at each other.

They remained in bed, but now wore matching terrycloth robes. Jacob reached over to a side table and grabbed the bottle of champagne. "To good times," he said, holding up his glass. He was determined to savor these moments with Raquel and to stop thinking about reasons behind his brother's death. The truth was that intrusive recollections of sibling rivalry fostered by their father frequently overtook him. Early on in life, he had learned that Esau was the favorite son.

"To good times," Raquel repeated, shaking him out of his thoughts.

Jacob's cell phone rang. "My parents," he said after looking at the display. He walked toward the balcony. "Better reception." Raquel nodded and indicated that she was going to go to the bathroom.

When she returned, Jacob was again lying in bed.

"My parents still call me to find out if I arrived safely." He laughed. "They told me to have a good time. To make sure you take me to all the good places for a nice time. They know me. Dad asked if I would be meeting anybody who knew Esau. I told them about Smith. Hey, there's more than enough time to learn about my brother."

Raquel touched him warmly. "Mama and Papa are eager to meet you. Mama is excited to have the cocktail reception for Señor Trumball. I've been busy on the phone, too. I called my parents from the bathroom. I told Papa that the artist must have his vodka. He drinks lots of it. Papa laughed and said he'd be sure to have plenty of Stolichnaya."

"Let's get dressed," Jacob suddenly said. "You can begin giving me the grand tour—well, a little piece of the tour. Let's have coffee and cakes in a café." He poured himself another glass of champagne. "How do you say, bottoms up?"

"We say 'salud.'"

"Salud," he said with a smiling wink.

They showered quickly. Jacob shaved, and when he got out of the bathroom, Raquel was already dressed and deciding on a scarf to wear.

He pulled a pair of gray slacks from his closet and wore his everyday blazer.

Downstairs, Ortiz drove the Mercedes up to the lobby door. Jacob motioned him away and told him that they were going to walk. Ortiz shook his head but proceeded to follow them slowly in the limousine.

When the beautiful Raquel Gingold and her American art dealer friend breezed by groups at outdoor cafés, many smiled in her direction. Raquel wasn't one to hide from the public, nor would she stop now and sign an autograph. She would never be imprisoned by her fame and she'd made that pledge to herself years before. Still, she silently criticized herself for choosing to wear a long scarf to hide her identity in her native town. More suited for New York and other international cities where she was far less recognized. She should have known that this disguise of long, navy silk framed her face, holding a spotlight to it. It did less to discourage or fool the celebrity watcher than those big and round dark sunglasses that she also favored. Both accessories brought attention to her glamour. And she knew it. She loved the attention, even as she pretended not to notice.

Inside the Café Tortoni they sat in red leather chairs around a round, marble table drinking café con leche. Writers, artists, and intellectuals, frequented the place, surrounded by bronze statues and decorative mirrors, arguing about the unstable economy. "We go back and forth between pesos and dollars," one voice proclaimed. "Soon it will be euros," said another. "Maybe we're better off with euros. Inflation is raping our lives." A mahogany grandfather clock struck once. At a small table, four young males and one female looking like holdovers from the '80s, argued and drank coffee. Their ponytails and scruffy appearance looked out of place to Jacob. Raquel avoided their occasional glances.

"I've sometimes wondered how I would show New York City to somebody who had never been there. I wouldn't know where to start," he said.

"The Statue of Liberty," she said.

"The Statute of Liberty. Maybe a view from the River Café under the Brooklyn Bridge," Jacob said lovingly.

Raquel's face lit up. Jacob reached across the table, holding her hands firmly. He had never seen her happier.

CHAPTER SEVEN

General De Solis' villa in Palermo Chico was a French-style, old stone house. The road to the front door required several bends through a deep forest, where armed guards with Dobermans surrounded the mansion and patrolled its manicured gardens. The general waited in his bunker, a concrete cave underneath this lush paradise. He refilled a glass of scotch and replayed his favorite newsreel of General Charles de Gaulle entering Paris victoriously in the summer of 1944. He sat in a leather chair, imagining his own triumphant march from the Casa Rosada, Argentina's presidential palace, down the Avenida de Mayo to the National Congress Building, where he would speak to his country's lawmakers in its great hall.

Four years ago, De Solis had met with the leaders of his country's drug cartels, proposing a drug distribution center in the United States. But where? Esau had introduced him to a man called Smith, who was then at the Argentine desk at the Pentagon. Smith had convinced De Solis that arms trafficking was where the action was and more profitable than drugs. Paramilitary forces were springing up all over the globe. Pariah governments like those in Syria, Iran, the Sudan, and Somalia were eager to offer safe havens for these people. Smith arranged the back-door dealings, and Esau laundered the profit successfully through Cayman and Swiss banks.

This morning, De Solis rocked relentlessly in his chair in a private corner of the cavernous bunker, shouting, "Una fiesta." A long-stem, five-bladed wooden fan hung motionless from the ceiling. A cigar nested in a thick glass ashtray on a round table next to him. On the old news film, a voice called out, "Viva La France!"

Finally, Smith arrived at the compound. He entered an elevator in a guardhouse about sixty feet from the front gate. Smith tapped a code on the polished brass–plated keypad, and a heavy steel door opened to allow his descent into the fortified bunker. The elevator moved slowly, and Smith wondered why De Solis wouldn't fix it. What if they had to enter the bunker in a hurry? "The man is crazy," he muttered to himself.

Smith entered the large room with rows of fluorescent lights. Teams of officers and civilians stood over tables with computers, maps, and cell phones recharging in tiny cradles on the desks. Tobacco smoke floated in spiral cones toward ceiling air ducts. Smith walked vigorously to the far end of the bunker where the former general held court with his bottle of scotch.

De Solis wanted everything to work with precision as he mentally reviewed plans. When circumstances changed because an opponent acted differently from what De Solis had imagined, he blamed the messenger.

"Señor, where's the painting?" the general snapped as Smith approached empty-handed. "Your mission was to return with the painting."

De Solis stood six feet tall, with deep-set, sleepy blue eyes, a long Roman nose chiseled perfectly against an oval face, and cheekbones high enough to be pronounced, but not feminine graced. His lips were pursed and plump, and their thickness worked like a vise on the mouths he kissed. Wavy, blond hair was styled with a side part and worn short.

These days the fifty–eight-year-old general hung out at clubs with a fast, young crowd and society women, and was a well-liked guest at dinner parties and functions at charitable institutions. He was the epitome of an officer and a gentleman in Argentina, a charismatic man about town. He was often seen with attractive women at fine restaurants or at the Colon Opera House. He danced the tango brilliantly. His body moved with exquisite balance.

At his desk, the former general busied his hands with bending a paper clip.

"A delay. A slight delay," said Smith.

"Explain."

"The artist is crazy."

The general fell silent, as if letting the idea of a crazy artist settle in his head. "The artist is crazy, you say? What does that have to with the painting?"

"I have everything under control."

"I must have that painting. Surely, you understand the rush!" De Solis shouted.

Smith nodded. "We'll get it in a few hours."

"A few hours."

"We'll get the painting when the artist arrives. Not before. That's how they set it up. It's crazy, I know."

"And Señor Rose. Does he know anything about the code on the back of the painting?"

"He said nothing to make me suspicious."

De Solis puffed on his cigar, blowing perfect smoke circles toward the ducts that ran across the ceiling. He was determined to play by rules he had arranged; no violence—instead, intense persuasion. He placed the cigar back in the thick glass ashtray and reached for his glass of scotch. He stared down at Smith. Another moment passed without comment.

As a young army officer in 1970s, Juan Domingo De Solis had helped the CIA by forwarding documents of Soviet arms purchases made by left-wing radicals. Subtlety and persuasion had been his tools then. By 1976, with inflation in Argentina at 800 percent and increasing civil strife, he had been one of the officers who spearheaded the bloodless military coup of that year, ousting the Perónist government. Then he had gone ahead to crush all cells of armed leftist subversion and to set up machinery to eliminate resistance. The military government had given way in '82 to the return of democracy and a defeat by the British over the Falkland Islands. De Solis had been among other military officers sentenced to life in prison and convicted for crimes against humanity. Suave and persuasive, he was released by presidential pardon after serving only six months. He had maintained his authority and power well into the '90s, clandestinely honing a vast network of corruption that he'd created. Five years ago, he had apologized to his country for the actions of the military during the junta, claiming he was following orders from superiors.

De Solis returned to his chair. "I must have that money. In seventy-two hours, the U.S. president's plane arrives in Buenos Aires." He leaned back. A smile crossed his lips. "Señorita Raquel calls me a ladies' man. What do you think of that?"

Smith nodded his head up and down a couple of times. "So my video cams and microphones are working well?"

"Too well."

"Why too well?" Smith seemed puzzled. How could his teams' work, bugging the hotel suite be too good?

"That information, I don't need to know."

"What the hell do you mean?"

"I know when he's making love to her. That I don't like."

Smith squared his shoulders and started to laugh. It was a rare moment that he joked with De Solis "There's an easy solution. Don't watch."

"I don't."

"Then what are you talking about?"

"I get detailed reports. I don't want her making love with the art dealer. Or any man in Buenos Aires. Do I make myself clear?"

"There's nothing you can do."

De Solis checked his watch.

A fat-jowled man broke into their conversation. "The art dealer is going to the Lavazzo Art Gallery. What are my orders?"

"Contact Señora Bertha."

"This will be done, General De Solis. Done."

"Instruct her to give us all details of his visit. I want every word of their conversation."

"I understand."

"I want to know what he knows. I want to know what the actress knows."

"We will be at our listening posts."

"See that I get written transcriptions of all talks between the art dealer and the actress."

"Yes, it will be done." The fat-jowled man saluted and returned to a desk teeming with the latest receiving devices, flat screen monitors, and various headsets.

"You, watch the Lavazzo Gallery," the general barked at Smith.

"Yes."

"Señor Smith, you told me that the art dealer isn't suspicious of anything."

"Yes, that is so."

"How can you be sure?"

"He asked about his brother. I don't think that means anything."

"Then why is he going to the Lavazzo Gallery?"

"We'll know shortly."

"What about the actress?"

"The actress was curious that she didn't know me. Nothing more."

"She is curious about you ... he asks if you knew his brother ... and he leaves for Señora Lavazzo's gallery." De Solis took three quick puffs on his cigar and glared at Smith.

"They don't know a damn thing. All he wants is the nine million bucks for the painting," Smith said. "And the gala celebration for the artist. And a romantic weekend in Buenos Aires with the actress. That's it, nothing more. That's enough to go on."

"We must lunch with all of them," De Solis said.

"You've arranged to be with them at dinner. I'll know exactly when the artist arrives. Then we'll get the painting."

"I will confront the art dealer," said De Solis, ignoring Smith.

"I'd advise against that. You'll put ideas in Jacob Rose's head. Now you'll make him suspicious."

"Time is moving quickly."

Smith was shaking his head. "I don't understand."

"We'll confront everybody at an afternoon luncheon."

"Confront them with what?"

"The truth," De Solis winked.

"That their painting has coded information, just like our forgery?"

"Yes. But instead of money, we will tell them that the codes are about a plot to kill their president. Oh, Americans are very patriotic these days. Once he hears this, he'll hand over the painting immediately."

Smith resented becoming De Solis' lackey. He wanted the money Esau had hidden, that's all. De Solis' rants pushed Smith to devise a plan in his mind. He would adopt a respectful approach toward Jacob. Not because the art dealer was his buddy's twin, but because he felt deep down that Jacob had knowledge of the whereabouts of the hidden money. Why not? After all, they were twin brothers. Smith cleared his throat. "Why would the art dealer believe you?"

"He might not. His lady friend will. I can assure you of that as fact."

"No. I don't like this. This is crazy."

De Solis blew more perfect circles of cigar smoke in the air. "I am certain the actress will believe this."

"Let me handle it my way."

"Your way?"

"Yes."

"And what is your way?"

"Seize the painting and start a fire in their suite to cover our tracks." Smith nodded in approval of his idea. Creating fright stimulated his passion. Just talking about it gave him a rush.

"That makes no sense."

"We'll make sure nobody is in the room. This way we'll get what we want. Quick and easy."

De Solis twirled his cigar. "What if the code isn't on the real painting? *Imbécil!* Did you ever think about that possibility? Or is it that you don't think?"

"The code must be there," Smith replied, but rapidly decided that the general might have a point.

"We'll do as I said," De Solis ordered. "We'll bait them with the assassination plot. Appeal to their patriotism. *Brilliante.*"

Smith frowned. "Yes, sir."

"Now, you have your work, Señor Smith and I have mine."

"Are you sure that's what you want?" De Solis didn't answer, and Smith knew that he was excused and that he must leave the bunker at once. When you lose a fight, he thought, you move on. Often, he had tried convincing Esau of that, but Esau was stubborn and would never accept defeat.

He left for the secret elevator to the outside world. Smith suspected that the general had ordered Esau killed, and almost accused him of it when he learned of Esau's suicide. He thought more about Esau, now that his twin brother was in Buenos Aires. Even so, an idea nagged at him. What if Esau had double-crossed him and had made a deal with Jacob? Despite the real grief that he felt at Esau's death, a suspicion of having been betrayed began to unnerve him. Smith looked grim. He would concentrate on Jacob's demeanor and his talks with him for any telltale clues. He convinced himself to be patient.

Later, about five miles away from the compound, he activated a device in his car to pick up conversations at Bertha Lavazzo's gallery.

CHAPTER EIGHT

They had been walking around the Plaza de Mayo, holding hands, then down Corrientes and Lavalle, past a huge portrait of the famed tango dancer Domingo Gardel and over to Florida for window-shopping. All the while, Ortiz, their driver, dutifully followed them in the limousine.

"Bertha would know something," Jacob said to Raquel.

"But you'll see her tonight ... at dinner."

"No. I have to do it now."

"You promised—"

"I can't wait for dinner," he said, cutting her off.

"You agreed, darling ... to relax."

"Please understand."

"I'm trying to understand. Really I am."

Jacob didn't know Bertha well at all, didn't know what her operation was like, though Trumball had encouraged him to engage her gallery as his Latin American representative. The impetus for this association came from Esau, who brought her gallery to his attention almost a year ago. Two women in my life now, thanks to Esau, he thought. Jacob stopped on the street and faced Raquel. "Look, I want to be with you every minute of the day. Things are troubling me. I need you to understand that ..." he said, his voice trailing off as he suddenly became aware that they had an audience. "God, I hate this. I can't even talk to you here without having everyone gawk at us."

Passersby looked at them as the two paused on the street, recognizing her, wishing to speak to her, but Raquel pretended that they were alone. "Fame can be an intimidating thing," she said. "Jacob, I'm sorry. Yes, I want to be with you." She understood that she couldn't constrain his impulse. "Okay. Go and talk about the art world with her. I'll walk back to the hotel. I'll be fine."

"Have you ever been to the Lavazzo Gallery?" he asked.

"No, never."

"I've got to leave you now, darling."

She shrugged. "Yes, yes." Bright-eyed and an eager tour guide, she stared at him earnestly. "Ortiz will know exactly where Bertha's gallery is."

"I'll be back in an hour."

Jacob motioned to Ortiz to pull up to the curb as he watched Raquel disappear down the street. Apart from her running a small gallery, he knew little else about Bertha Lavazzo. Bertha's origins, like so much of her life, were mysterious. The most that anyone had known about her was that she'd landed in Buenos Aires sometime in the 1970s during a brief marriage to a Milanese banker, whom she'd reputedly met in New York. They were newlyweds, it was said, when he was posted to Argentina. Two years after their arrival in Argentina, he met a sudden death, drowning in a boating accident with a group of four friends including his alleged mistress at the time. According to the newspapers, his fifty-six-foot schooner simply blew up, tossing him and his guests out to sea in the explosion, helpless amid thrusting waves that would later claim them. The investigation was hobbled by the disappearance of any evidence to suggest tampering, and since no one survived, little was ever known of what actually had happened. So, with what little inheritance her Milanese husband hadn't gambled away, the widow Lavazzo had opened Lavazzo Fine Arts Gallery.

While Bertha had always run with an art-world crowd, mostly as a groupie of sorts, she could now claim some legitimacy to her interests when she became an art dealer. Given to fanciful self-delusions—one being her reputation as a figure in the art world, a self-proclaimed doyenne—she leapt at the chance to pose for Laban Trumball twenty years ago. The result was *Nude Reclining on a Le Corbusier Lounge*, the large canvas of a naked, heavy-set woman that hung above Jacob's desk at the Rose Gallery in New York. The artist had originally named the painting *Madame B. Reclining in Her Studio*, but Bertha had protested. Trumball had captured her corpulence in all its fleshy detail. Bertha had found the appellation objectionable and had thought it was ambiguous and demeaning, both to her physique and her lifestyle. "I like it. It's you. You in all your flesh and glory," the artist had protested. No, Bertha would not accept Trumball's attempt to persuade her. She had accused him of thinking of her as a madame in her brothel. "I assure you, Laban," she'd scolded, "that title is an insult." Bertha had delivered her reply with a straight face back then, but soon enough had erupted with vigorous laughter. They had both turned to laughter, then champagne, and then left the artist's studio for a rollicking night on the town, and as always wound up for late-night partying at Studio 54 with Andy Warhol and Liza Minnelli and their group of hangers-on.

CHAPTER NINE

Fifteen minutes later, Ortiz slowed the limousine as they approached the turn onto the 1400 block of Avenida Corrientes, just west of Avenida 9 de Julio. Small, single-floor bookstores, a few art galleries, a dress shop or two, and three old movie houses filled the street. Bertha's gallery, a small storefront directly on Av. Corrientes, stood in the middle of the block, conspicuously dilapidated among her neighboring merchants.

Lavazzo Fine Arts resembled a pawnshop. Esau had always portrayed Bertha's operation as strictly first-class, yet even the sign on her façade hadn't seen a coat of paint in years. Perhaps Madame B. was more concerned with discretion than new business. No matter; her reputation preceded her in this town, and she had represented the world's best artists to this area of the globe for many years. Reverse snobbery, he concluded, as he closed the door behind him and adjusted his jacket.

Inside, various threadbare Persian rugs in the center of Bertha's salon made it resemble the interior of a fleabag hotel in the Far East. Dust seemed to inhabit every surface, and the stale scents of body odor and an obstinate perfume wrestled with one another in a pungent attempt at victory. Bertha's gallery appeared to be in mid-exhibition. "That's a good sign," Jacob murmured to himself, as he inspected the walls flanked with a dozen or so contemporary canvases by local artists. These were mostly landscapes, country scenes of ranch life, and herds of cattle, or the nearby mountains outside Buenos Aires.

An assistant, a scrawny, middle-aged woman with sallow, sunken cheeks and a brittle frame, seated Jacob in an upholstered chair covered with brocade remnants and faded tapestries. She introduced herself as Alice Drukwald, Bertha's assistant, and informed Jacob that Bertha was still meeting with her tarot card reader.

"She will finish in a few minutes, señor," Alice said almost sternly, and offered Jacob a whiskey. He accepted and smiled politely, bowing slightly. The side table next to his chair held a stack of magazines from at least a decade ago. She returned Jacob's smile awkwardly and handed him a glass while she took a seat opposite him, looking sideways toward the back room and drinking from her glass in nervous sips. Every once in a while, Alice would sneak a peek at his face.

"You are a very elegant man, señor," she offered. He seemed surprised by her sudden gust of warmth. Maybe it was all the whiskey and champagne he'd already drunk this day. Alice was nodding her head. "I see what Bertha thought—well, shall we say, strange?—about you and your brother." Her accented English wasn't Spanish-inflected; it was more European—Austrian, perhaps, something decidedly Germanic. More mysterious was Alice herself: out-of-date and over-the-hill, yet somehow a little girlish by her choice of childlike attire. Her auburn Buster Brown haircut revealed not one gray hair in its frame of her ashen skin, lined and devoid of any cosmetic care. Nor were her hunter green corduroy jumper and plain white blouse with its Peter Pan collar out of context with the white cotton, knee-high socks that arose from the crosshatched shoes he'd recognized on the feet of parochial-school girls from at least two generations ago. Most eerily of all, there was nothing ironic about this woman's attempt to dress this way.

"Strange?" Jacob paused as he said this word, considering its source. "How do you mean?" He continued to sip his whiskey as he stood up and moved about the small gallery space. Jacob had never liked making small talk, and the woman's bizarre appearance left him completely ill at ease, despite her evident familiarity with Esau.

"Yes, strange," she emphasized. "Were you not twins?" Like a cat eyeing a spool of thread, Alice examined him up and down. "You don't look exactly like one another. I recall that your brother had red hair."

"We are twins," he said.

"I am sorry about Esau. Bertha was in tears for days when she learned about his death."

Jacob said nothing and stared straight ahead. To pass the time as he waited for Bertha, he took note of how primitive the hanging landscapes appeared in comparison to the abstractions of the New York art scene.

"Another drink, señor?" Before he could respond, Alice was back at the bottle refilling her own shot glass. He extended his glass without so much as a glance in her direction, and she topped him off. He wandered over to the beaded curtain that separated Bertha and her mystical counselor from the rest of the gallery. Through the curtain, he caught sight of a few photographs hung in black frames; they appeared to represent Esau, a military man, and Bertha. They seemed to hang haphazardly. He knocked back his second whiskey in a gulp.

"Yes, yes. I shall do so," an impatient Bertha replied in the dramatic affectation of British English once common to theatrical stars. She was speaking to a very lean man, whose spindly back was turned toward the curtain.

"Another drink, Mr. Rose?" Alice seemed to startle him without even trying.

"No. Thank you." Jacob observed that she dropped señor for Mr. Rose, which affirmed that Alice's Spanish was an affectation.

"Bertha has had spiritual guidance for many years, you know. I suspect that you aren't a spiritual person. Or are you?"

"You were right the first time," Jacob said, returning to his seat. "Chance is a part of life. It's a roll of the dice out there. You sleep in the bed that you make for yourself." He frowned at the cliché he had uttered and vainly tried to sip from his empty glass.

Bertha finally made her entrance through dangling red beads as the clock on the mantle read 2:35. A young man, no more than thirty, in a wrinkled, steel grey polyester suit and with scraggily wisps of muted brown hairs on his chin smiled nervously, nodded to each of them and scurried out the door.

Bertha Lavazzo was a vision of buxom excess in every direction. She was broad-shouldered like a man, in her late sixties, and yet she was serenely feminine and curvaceous despite her bounty of endless flab. Jacob's father might have called her *zaftig*. Her breasts were barely contained by her undergarments. Her expanded waistline was scarcely concealed by the overflow of material that was necessary to construct her dress. Most Americans, however, especially the body-conscious art world snobs of Jacob's life in Manhattan's Chelsea area, would simply dismiss her as matronly. Her dark hair, thick and wavy, was swept into a French twist, just as when he'd first met her, though now it bore multiple strands of gray that age had provided her. In mock anticipation of seeing Jacob after so many years, she swung her large jowls forward to receive a kiss.

"You certainly haven't changed, Bertha," Jacob said, sinking his lips into each portly cheek. "You look terrific!" He wouldn't judge her by what she wore, but how she remained in character in those clothes: large, sweeping, enigmatic, and shabby.

"Even with my clothes on?" She let out a hearty laugh and smacked him on the back.

"Even fully clothed, Bertha," he said, visualizing the painting that hangs above his desk in his New York. She waved him back into his chair and plopped herself on the aging, navy velvet sofa that was opposite him. Alice appeared to have taken her leave, though in truth she sat huddled behind an old rolltop desk, busying herself with the audible task of paperwork. "May I get you something to drink, Jacob?"

"I'm just fine," he nodded toward the empty glass he still held.

"Your name has appeared in our newspapers, you know."

"I didn't know. Why is that?"

"Because of Raquel. She is one of Argentina's most famous actresses."

"Raquel isn't the reason I'm here."

"I'm sure. And why are you here?"

"To see your operation. And I want to speak to you about Esau."

"Of course!" she bellowed, so seemingly concerned. "Señor Esau was a gentleman of the very first order." Suddenly pained, she turned her head away. "Oh, how I miss him."

"Yes, I can see that." Jacob stood stone-faced, and perhaps secretly resentful that he, Esau's twin, could not share in this sense of affection. There was no point in suppressing the small grudge he held toward Raquel, and now Smith and Bertha. They were part of Esau's adult life, and he was not. Jacob's early sense of Esau as a generally active frat jock and party animal was all that he had to hold on to, and now that image seemed as outmoded as Alice's costume.

Jacob instantly recalled that Esau's suicide elicited a statement from the president. Esau had become a big deal in politics as a fundraiser and had chaired the president's re-election committee. His résumé was impeccable in government circles. His peers accepted that the missing years on his curriculum vitae involved secret government work and never questioned those lapses in time. He had a way of disarming people with friendly, backslapping habits. After all, he was a jock at heart and a sports enthusiast, from football and basketball to the star drivers of NASCAR racing. Sure, "*Esau was every inch a man's man. Why De Solis and why Smith? Who are these people? Art connoisseurs? Friends?*" Jacob asked himself.

Jacob quickly gazed at various paintings on the walls of her tiny gallery. "You must also miss ... his connections to the art world." He was not sure if Bertha caught his snide remark.

"He delivered paintings promptly, and always in person," she said. "He helped me with new clients."

"Particularly De Solis, no?" he asked. "Hasn't he been one of your more important clients?"

"I suppose. General De Solis entertains a great deal."

"So you are an eager supporter of the general?"

"He has a splendid villa with a most marvelous art collection."

"He's a frequent patron?"

"Yes, he's bought works by many of my artists."

"Though he returns more paintings than he keeps." Jacob pointed his glass toward Alice.

"The good general likes to impress his guests," Bertha replied.

"At little expense to himself, when it pertains to art." Jacob shook his head with a sense of displeasure.

"What does that mean?"

"You're a more tolerant dealer than I am regarding these matters."

"Truth to tell? He pays me a bit of cash for my services whenever he decides to return a work of art."

"I didn't know that."

"The general calls it my 'grievance commission.'" She smiled. "But I thought you wanted to talk about your brother. Now then, how ever did we get on the subject of the general?"

Jacob recognized that Bertha was running a consignment shop at best. The days when she could operate as a representative of the world's best artists to wealthy South Americans were long gone.

Bertha had held onto Trumball, to be sure, but that had more to do with De Solis' demand for the old man's work as well as Esau's brokerage between the Rose Gallery in New York and Bertha's minor operation. This time, Jacob had negotiated *Lea with Two Love-Apples* directly with De Solis, eliminating the need for Bertha, which led him to the conclusion that today's visit would likely be his last piece of business with her.

He sipped his drink slowly. "Yes, then. Esau."

"Esau was a true friend."

"Did you see him much when he was in Buenos Aires?

"Mostly for purposes of business."

"I see."

"He'd bring me a painting from your gallery."

"I understand." Suddenly, things all made sense to Jacob. *Esau was involved in forgeries with Bertha and the general.* He believed now that he discovered the motivation for Esau's admission to him almost a year ago that he'd been making copies of lithographs. Apparently, Jacob's rebuke to him to end this activity immediately hadn't been taken seriously. "Let me ask you a question."

"Yes, please ask."

"Were you and Esau socially involved?"

"A few times, socially."

"Bertha, now indulge me. Was my brother involved in anything illegal?"

"And you think I'd know?" She seemed genuinely surprised.

"I don't know what—but it may be tied to his death."

"I remember your brother with fondness. I'm very sorry about his death."

"I hoped you might offer a clue or clues about his life in Buenos Aires."

Bertha listened closely and chose not to reply. "When does Señor Trumball arrive?" she asked, switching the subject.

"Shortly. He might already be here."

"Splendid. Then why don't we pick up this conversation this evening at dinner?" She glanced gratefully at the telephone as it rang.

"Your tarot card reader," Alice interrupted. "He has an urgent word for you."

"Excuse me, Señor Rose. I must take this in private."

"I'll have some more of that whiskey." Jacob motioned to Alice again with his glass. Alice filled his glass without careful consideration of its rim. The whiskey spilled across Jacob's hand. He grabbed a tissue from the table near him and wiped his hand before he could throw Alice a dirty look. Within moments, he could smell that perfumed scent as

Bertha emerged once more from the back room. She was visibly shaken and agitated, her cheeks were ashen white.

"Now, then, where were we?" Bertha asked.

"That was a quick phone call," he said.

"So it was," she said, as they exchanged awkward glances. Alice had ventured back to her desk. Any remaining color abruptly vanished from Bertha's cheeks as she took a deep breath and checked the clock. "Before you go, why don't I give you a quick tour? I'm very proud of this exhibition. These artists represent the hottest crop of new Argentine pastoralists."

"I suppose. You know, I spotted several photographs on your office wall back behind the beads."

"I just love documenting events.

"Esau is in some of the photos."

"Well, he was a part of my life. Please, have a look at the photographs," she said, gaining her composure and ushering him to follow her.

Jacob swept past Alice without as much as a glimpse. He could feel her eyes trail him past the beaded curtain. Bertha stood smiling. "Here is a very young me." She recaptured her previous animation as she stood before a yellowed photograph of a group assembled in evening clothes.

"My God, that's Trumball in the picture with you. He was crotchety even back then, wasn't he?" Jacob observed the artist's characteristic scowl.

"Yes, he was. The photo was taken in New York in the early 1960s. We were at the Waldorf at a reception in the Towers given my Mrs. Douglas MacArthur."

Jacob chuckled. "So, Trumball ran in those lofty circles. Though, the old man has more war stories than a four-star general." By now, he had loosened up a bit. He couldn't remember how many shots of whiskey he had had, on top of the glasses of champagne that he had drunk earlier.

"Oh, yes, we ran with a very exciting crowd in those days."

"Were other artists in your group?"

"Yes. Here I am with Salvador Dalí, again in New York. Salvador drew a shoe for me, silly goose. A shoe. On a yellow sheet of lined paper."

"Why a shoe?" Jacob had little interest in this trip down memory lane, but was determined to humor her if he was going to unravel information on Esau's thorny business dealings.

"I never knew why," she said, shaking her head. "Then he signed it. I still have it upstairs."

"I'm sure it holds a great deal of personal significance."

"I wasn't asking you to appraise it," she snapped.

Jacob held back. "Let's talk about the photos with Esau."

"Yes. Fond, fond memories for me. It's as if the photos were taken only yesterday."

"When were these actually taken?" he asked, pointing to a few photographs that appeared to be falling off their hooks.

"You're jumping ahead of me."

"Humor me."

"In the early '80s."

"Esau had just arrived then in Buenos Aires."

"Yes."

"Now you remember that I had a few questions to ask?" Jacob queried.

"I suppose. This photo is like a family picture of the time, you might say."

"There's Smith. I met him today."

"Yes, Esau and Smith were terribly close friends. That's General De Solis and a much younger, far more voluptuous me, don't you agree?"

A moment passed without any further exchange. He accepted that he wasn't getting anywhere with Bertha. Well, she'd lost touch with reality. "All right, then, answer this for me."

Alice filled her glass again, which Bertha gulped down quickly. "Yes, go ahead, please."

"Were Esau and Raquel involved back then?"

"You won't let go, Jacob, will you, my dear."

"Indulge me. Okay?"

"What did Raquel tell you?"

"That they were friends, just that."

"And you don't believe her?"

"I never pushed her for an answer."

"You're not a terribly trusting individual."

"Maybe I'm not." Though Jacob knew that despite his business cunning and achievements, he'd always been too trusting.

"Someday you will be tested," Bertha warned. "I assure you, you will be tested," she said, shaking her finger.

He brushed his hair back with his fingers. Jacob was quickly losing patience, but managing to control his anger. "I don't believe in karma, so spare me any bull about this New Age nonsense."

"Then let me be more direct."

"Finally. Yes, I would appreciate that."

"Dear," she hesitated and seemed to search her mind for the best way of phrasing her next remark, "your brother was a homosexual."

Jacob turned to Alice and returned to stare at Bertha. The air between them seemed compressed into a huge block of ice. He looked almost belligerent at this information, as if it were an accusation of his family's honor. "I'm sorry. Are you telling me that my brother was gay?" The suggestion that Esau was gay struck Jacob as impossible. I would have known, he told himself.

"Didn't you know that?"

He sipped his whiskey, almost biting the glass, barely able to control his hand, which was shaking with rage at her bold-faced lie. Finally, he turned to Bertha. "Raquel never told me." He wouldn't let her off the hook with what he perceived was a dirty and disparaging remark. His voice remained sharp. "Don't muck up my brother's reputation for your own advantage. You're taking payoffs from General De Solis, but leave my brother out of this."

"Please, Mr. Rose! Don't get angry. Why should Raquel, why should anyone think to tell you? She probably assumed you knew. After all, you were twins."

"Well, I didn't know."

"So now you do."

Her response did it for him, pushing him over the edge. "There's little here that I can find to my liking."

Jacob decided against asking further questions. He was going to have to come back when he was calmer. He would have to leave the gallery with more unanswered questions than when he arrived. There was his puzzlement over his brother's sexual orientation, and Bertha's frown, as if she achieved her goal of covering up her role in whatever play they were enacting. Jacob left the gallery without waving a good-bye to the two of them. Alice came over to find Bertha weeping desperately.

Minutes earlier in an alley several streets behind the gallery, while Jacob reminisced with Bertha about the old days in New York, the tarot card reader stopped, grabbed his cell, and phoned Bertha.

"Lavazzo Gallery," Alice answered.

The tarot card reader's heart pumped quickly. "Get Bertha on the phone, please. He pulled out a candy bar from his pocket and began chewing as he waited for Bertha. Finally, Bertha answered.

"I have creepy feeling that I'm being followed."

Smith, wearing aviator glasses with dark green–tinted lenses, approached the young man. "Can you tell me what time it is?"

"I don't have a watch."

"Look up to the heavens. Can't you tell me what time it is?" Smith sneered.

The young man froze with fear. He let out a shuddering breath of air and began to squeeze his hands. "I don't wear a watch.

"Hello, hello. What is going on?" Bertha called out.

"Bertha, get help! Quickly! Hurry!"

Smith stared through the dark green glasses. "Well, now you'll know eternity firsthand." Smith swiftly jerked a piano wire from his pocket and with brute force wrapped it around the man's neck, twisting the wire and snapping his windpipe. He pushed the body into a garbage can, poured gasoline, struck a match, and watched it ignite.

Outside Bertha's gallery, Jacob took a deep breath. He slid into the backseat of the limousine. For all his good intentions, in playing detective to uncover events that led to Esau's suicide, Jacob didn't notice the black Lincoln Town Car parked across the street, or Smith jaywalking over to the Lavazzo Gallery.

CHAPTER TEN

Chelsea, the area in Manhattan where his art gallery was located, had become a Mecca for the gay world, attracting young, handsome, well-groomed types, walking around at night with lovers. Was Esau like that in public with another man? Jacob doubted that. Esau probably just tested those waters. This seemed to be more to Jacob's liking, an easier pill to swallow, for now. He pulled the yellow sheet of paper from his pocket and stared vacantly from the rear seat of the limousine. He placed the paper back in his pocket and instructed Ortiz to drive straight to Avenida 9 de Julio, at the 1000 block. He had a hunch but wasn't sure what he'd find as he looked blankly at the sights.

"Anyway, it just does not fit," Jacob murmured. As the limousine made its way down the boulevard, Jacob settled back, but after a moment felt a bit of unbearable shame, like a blow to the stomach. Esau had been an athlete at Cornell, and the many coeds who sought his affections accounted for his brother's active social life in and out of their fraternity. Esau had been, in today's slang, a *babe magnet*. Jacob smiled, finally. *A babe magnet*. That was a term one of his younger and very brash artists had used to describe himself. Jacob thought the artist a blowhard who couldn't possibly charm the many supermodels he had claimed to have slept with. He was a respected painter, and Jacob had already made a tiny sum from his first two shows. *If the artist wanted to brag about his prowess, who was he to care?* He did care about Esau, and while the art world cured any lingering homophobia that a man like Jacob might have once harbored, it wasn't easy learning that his twin was gay, especially when the news came from the mouth of the pathetic Bertha Lavazzo.

"We are very close to the address you asked for," said Ortiz. Abruptly ahead, Jacob was intrigued by what he saw. A public monument of sorts, clearly monolithic, and it appeared to stand right in the center of town. Its marble skin bore an inscription, too, but from the speed that the car traveled, all of that was illegible. As they drew nearer, there was no dispute about this statue's phallic impression. He remembered that they passed the monument this morning, driving to the hotel. *Where the Obelisk meets the sky*. Ever closer, Jacob sat upright as they wove past the roundabout with its obelisk at the center. Another kind of ominous feeling lodged in his gut, just as it had since he'd left Bertha's gallery. Now it felt more discernible. Esau had been trying to tell him something in that irritating note that Jacob was convinced he could show no one. So its unclear messages might have been more than the scribbles of a man on the edge. If Esau hadn't revealed his sexual orientation in that letter, he was certainly trying to expose something.

"Stop right here," he directed Ortiz, who screeched to a halt in front of a group of parking garages that bore the number 1970. Was this a date in the letter, or was this an actual address? Was it this address? Or was Jacob being tested, as Bertha suggested he would be one day? He would find out soon enough if Esau's note had meaning.

Inside the garage, a short, squarely built man sat in the tiny booth. He was engrossed in the newspaper, cursing the soccer scores of the sports section, when he looked up at Jacob, confident that he'd recognized him.

"Do you speak English?" Jacob asked the man who leaned out from the booth.

"Yes, señor," he answered in a halting Spanish accent. "How can I help you?"

"This may sound crazy ... loco," Jacob offered, "but did you know a man whose name was Esau Rose? He looked like me. He was my brother and he had red hair. You might remember his hair color. I believe he was here before."

The garage attendant listened intently and turned over possibilities in his mind's eye. "*Aiii!* Sí, señor." He nodded, briskly. "I was thinking something was familiar with you."

Jacob could only smile in anticipation. Perhaps this man might share a fast clue, so that Jacob could be on his way.

"I have your brother's ticket. You pay me for him?" Jacob nodded yes. "I am owed, let me see. Well, we will say it is 700 American dollars. I charge you by the month. That is fair, yes?"

Jacob studied the ticket. Esau had apparently owned a car that he'd parked here on 9 April. Not exactly the jackpot of clues, but at least Jacob felt he was on to something. He warily agreed to the price and handed the man his platinum card, while the garage attendant handed him the keys.

"The car is parked on the third level, Area C," he said, pointing upwards toward its location. "Number thirty-six."

Jacob walked up a beaten concrete ramp to a small elevator. He entered and impatiently pressed three on the elevator panel. Park a car on 9th of the month and on 9 July Boulevard? *Where was Esau taking me with these puzzles?*

Reaching level three, he stepped out onto another concrete ramp that led directly to Area C. Parking garages, he marveled, must be identical the world over. Jacob pulled the keys from his jacket as he counted the spaces to thirty-six, where a shining, black, brand-new Lincoln Town Car sat quietly among a fleet of compact foreign imports. "I would never have guessed," he snickered. He noted three keys on the chain. Okay. One for the door and one for the trunk or glove compartment; the other for the ignition, he figured.

Jacob inspected the car inside and out. Its standard, black leather interior still smelled of that new-car scent, and it contained no papers or other personal effects. He slid the keys back into his jacket pocket. It could have belonged to anyone; but it was Esau's, though nothing about it suggested his ownership except for the parking receipt that Jacob held in his wallet. He flipped open the trunk. Suddenly, he saw through the corner of his eye a car turning around the bend, heading quickly toward him, an identical car, gleaming in brilliant black, its windows impenetrably tinted to match. A quick look persuaded him that the trunk was empty

"Move it, move it," shouted a ski-masked thug, poking his head out the tinted passenger-side window to warn Jacob in distinctly American English. Jacob backed away from the Lincoln and began to run before the approaching vehicle could trail his rear any closer than the twenty feet that seemed to separate them.

"Hey, asshole, what are you trying to do?" he shouted back, running as fast as he could down the ramp to the next level. As he looked back at the car speeding toward him, he could see at least five men smashing Esau's car, ripping apart the seats and doors, and breaking open the trunk lid. It was as if they came from out of nowhere because, as far as Jacob could recall, the vehicle never stopped to let anybody out. No, he figured, they must have been hiding in a nearby vehicle. And they signaled the Lincoln to chase him out of the garage.

Immediately Jacob heard some sort of announcement in Spanish that confused him. "Evacuate the garage!" a voice finally blared in English from a loudspeaker. "This is a drill. You must leave now. Do not use the elevator. Do not panic. Follow the stairwell to the exit below." The voice sounded robotic, computer-generated, somewhat official to Jacob's weary mind, though he wasn't about to trust anybody here. A siren blared. He thought it might be the police. "Good." He felt relieved, if only temporarily. No, he wouldn't use the stairwell. They might ambush him there. He continued to as run as fast as he could, keeping to the sides of the descending ramps as the Lincoln followed his trail, now even closer, within at least ten feet of him.

As he got to the exit, the burly man in the booth was nowhere to be seen, but Ortiz was there, not far from the limousine, craning his neck and body to see what all the frenzied noises he could hear from inside were about. Jacob got to the entrance of the garage, his arms flailing, and he motioned Ortiz to get into the car and move fast, just as the speeding Lincoln exited in the other direction.

"Go, go, go!" he yelled to Ortiz, who sped into a U-turn to trail the car that Jacob had thought was following him but was speeding ahead. Jacob careened back and forth in the rear seat, barely catching his balance or his breath. Sweat poured from his brows, and his shirt was wet. He removed tissues from a box and dabbed his forehead. He was resolved to find out who was driving that monster vehicle and where it was headed. He even thought about turning around and driving into that garage to find those men who'd destroyed Esau's car. But what was the point? The car was clean, and those hoodlums might be armed. Better to be outside, he reasoned, chasing crooks on the open road, rather than return to the third level of a parking garage, where any cry for help would never be heard. Still, he had the daylights scared out of him. He wasn't about to tolerate this kind of assault on his life.

"What happened, señor?" Ortiz inquired, excitedly.

"I don't know. Those crazy guys chased me out of the garage. Just keep following them."

"Oh, señor. We are losing them. You are lucky you did escape."

"I've got to find out what the hell is going on here."

"Sí, Señor Rose."

"Catch up to them."

"Señor, I cannot drive any faster. I think it is dangerous to find them. We should; we go to the police, no?"

"No."

"You don't want to report this to the police?"

"Later," he said anxiously, all very confused. "We have an appointment at the museum to meet with the director. I need to think about this. Head back to the hotel."

"Sí, señor. As you wish."

Ortiz pulled up to the hotel entrance and Jacob flew out of the car, telling the driver he'd be down in twenty minutes with Trumball.

Passing through the hotel lobby, he tried to collect himself, smoothing his hair, and dabbing his forehead again with the few dry tissues he still held in his hand, but his shirt remained drenched. He'd have to change his clothes, now thoroughly wrinkled. His appointment with Señor Mendoza, the museum director, was only a half hour away, and he prayed that Trumball would be ready and waiting for him upstairs.

So far, Buenos Aires felt inhospitable, even dangerous. "Damn that brother of mine. What had Esau been up to? Why would he have done business with Bertha Lavazzo in the first place? Esau must have known how dilapidated her gallery was. What was his connection to the five men who ransacked his Lincoln? Had someone been out to get Esau? A former lover, perhaps?"

Jacob thought about Esau's sexual preference as a possible clue to this puzzle. He wouldn't rule out anything, though. Not now, especially when he wondered whether he had become the target of Esau's legacy. He needed a drink, and possibly days to think through his situation, yet he had only minutes before his next appointment.

Jacob swept into his room to find Raquel sitting with Laban Trumball. At six feet four with a slight hump on his back from osteoporosis, a hawkish nose, and unkempt, thinning gray hair, the artist looked like every one of his eighty-eight years. Trumball and the actress seemed to be watching television.

"Maestro. Why do you insist on watching the television without sound?" she asked.

Trumball scowled. "I don't watch TV. I watch colors and shapes."

Normally Trumball's remark would have amused Jacob, but the events of this day had left him humorless.

Raquel looked on as he unsteadily poured a glass of white wine. "Darling, what's happened?" she cried out. "You look so ... so, on edge."

He paused. "I visited Bertha's gallery, a flytrap if ever I saw one. Oh, she offered me some very revealing news. Her assistant poured me three shots of whiskey. At least I think it was three. After that, I was forced to run for my life, chased by a speeding Lincoln through three levels of a parking garage. Yeah, that about sums it up," he said sarcastically. "How was your day?"

"You were what?" Raquel asked. Trumball continued to watch his soundless television, oblivious to the conversation.

"Just what I said."

"You were chased ... by a car?"

"I'll tell you all about it later!"

"Don't be angry with me."

"I'm not angry with you."

"You're yelling at me. Please don't do that."

"I don't have time now. We have an appointment with Mendoza, the museum director. That is, after all, why we're here. The big celebration. Isn't that right, old man?"

"Don't go disappearing on me again," Trumball snapped. "I've been sitting here waiting for you."

Raquel ignored Trumball's remark. "Please, don't talk to me like that. Don't dismiss me." She whispered, not wanting to stir an argument.

"My brother mentioned the 9th of July 1970 to me a while back. In New York." Jacob didn't feel he was lying, even if he had fabricated Esau's verbal statement.

"Don't get upset. Calmly please," Raquel pleaded.

"I know. I thought it was a day of the year, an anniversary, birthday or something.

"Nueve de Julio?"

"Yes. I learned it was an address for a parking garage, here in Buenos Aires."

"How?"

"Because he told me the date. He mentioned a new car he'd bought. I figured that that might have had some relevance to his having lived here."

"Why didn't you tell me about this before?"

"I don't know. I didn't think it was important. So I went there. To the garage. After visiting Bertha's gallery."

Puzzled for the moment, Raquel asked, "Would Bertha have stirred your thinking?"

"Yes. Just let me continue."

"I'm sorry."

"When I found Esau's car, thugs peeled out from nowhere. They chased me away, down the ramp, and ransacked the car."

"My God."

"They destroyed it. This brand-new car."

"You interrupted a robbery."

"I don't know."

"Did you contact the police? My goodness. Are you okay?"

"I'm not okay. I must get the old man to the museum."

"Please, Jacob, let me get you something to eat. You're probably hungry, aren't you?" She spoke nonstop, hugged him with a gentle squeeze, and showered him with tiny kisses.

Trying to bring some order into his chaotic universe, he turned to her. "Don't worry about me. I'm okay."

"No, you're not! Don't play the macho tough guy with me."

"Honey, please. Trust me. I'm fine. I can handle this." Jacob still wouldn't reveal the note or its contents. For whatever it was worth, he was holding onto a piece of Esau that he'd chosen not to share with anyone else. "Look, Trumball and I have an appointment to meet with Mendoza. I said that, didn't I?"

"I must call Juan Domingo" Raquel insisted. She glanced at Trumball, who hadn't flinched in his attention to the TV.

"Don't bother him with this."

"If we are his guests, he should look into this and see about our safety." Raquel pressed the digits to General De Solis' compound. She asked for the general, who quickly got on the phone. They spoke in Spanish, but she interrupted the conversation to ask Jacob if he had recognized any faces. He told her no, that they'd worn ski masks and that it all had happened very quickly. "Juan Domingo wants to know if you saw anything in the car, such as evidence of any kind or anything that would make you suspicious. Anything, darling. Think hard, please."

He shook his head no. "The car was totally empty."

She repeated, "Esau left behind an empty car. There was nothing in the automobile." They spoke for another moment in Spanish. She turned toward Jacob. "He agrees that you might have interrupted a robbery. Just bad luck. Oh, you could have been hurt. Thank your lucky stars. I'm so sorry that this had to be your introduction to Buenos Aires." Raquel touched her lips and hung up the phone, assuring Jacob that General De Solis would check into the matter.

"It happens," he said. "Shit happens. I'm lucky, I suppose." Jacob couldn't believe that the garage episode was chance, nor the robbery scenario, not when the letter referred to that address.

Raquel hugged him again.

CHAPTER ELEVEN

More and more U.S. Secret Service personnel, accessorized with earpieces and aviator glasses, crowded the hotel lobby awaiting POTUS' arrival. "Sunday, seventy-two hours to Trumball's gala, and a president on a mission to Buenos Aires," thought Jacob. Tight security made him feel both uneasy and secure, and at moments he wished for Monday. Jacob straightened the old man's collar before pushing him through the revolving lobby doors. It was 3:15 and they were on their way to a meeting with the museum's curator.

Ortiz quickly sprung from the limousine's driver's seat, where he'd been patiently waiting, and held the rear passenger door for them. "And the lady?" he asked, looking around.

"She's relaxing," said Jacob quickly. *And the lady?* He turned the phrase over in his mind as the car drove off.

He grabbed the phone and called Raquel. "I'm sorry for being such an asshole. Are you okay?"

"Yes, I'm okay. Don't apologize. You have nothing to be sorry about. You could have been hurt. Are you sure you're okay?"

He scrunched his lips to make the sound of a kiss, self-conscious, in front of two gawking spectators. Hearing her voice lifted his spirits.

He readily admitted to himself after only a few weeks into their relationship that Raquel was a major part of his life. Last month at a performance of *Tosca,* by the Metropolitan Opera Company on the Great Lawn in Central Park, she had asked a question that he still wrestled with. "Do you love me, or are you in love with me?" He remained puzzled for the moment and recalled answering, "I am in love with you."

"Oh, that's your answer," she said, smiling seductively at him. He remembered vividly now how he had felt a stirring, gut-wrenching affection for the first time in years for a woman he wanted. That evening in the park, she wore a lipstick red dress that clung to her gorgeous body, and her brown hair, pulled back with white barrettes shaped like roses, floated above her shoulders.

Jacob asked what her response meant. She lifted her shoulders and told him she didn't know, but hoped he could distinguish between the two. He rubbed her leg, and she snuggled next to him. He felt his heart going out to her.

Trumball interrupted his thoughts. "So the big shot New York art dealer is a romantic, after all."

Ahead of them, the museum of the Moderns of Buenos Aires, a columnar, classical building, an architectural treasure to the glory of Argentine civility, stood as a proud fortress of South American culture. When the car drove up and Jacob poked his head through the window, the director, a man with lacquered, brown hair and a manicured mustache, hurried to greet them. The director appeared slick in a dark blue pinstripe suit. "Check out our Argentine Gatsby," Jacob nudged the old man.

"I'm Señor Reuben Mendoza," the man said to Trumball, whose arms opened wide for an embrace.

Mendoza led them through a grand hall within an atrium of several stories. Silver lamé balloons like gigantic plastic pillows already floated amid the arched ceiling in preparation for the Trumball gala. The main rotunda was enormous. Large windows looked onto lush gardens of tropical trees and gigantic sculptures by Henry Moore. Nudes by DeKooning and Trumball hung on the broad white walls below.

The trio entered Mendoza's office on the second level and on the right side of the atrium—a geometric room with Bauhaus furnishings and several rare daguerreotypes by Atget and Nadir on the walls. "Gentlemen, shall we drink an afternoon sherry while we discuss the arrangements?" the director asked.

Jacob nodded. He was captivated by Mendoza's aesthetic. He hadn't seen so many good, modernist pieces assembled in one room since he'd visited a colleague during the art fair last summer in Basel.

"You must approve what we have planned. Sí?" Mendoza said.

"Excellent," toasted Trumball, who seldom if ever drank anything but vodka and held onto the glass of sherry awkwardly.

"You'll arrange to bring the painting here later? Or did you bring it with you, Señor Rose?"

"Later. First, I'm showing the painting at the house of some friends, hosting a private party for Mr. Trumball."

"The cocktail party at Señorita Gingold's parents' home tomorrow evening?"

"Indeed," Jacob said.

"I shall be there." Mendoza directed their attention to his desk as he unfolded a large layout sheet for the dance in the hall of the rotunda. The plans called for a dais installed in front of a large wall that would feature an enormous black-and-white portrait of Trumball photographed ten years ago by Richard Avedon for an essay on the artist that ran in *The New Yorker*. A small, revolving platform would sit in the center of the hall. After the luncheon and various welcoming remarks, the painting would be lowered from the ceiling, along with two huge canvasses—early works of Trumball's on loan to the museum from De Solis' collection. Mendoza explained how he wanted Trumball to stand under *Lea with Two Love-Apples* as it was lowered, catch it, and then turn it for all to see.

"Elaborate, isn't it?" Jacob pictured Trumball spinning on a carousel in an amusement park. Just the medicine he needed to take his mind away from his run-in earlier with thugs at the parking garage.

"For Señor Trumball and *Lea with Two Love-Apples*,—a ceremony worthy of his greatness. Before the painting is lowered," the director continued, "I've arranged for all lights to be extinguished. Señor Rose, you will lead the artist to the stage in the dark. We will have safety lights in place to assist you.

"Once you have reached the platform, the orchestra will begin to play Sir Edward Elgar's 'Pomp and Circumstance.' Then, a pin spotlight will focus on Señor Trumball while the painting is lowered into his hands. I'm sure Señor Trumball will get a standing and thunderous ovation."

"I'm impressed." The old man stood, bowing clumsily, as so many Americans do when greeting Japanese business people. "I accept your plan gratefully, Señor Mendoza." With that said, Trumball placed his untouched sherry on the desk.

"Señor," Mendoza turned to Jacob, "it will be your responsibility to introduce the artist from the dais. There will be several prominent speakers before you."

"I'll be prepared with a speech."

Mendoza outlined the menu: "Sliced melon, chilled cream of cucumber soup, whole wheat baked lasagna with spinach, and then an assortment of cheeses with a fine port wine, a choice of four sorbets, and magnums of champagne to flow freely throughout the luncheon." He smiled intently as he offered up this grocery list of details. "After the luncheon, we will have dancing to the Lopicito Orchestra and a special tango performance by Ilde Pirovana and Diego DeSota as part of the festivities," Mendoza beamed. "And a chorus will also perform."

Jacob felt good for the old man, who soaked up this moment of international praise that for too long had eluded him. As he expected, Mendoza already had assigned reporters and photographers to cover the gala at the museum.

"It would be great, wouldn't it, to get our president here with Trumball? What a photo op. We would be in the footage of every news organization in the world," Jacob said.

Mendoza hesitated, then nodded. "Concepto occurrencia, señor. I've already invited your president through your ambassador, but they have not given me a definite answer."

"You're ahead of me. Good thinking." Jacob smiled. He relished the picture of the artist shaking the hands with the president of the United States.

"A toast to Argentina." Trumball raised his glass.

Trumball hadn't always been this outgoing. He'd been diagnosed with clinical depression years ago. When he jumped ship to the Rose Gallery, Trumball confided to Jacob that he'd feigned depression simply to get out of his contract with the Leopold Katz gallery. Ironically, he'd descended into an actual depression shortly after signing with Jacob. To lift Trumball's spirits, Jacob had rounded up his younger artists and students from NYU, Cooper-Union, Parsons, and the like, inviting them to storytelling evenings at Trumball's bedside, where the artist had remained most days, miserable and glum.

Trumball had come to enjoy the attention and to instruct younger painters in his ways of seeing. He had reminisced about the great painters he'd hung out with in Montparnasse in the '30s and with a then young DeKooning and Pollack in New York in the '50s. Jacob had kept those evenings alive for the next few years, restoring Trumball's sense of purpose. The result: the artist had begun to paint with a fury, resulting in six brilliant pieces that were now in the Guggenheim's permanent collection.

"One more thing," the director said. "As you know, the luncheon honoring Señor Trumball will be a black-tie affair."

Jacob bit his tongue. "Yes, of course. For Señor Trumball. A black-tie luncheon."

CHAPTER TWELVE

When the two returned from the museum, Smith approached them in the hotel lobby. "General De Solis has urgent business to discuss."

"What's so urgent?" Jacob felt that events might not go as smoothly as he had hoped.

Raquel joined the group

Jacob had not yet met General De Solis, though they had talked over the phone and had communicated through e-mails to finalize the sale of the Trumball painting. His gut feeling about the general was not positive. Regardless, Jacob wanted something much more than a comfortable feeling from the man. He knew that when he shook De Solis' hand and received final payment, he would smile and forgive the man's insolence, for he would have sold a painting for the largest sum ever for a living artist.

"This way, please." Smith escorted them to the rear of the hotel's Cardinale Ristorante. General Juan Domingo De Solis sat in a corner booth. When they approached, De Solis stood to give them all a slight bow before embracing Raquel. There were no smiles or handshakes as Smith introduced Jacob and the artist to the general.

De Solis stared broodingly and with a menacing intensity. "I must have the painting no later than half an hour from now, and in my possession for the next seventy-two hours." He spoke unmistakably.

Jacob's back tightened at a demand issued no more than ten seconds after introductions were made and before he was seated. "With all due respect, sir, there are additional considerations."

"Which additional considerations?"

"We'd discussed that the transfer would occur after the reception at Raquel's parents' house and after the gala at the museum."

General De Solis shook his head. "No, no." He quickly looked around to ensure nobody was listening in. "The urgency of the situation forces me to come to the point. There is coded information about a military coup, written on the back of the canvas. I will return the painting in time for the museum gala. I assure you my meetings begin immediately. Secret meetings, I might add."

"Coded information?" Jacob queried, baffled at what he'd just heard.

Trumball suddenly perked up.

"Juan Domingo, what are you telling Jacob?" Raquel asked.

"On the back of the painting, in the same lines as your artist's meandering shapes, colors, and numbers, is a list in code of names of renegade Argentine military officers. Rebels are plotting to overthrow the leadership in my country. These scoundrels will detract attention by an attempted assassination of your president."

Jacob could hardly believe what he heard. "What will you do?"

"Stop them. The code on the painting includes location coordinates. We won't know where these men are positioned until, and I repeat—until—we break the code."

The art dealer leaned back. "You're joking, right?"

"No, he's not," Smith said.

Jacob gave Smith an odd look. "Then maybe I'm not following."

"Your brother infiltrated certain rebel groups. We believe he secured the information and placed it back of the Trumball canvas, before he took his own life," Smith said.

Jacob remained silent for several seconds. "This is some kind of a sick joke."

"I'm most serious, Señor Rose" the general responded.

"Then why don't you just talk to the Secret Service agents. They're hanging out all over this damn restaurant." Jacob pointed to several agents lounging at the bar.

"I said these rebels are planning a military coup. To cover their tracks they will fake—yes, fake an assassination of your president to create chaos and seize power."

"Why should I believe you?"

"In the first place, it is my painting."

"Not until your final payment is presented," Jacob corrected.

"Maybe these murdering officers are not so stupid. Maybe when they use your president's arrival as a cover for their coup, their trickery will succeed." The general's eyes grew fierce; his violent temper was beginning to stir itself. "Your president is about to land in our country. There are soldiers on the rooftops."

"And you want me to accept this bag of shit."

"Soldiers, I will add, who are disloyal to the Argentine government. They take orders from certain military personnel whose names may be listed on that painting."

"You want to steal the painting, that's what I'm thinking, General De Solis." Jacob grew even more annoyed. "You've invented this story."

"Jacob," Raquel pleaded, "what is the harm in helping Juan Domingo?"

"You can bring the copy that I own to her parents' home." The general paused, looking at Raquel now.

Jacob's face lit up, as his anger flared. "You're telling me that you have a forgery?" Jacob knew now that his earlier suspicions were justified.

"Sí, Señor Rose."

"I don't believe this." *Was Esau indeed involved with forgeries and blackmail?*

"I will give you the forged canvas. I'll return the original in plenty of time for the museum celebration," De Solis promised. "I am asking you to commit only a little act of deception."

"A little deception?" Jacob turned and frowned at Smith

"For a short while," said Smith

"There's a fake *Lea with Two Love-Apples*? Do you hear that old man?"

"I've heard everything!" Trumball snapped.

"Well, then, you understand what General De Solis is attempting here. He wants to steal your work."

Trumball stared at the general for a moment. "Let me see the forgery. Are there others? Jacob, if this gets out I'll be a laughing stock for switching over to your gallery."

"So much for loyalty for working to revive your career as an artist. And I'll be ruined."

"Esau was playing games," said the general.

Jacob stood suddenly. "I won't get involved in this deception."

"I must have the real painting immediately to decipher the entire code," De Solis snapped.

"May I suggest, General De Solis, that you go to the American Embassy and tell them immediately about your assassination theory?" Jacob made up his mind. He would not give up the painting to a crook.

A hush fell when the waiter came over to fill their glasses with water and to take their orders. Smith waved him away. Jacob was shaking his head, thinking back to the day Esau told him about this deal to sell the Trumball painting. He jumped on it then. "What a pile of shit I have stepped in to," he thought.

Raquel leaned over to touch Jacob's hand. "I know Juan Domingo. He is telling the truth. Jacob, the portenos, our local citizens love him."

He fixed an angry stare on Raquel. "I understand that you trust him. But I don't."

"Why are so stubborn!" Trumball said flatly.

"Take these facts, General, to the proper authorities. I gave up a chance to sell the painting in New York only to go through this spectacle. I was duped. I'll take my losses and move on."

De Solis leaned across the table almost in Jacob's face. "I don't enjoy repeating myself. I have a forgery of the painting, señor. An excellent forgery, which we will exchange."

"Did you know anything about this?" Jacob asked Raquel.

"No."

"Take General De Solis' offer," Smith said.

"I am asking you as politely as is possible to switch the fake with the original. That is what I must have you do," the general demanded.

"That's all you'll have to do. It's that simple," Smith added.

"Your president's Air Force One is on the television now," De Solis observed. "Look, Señor Rose." He pointed to the large projection television above the bar. "Will you help me, and help history? My thoughts are for saving your president's life. This is my agenda now."

"My painting will save the president from an assassin's bullet. Where is your patriotism, Jacob?" Trumball grunted.

"I won't step into subterfuge."

"We'll meet back here, one half hour from now," De Solis ordered. "I strongly urge you to consider my proposal."

"Let's get out of here, Raquel. This place stinks." Jacob's neck turned red as he reminded himself that although De Solis wore a uniform, he held no real power.

When they left, De Solis spoke calmly. "Do you think I've persuaded him?"

"Maybe," Smith said. "You've got a strange formula for getting results."

"He will agree. I promise you."

"And what if Jacob is a partner with Esau and there is no code?"

"We'll get Jacob to lead us to the money."

"And if he doesn't cooperate?"

"Then you will kill him."

Smith nodded and glanced at the general. "We'll wait for them to return."

CHAPTER THIRTEEN

The elevators to their suites were at the opposite end of the lobby. Bellmen with new arrivals hovered around them. Trumball leaned against the wall. He had absorbed the setting in the restaurant a moment ago with General De Solis, but now after hearing both sides, De Solis' and Jacob's, he could no longer hold back.

"If my painting will save the life of the president of the United States, then we will cooperate."

Jacob shrugged. For the moment, he didn't know whether to laugh or cry. "Laban Trumball, American Patriot." He tossed his hands up, not yet prepared to yield to the inanity. "When this all turns out to be a scam, who then will guarantee my business. Who will guarantee my profit and my life?"

"I will," Trumball said. "Raquel is my witness. You can keep all the money from the next two sales of any of my works. How's that? Your crazy brother created this mess. Your crazy, son-of-a-bitch brother. He forged my paintings. I give you my word that you won't suffer any financial loss."

"This doesn't solve my problem. Or yours."

"I'm offering money. You deal with the shit."

"And if other forgeries pop up?"

"Why ask me? I didn't instigate fakes."

Jacob walked a few feet away from them and stood beside a Regency scroll desk with a glass vase holding a large display of white tulips. Above the desk, he readily recognized a mahogany, framed, seventeenth-century Flemish landscape. He detested playing games of duplicity. Jacob's inherent abilities had been in the art of the sale, decisive and direct. Whenever he brought a client up to his office for a final decision, he'd always sit up straight behind his desk—yes, the painting of Big Bertha above him—and spoke with an excitement about the canvas in hand with bursts of enthusiasm. Jacob was shaking his head as he approached them, hardly able to believe himself. "I'm consenting to this deception because of her," he replied pointing to Raquel.

"I'm sure it's the right decision," Raquel said. They walked briskly past groups of onlookers, back toward the restaurant. Trumball traipsed behind. He held his head high, as they approached the table from which they'd so hurriedly fled only moments before. De Solis stood as rigid as a defendant does, waiting for the foreman to announce the jury's verdict.

"Be seated, everybody," Trumball said. He slowly eased into the booth.

"Can I refresh your drink?" Smith asked.

"Of course," the artist mumbled. "May I remind you, Señor General, that you were imprisoned for horrible crimes during your junta period? I know history."

"I've been pardoned by my president. I admitted that what we did was wrong. We chose an inept policy for Argentina. I admitted that."

"Yes. Yes. And you are working for justice?"

"I'm working to right the wrongs committed by military officers who have murdered my countrymen."

"Why should we believe you?" Jacob interrupted.

"I'll explain for him," said the artist. "My *Lea* painting will get worldwide recognition. General De Solis believes there is information on the back of the canvas, Jacob, that will save lives, prevent murder." Trumball placed his hand on Jacob's arm. "I believe the general. Don't be stubborn."

Jacob met this prospect with complete disgust. "You see those men in nicely pressed suits? Earpieces in place? These agents are receiving messages, instructions from their superiors. This isn't the time to keep silent if an assassination attempt is even hinted at!"

"We're here to help you, Señor General. My painting is at the center of this historic moment. Let's keep to the main subject of this meeting." Trumball knocked back a shot of vodka and turned to Jacob.

"You are so correct. Your assessment of our situation, Maestro, is ... you hit a bull's-eye," De Solis said.

"You're a money-grubbing son of a bitch." Trumball glared at Jacob. Raquel gasped. "You would think differently, Jake, if you were a creative person. No. I don't think you have a creative bone in your body. General De Solis is offering you the chance to change history."

Jacob glared at Raquel, incredulous at what he heard. "Creative people," Jacob mimicked, "have not been the ones to take up arms against oppression. They write, they paint. That's what they do!"

"I'm sorry, darling. That was a mean thing for me to say. But you are not a creative person."

"Bring the painting downstairs in five minutes," De Solis commanded.

"We won't have to go up for the painting," Jacob replied. "It's in the safe at the front desk."

"My bodyguards will escort you. The car is waiting for you at a side exit." De Solis moved quickly. As he passed certain tables, several bodyguards jumped to his side and followed him out with Smith. De Solis drove back with several guards to the compound in an armored Hummer. Jacob, the old man, and Raquel walked out of the restaurant escorted by an armada of six burly Argentines. Jacob stopped at the front desk. "My film container," he told the desk clerk. "Of course, Señor Rose. Here it is," the clerk said, after opening a locked cabinet under the desk.

Within moments, they were inside the car. The darkened windows of the general's Bentley hid their identities. An aide handed each of them black hoods. Jacob clutched at the film canister containing *Lea with Two Love-Apples* rolled neatly up inside.

He said nothing. Raquel curled up beside him.

"Wear these hoods over your heads," a bodyguard ordered as they approached the gates to the villa. "We're entering a secret location on the general's grounds."

"Well, you can forget about me wearing this," said Jacob.

"Mr. Rose, we'd appreciate your cooperation," the driver called out.

"Listen, Jake, you agreed to the exchange. Now put the damn thing on your head," Trumball snapped.

The car pulled off to the side of the road and progressed no further. The dismay with which Jacob donned his hood persisted as they approached the villa in Palermo Chico. It sat on area as large as Central Park. With hoods on, they entered the compound through the electric gate. The Bentley moved up a long driveway, then swerved right and stopped short. They backed up a bit. Soon, Jacob felt the car descend as if into a huge elevator. When its movement halted, a bell sounded and they exited the car. They were led into a vast underground room, where soldiers removed their hoods.

De Solis, leaning against a huge rectangular table in the center of the room, greeted them. He spoke quietly and methodically. "You are a gentleman, Señor Rose. I congratulate you."

"Yes. Do me one great favor."

"And what is that Señor Rose?"

"Make sure your code analysts are careful with the painting."

"We will be extremely careful, I assure you." Jacob handed De Solis the film canister. The general handed Jacob the forged painting and a large brown envelope.

Later the trio sat in the Bentley again, their hoods in place. Smith rode up front with the driver. "Don't open the envelope until you're in your suite."

Jacob wondered if there was money in the envelope.

At the hotel a half hour later, Trumball unzipped the black garment bag that held the painting, while Jacob poured himself a tumbler filled with vodka over ice.

Trumball held the phony painting up to the light that poured in from the window. "Esau knew my every stroke. Damn, he was a genius."

"My brother was a crook, not a genius."

"I painted this over years. Hard-working years. Layer upon layer. Erasing, painting over early sketches and lines, and he forges it instantly like … like…." Trumball was gasping for air in his enthusiasm. "Do you think he faked much of my work?"

"No, Trumball." Jacob opened the manila envelope. It contained instructions, precise timetables, and a set of phone numbers. He thumbed through the envelope, noting two small packets. One was marked, "Open in the event of the death of General De Solis." The other packet held two pills and an inscription, "Swallow if captured."

Trumball sniffed the pills. "Cyanide, Jake. Flush them down the toilet. Here, give it to me."

"Let's get the hell out here," Jacob said. "The situation is crazy. Let's get in the car and leave for the airport." Jacob stared blankly out the window and at clock tower across the way. The giant hands of the clock atop the lit-up red brick building pointed down, reading six thirty-two. The scene he noted, men with machine guns on building roofs and on patrol in the street, was commonplace now. A shadowy figure stood in front of the clock hands with a pair of binoculars pointed toward their window. In another time, in any other place, he might have thought more soberly, but logic was nowhere to be found in Buenos Aires. Had this been New York, he would have called the FBI, the Art Dealers League, the police, and the media. He would not have tolerated any of this nonsense. But this wasn't New York. This was a city not his own, where he had no influence. He wasn't on the A-list here. All he could do now was to listen anxiously to the whirling sound of a couple of cyanide tablets that the artist flushed down the toilet. Minutes later, he looked across the room. Trumball was fast asleep.

Raquel stood beside him, her arm in his.

"Are you a part of De Solis' plot, too?" he asked.

"No, darling, of course I'm not."

"Did you have any clue as to what De Solis wanted?"

"I never suspected a thing."

"He's nuts if he thinks I'm going along with this."

"You already have. And he's not nuts, I assure you."

"And what about Esau?" Jacob walked back into the large room. Raquel followed. "Was he murdered by De Solis?"

"Don't talk foolishly, darling."

"Why is it foolish? Why are you so trusting?"

"Esau's death isn't on De Solis' hands."

"Do you know that for a fact?"

"No, but I know JD is sincere."

"You're siding with him, Raquel."

"I understand why you're suspicious, but you must trust me."

Jacob's jaw tightened. "How do I know this isn't a trick?"

"Would you feel better if it were?"

"Raquel, this is a frightening situation." She said nothing for what seemed an eternity and walked over to a dresser. She took her hair down. "Jacob, we're safe. I know my own country."

"Nobody's safe now. Let's get the hell out of here. Out of the hotel. Away from Buenos Aires. Out of Argentina."

"Are you without a shred of courage?"

"Damn it, no."

"Why are you running?"

"This isn't a test of my courage.

"I believe it is."

Jacob shook his head. "No. No. It seems in Argentina all you talk about is that I will be tested. For what? This is just New Age shit."

The silence between them heightened the sound of whirring sirens below.

Raquel stared vacantly. "Yes, you're being tested. Maybe for once you'll have to square things with yourself. Jacob?"

"What? What are you trying to say?"

"You're in the middle of this now, so open yourself up the events surrounding you."

"Damn it, Raquel. I'm not into this poetry crap. I'm being asked to pass a fake onto a major museum. Think about that for a moment."

Raquel turned to him with an incredulous look. "You're missing the point."

"What point? And if I go through with this charade, what are my chances of selling to the Modern in New York? It won't matter when I'm sent to prison, will it?"

Raquel sat brushing her hair. "You can only go along with them."

"What are you telling me?"

"JD is a powerful man." Jacob didn't respond. "Esau was a colleague of Juan Domingo and Smith," Raquel went on.

He looked directly at Raquel's reflection in the mirror as if trying to read her mind. "Are you trying to taunt me? Let's get the hell out of Argentina."

"I thought you were a fighter."

She got up and walked away, avoiding his glance.

"This is real life, not a film location." Jacob wiped his forehead with a breakfast napkin that still lay on the table. "You know, deep down, I believe he devised this plot to steal the painting. That is my feeling. I can't change how I feel. Those are my instincts. De Solis is a con man."

"Do you trust me at all?"

He was silent.

"Don't you trust me?" Raquel asked again, as she took his hand and led him to the sofa. Tears filled her eyes. "I would never deceive you, darling."

"I'm not much for politics that aren't mine."

"I respect history. What this means to me, darling, is that we must believe in what Juan Domingo is doing."

"I don't see it. I know he's an old friend, but he's a con artist."

"No, Jacob, he definitely is not."

Jacob paused. Did he trust her? She'd withheld the truths about Esau. Now he had to consider the ramifications of following through with De Solis' plan. Would De Solis complete his mission to decode the canvas in time to swap the fake for the original? Jacob confronted the prospect of presenting a forgery to the museum. No, he had little time to dwell on that occurrence. He was determined to break whatever hidden message was contained in his yellow sheet of paper that he held in his jacket pocket. He was convinced that Esau's note was a code of sorts.

"I need time by myself," he told her. He went down to the hotel bar, leaving Trumball's snores to serenade Raquel.

CHAPTER FOURTEEN

Jacob sat in the lounge flipping through the day's international edition of the *New York Times,* but his mind was on Esau. *So, his brother had a secret identity,* Jacob thought. *Why didn't I know of his? What happened to Esau in Nam and Cambodia?* He came to no conclusions and returned to the suite almost an hour later to change into his tuxedo for tonight's dinner party with General De Solis. Trumball, refreshed from his earlier nap, knocked on their door. He already was dressed for the evening, wearing a slightly bedraggled tuxedo that played down the hump on his back. The old man walked straight ahead to the balcony, stretching his long, gangly legs as he sat and absorbed the river breezes. Jacob joined him. They waited for Raquel. The two didn't speak, but seemed to prefer to remain with their own thoughts. Jacob got up, walked to the balcony's railing and glanced at the avenues beyond. Soon enough it was 9:00 p.m., and street activity increased.

Because Buenos Aires is much like a European city, its dinner activities begin later in the evening than in New York. People below didn't rush. Strollers moved in and out of coffee houses or browsed through bookstores on Avenida Corrientes. The night air smelled of a mixture of diesel fuel and brewed coffee. Breezes wafted leisurely, slowing people's pace, it seemed to Jacob, and lulling them into quiet walks.

Raquel stood in the doorway, resplendent in her black Versace. Her hair was pulled tight, secured by a bun that held a single, fragrant red rose. Jacob smiled and winked. "You look damn good," he said, and poked the old man to get up out of his chair.

Downstairs Ortiz waited and held door to the limo, then whisked them away to the Recoleto barrio.

With its neo-Impressionist paintings, maroon velvet banquettes, soft candle lighting, and antique cutlery, the restaurant on Vincente Lopez was a particular favorite of General De Solis. At 10 p.m. on the first evening of their four-day holiday, and in the last banquette along a corridor of similar seating, Raquel and Jacob were seated opposite Smith and De Solis for the dinner engagement that Jacob now rued. Trumball anchored one end of the booth, and Bertha Lavazzo, ablaze in a fiery red taffeta dress that fell to the floor, occupied the other. Jacob fidgeted at his seat, facing De Solis and Smith, still obsessing over his capitulation to the general, whom he now despised as a diabolical tyrant who forced a fiction on them in order to swap the canvases. Raquel, seated to Jacob's left, tried to counter the tension as best as she could. She talked about Buenos Aires, its nightlife, and its fine restaurants, to lighten the mood. Jacob was unmoved, even as De Solis—bedecked in full military garb with decorations and in contrast to the other men in black ties—bestowed an amiable but singular focus on Jacob's lady friend.

"Señor Mendoza told me that you approved all his arrangements in your honor," De Solis said. The artist nodded.

"You must feel proud," said Smith, looking directly at Jacob. Without his sunglasses on, Smith's eyes were large and a vivid smoky blue.

"I'll feel better when this is over," Jacob replied.

"He can't get over the fake you gave him," Trumball said

"Señor Rose, you are not wrong to feel the way you do," De Solis said.

"I prefer truth to lies"

"If you want my personal opinion...."

"You'll pardon my manners but frankly, I don't want any more opinions," Jacob said.

"I think that you are too hard on yourself, Señor Rose."

"Enough with opinions. We're already engaged in this deception."

"You will come to realize that you are a hero for doing what you've done," De Solis continued, ignoring Jacob's conclusions.

"What fake are we talking about?" Bertha asked.

"The painting that Esau delivered through you to General De Solis," Smith said.

"Was it a forgery?" Bertha sounded almost genuine, though Jacob mistrusted her. She had to be in on this, he thought. And he intended to get her to fess up about Esau in due time.

"Señor Mendoza has told me that three hundred people will attend the celebration," De Solis added.

"Quite an honor, Maestro," Raquel said.

"My experts hope to break the code shortly. I assure you that this will take place in time for the reception honoring Señor Trumball." De Solis folded his arms in front of him.

Bertha, who sat nervously throughout much of the conversation, suddenly announced to the table, "All the right people are aware of this honor, Señor Trumball."

"Why is that any source of comfort?" asked Jacob.

Bertha replied resolutely. "Laban, you'll be fêted for the significant artist that you are."

De Solis gave an odd look as he addressed the table, glaring at each of his guests." Allow me to add two things. One, it is best, not to mention the codes to anyone outside of the people at this table."

"And what's the other?" Jacob asked.

"That this evening," De Solis paused, "we celebrate! Salud."

"Bertha this also applies to you," Smith warned.

Raquel massaged Jacob's arm, looking into his eyes. The waiters refilled their wine glasses. With every refill of his wine, Jacob ordered a shot of vodka, while Trumball requested doubles. "To Raquel and her film project," Jacob said easily, resigned as he was to get through the dinner.

"Salud!" General De Solis raised his glass, and everyone followed again.

Jacob turned eagerly to Raquel. "How do you plan to portray the general?" Raquel was producing a film on the junta period, "the dirty wars," and the "disappeared ones." De Solis had volunteered to be her technical advisor.

"According to history."

Bertha fidgeted her thick fingers around the base of her wine glass. She probably knew that Jacob would press her for what she knew about

Esau's participation in their collusive business of art forgery. For now, she chose to ignore him.

"Well, you'll have to extend the story line," said Jacob.

"I don't understand," Raquel said.

"Well, the old man's painting here has played an important role in U.S. and Argentine politics."

"Jacob, you are well aware that the film is about the 'disappeared people,' who were rounded up by the former fascist regime. Many were murdered, many tortured, never to be heard from again. It isn't a subject for sarcasm. And my film is not about today's events."

De Solis acknowledged his upcoming role and turned his attention toward the large room, receiving the nods and hand movements from various patrons who appeared to be eavesdropping. "Get Señor Mendoza on the phone," he ordered Smith. "It would be good to invite the president, if security permits."

As Smith rang up Mendoza at home, De Solis took the phone to speak to him in Spanish. Jacob watched Raquel smile, as if these circumstances were entirely normal. He understood only the word *presidente*, and he suddenly felt as if a conspiracy had been perpetrated against him.

"Which president?" asked Jacob.

"My president, of course," De Solis said. "I cannot speak for the American government. Señor Mendoza has assured me that everything has been taken care of, and if our president isn't able to attend, your ambassador will make a special presentation to Señor Trumball. To the artist. Salud!"

Suddenly Raquel, Smith, and Bertha joined the general in applause as the old man gave a seated bow, missing the salad placed before him by a hair. Waiters scurried about carrying different plates filled with an array of pastas and vegetables, while the sommelier poured a red bordeaux into the goblets of each place setting.

"Have you made a final decision for your screenwriter?" the general asked Raquel.

"Yes, I have, Juan Domingo."

"Let me guess." De Solis moistened his lips as if he were about to make an important announcement: "Luis Puenzo."

A smile grew on Raquel's face. "Sí. That is correct."

"A great intellect, I might add," De Solis said.

Jacob swirled the wine in his glass and studied its color. He grew impatient with each minute, and suffered the agony of dining with those he suspected were out to undo him. It did not help matters that Raquel, who never told him that Esau was gay, was now placating the general.

Across the table, Smith took a deep breath and looked at Jacob. "I thought of Esau as my brother."

De Solis interrupted. "The business of art in America. I cannot accept the materialistic aspects your buyers place on art."

"And what might that be?" Jacob asked.

De Solis shook his head. "We intellectuals must remain the conscience of the human race. Don't you agree?"

Jacob caught Raquel's eye. She winked as if to suggest that everybody gets intoxicated occasionally. "What a pretentious ass," he whispered to Raquel.

The general addressed the table. "There is good and bad in all individuals."

Bertha glanced at Trumball. "Yes, it is true; that is what makes us all artists and poets."

"We must break the shackles that bind us to the past," De Solis declared. "Do you all not agree?"

"I see that you are interested in history," the art dealer said.

"Very much so."

"Then you are a master of many trades," Jacob said.

"I'm an art historian. Let me speak frankly," the general went on. "As a boy, my father told me about the several visits Hitler made to my grandfather's house in Vienna."

Jacob's face stiffened. "Who was your grandfather?"

"An artist interested in light and darkness, not form, not shape."

"Juan Domingo." Raquel's displeasure surged. "You are equating good and bad with artistic properties in that murderous time. When one does that they diminish the horrors."

"I don't equate good with bad," De Solis grumbled.

"I don't follow you," said Jacob.

"Art to my grandfather was just that. Not color, not shape, not form, but light and darkness."

"Juan Domingo, please. Do not find virtue in the murderers at the victim's funeral," Raquel replied, with an intensity in her glare.

"Imagine how exciting these stories of the German youth movement and the Nazi uniforms were to a boy?" De Solis reached for his wine glass, and then blotted his lips with the white linen napkin.

"As a little boy you admired stories about Hitler. Yes?" Raquel added.

"Sí."

"You envied the uniforms and the songs the teenagers sang, so spirited and nationalistic. Yes?

"Sí, yes, get on with what you wish to say."

Raquel eyed him. "Why don't you accept that you and your family were wrong!"

De Solis' expression turned to anger. "My dear Raquel, I was a young boy then."

"You were misguided. You can admit to that. You don't have to come up with semantic twists and turns."

The general paused, then raised his glass, "Salud!"

Trumball closed his eyes, while Bertha listened attentively. Smith wandered off a moment before and was talking to a brawny figure with pockmarked skin and a gray, receding hairline. Jacob watched a controlled fury overtake Raquel's face that he'd never seen before. How brave of her, he thought. If there was one moment that cemented his love for her, it was then, for Raquel showed her passions. He worried that he was disappointing her in not making a pointed comment. What could he possibly add to enhance what she said? No one spoke for the next moment.

"I do not think we should discuss this any further," De Solis said, throwing up his hands. "If I said something unpleasant, my apology."

Smith returned motioning to De Solis. "It's all set."

After dinner, the man Smith spoke with moments before lumbered toward them to announce to the general that everything is ready as planned. De Solis told the group that he had arranged surprise entertainment. "I must say good night. I have urgent work. Smith will ensure that you all have a pleasurable evening."

"If you've all had enough to eat, please follow me," Smith ordered, never once taking his eyes off Jacob. The art dealer got up only hesitantly, and was brought to his stance by the tender urging of Raquel, while Trumball had already offered his arm to Bertha, who nearly knocked her chair over as she lifted her bulk of taffeta to receive the towering older artist.

They passed through heavy mahogany double doors and into a square-shaped room with mirrored walls and densely carpeted floors. As the huge doors locked behind them with a quiet and abrupt finality, almost as if this enclosure were vacuum-sealed, they walked over to a colorful roulette wheel and the adjoining card table. De Solis' favorite restaurant concealed a members-only casino.

Smith placed an even stack of chips in front of his guests. "Compliments of the general, to start off your entertainment. Enjoy."

"I don't gamble anymore, Smith, darling," Bertha said, gently pushing her pile to the center of the table.

"Well, then you will watch us," Smith said.

"I will root for Señor Trumball to win lots of money," Bertha said. The artist bestowed a Continental kiss upon her plump hand.

"May I order us all a cognac?" Smith asked.

"A vodka," noted Trumball, who was busy reminiscing about the old days in New York when he and Bertha were the toast of society.

"Still a vodka man, Laban?" recalled Bertha, who chuckled as she remembered the night when Trumball went glass for glass with Richard Burton at Leonard Bernstein's social gathering for the Black Panthers.

"Allow me to introduce your esteemed card dealer, Señor Eduardo," said Smith, before conferring with the waitress on their drink orders.

Eduardo the card dealer evinced menacing body language, and no tuxedo could conceal the gun bulging in his jacket pocket. His mustache was as waxed as his brilliantine black hair, slicked to immovable perfection, a crown above pale white skin and an aquiline nose, whose nostrils flared with copious inhalation. His lips were thin. His hands, taut and muscular, were heavily veined, and he shuffled the cards with unerring skill. Jacob disliked him at once.

The cognac arrived on a silver tray carried by a young attendant, small-breasted and blonde by a bottle. She playfully placed the cognac before Jacob, her red nails caressing the snifter in a suggestive way, but he hardly noticed; he was there to play cards.

After watching Jacob play a few perfunctory rounds of blackjack, Raquel wandered off with Bertha and Trumball to watch a cluster of people playing craps.

Jacob's rule for playing blackjack was always to stop at thirteen, never take another card, and never be tempted. Experience taught him that he would bust if he asked for a card over that number. Tonight, he felt he could afford to take more chances, and luck flew his way. By his second glass of cognac, his stack of winning chips piled high in front of him, but several hands later, Jacob's hefty stack had diminished. He'd pressed his luck. This streak was too good to be true.

Just then, Raquel appeared as his lucky charm.

"In a funk, darling?"

"In a funk? No." Despite his last three losses, he was determined to control the game.

"Just checking." She kissed him playfully.

Jacob smiled as Raquel returned to the craps table. He looked up to receive Eduardo's icy stare. Smith looked blank, but Jacob was undeterred. He'd show the bastards how blackjack was played. Jacob seemed to act as if his life depended on it. This had become more than just a few rounds of cards. He was playing on enemy turf, and the victories would be made sweeter each time he took a hand. Yes! He'd just captured his fifth sweep. The chips looked like a skyline, the skyline of the city in which he knew only success. This game, like New York itself, felt his, all his. He couldn't help disguise his glee in front of Smith, who was losing heavily.

"Nice game of cards you got down here," he snickered. Eduardo, perhaps owing to his lack of English, stared straight ahead at Jacob. Smith remained indifferent.

"Easy come, easy go," Smith said. "You do know that saying?"

"Sure, I do," Jacob said, laughing as he took the sixth straight hand by sticking at eighteen, and taunting Eduardo to produce another jack to bust the dealer's hand. Jacob was still snickering as he sipped another glass of cognac, when he noticed Eduardo's strong fingers moving swiftly from beneath the deck. Did he think he could shuffle from the bottom of the deck and not expect a hawk eye like Jacob to notice? "I know I'm winning." He paused. "But this man is cheating."

The card dealer heard the remark and reached into his jacket, but Smith lunged across the table and averted any chance of foul play. Smith shook the dealer by the shoulders. Like most Latin Americans, he took this insult as a slight to his honor.

"Are you crazy?" Smith yelled at the dealer, who simmered long enough to return to shuffling the next hand. Eduardo refused to deal to Jacob.

Jacob tossed his cards across the table, scattered his chips and walked away.

"You are a most ungrateful guest, aren't you?" Smith said. The dealer's face wore red. "We're here to make your weekend a wonderful time. Eduardo was not cheating," he insisted. "He was instructed to help you with your enjoyment." Smith chided Jacob. "Apologize, please. At once."

"Cut the shit," Jacob said, and quickly walked to the craps table. "We're leaving," he told Raquel and Trumball. "I thank my hosts for their hospitality," he said to no one in particular. "It's time to go."

Smith stared harshly at Jacob, but ordered the doors unlocked as Jacob left for their waiting car. Raquel, following closely behind, glanced back at Smith and Bertha, perturbed and embarrassed, while Trumball offered multiple, quick bows to both of them before joining Jacob in the backseat of the limousine.

"He's nothing like his brother," whispered Bertha to Smith, as they stood dumbfounded.

"He's definitely overstayed his welcome," Smith replied in a voice that sounded more like a hiss than a whisper.

CHAPTER FIFTEEN

Trumball's head bobbed and he snored lightly as the limousine drove on. Jacob pulled his phone from his pocket and began pressing numbers. He suddenly wished to confront Bertha once more. As they sped toward the hotel through the lively traffic on 9 de Julio, Jacob concluded that Esau wanted to deliver information to him. "The goddamn yellow sheet of paper holds a key," he reminded himself. Although Bertha feigned ignorance about the existence of De Solis' fake, she would know something that would help him uncover some meaning in Esau's note.

"Who are you calling?" she asked.

"Bertha, I'll be at your gallery at eleven sharp," he spoke into his phone. "I must see you."

"Why do you want to see her? You've just been with her."

"In case they forged other paintings." Feeling a quiver of fear for the moment, he was beginning to realize that he was trapped in a cabal of sorts. Esau had been involved in forgeries, and De Solis wanted the money for this.

"Who? Which forgeries?"

"There were two other paintings that Esau brought to Buenos Aires. For the general."

"Did Juan Domingo buy them?"

"No. Esau returned the paintings to my gallery."

"Why do you think that he made copies of these pieces?"

"I don't know. I want to be sure. That's all."

She shrugged, looking dismayed but concerned. "You're beating yourself up with this. Let go of Esau. You sometimes have a one-track mind. Juan Domingo meant well. He wanted you to have fun, especially after the traumas you experienced."

He hesitated for a moment. "You still think De Solis is on the up and up?"

"Yes." Raquel looked over at him. "Maybe, Bertha is responsible."

"She's a pawn."

The car pulled up to the hotel. Jacob thought the whole night had become a kind of freak show, where nothing was predictable. Jostling the old man from his sleep, he led Trumball to his suite. Jacob took the old man's clothes and shoes off and put him to bed. Trumball never stirred, but snorted, as if to catch his breath.

Returning to their suite, Raquel was blunt. "Do you hate your brother for killing himself? Isn't that what's at the heart of all of this?"

Jacob understood her question, but was surprised to hear it. He could never admit to hating Esau for killing himself, though when he tried figuring out who Esau really was, he hated himself for not understanding. Tonight he could no longer be silent. "I'm trying to reconcile all the things I'm learning about him with the picture of that kid I shared a room with at Cornell. I feel like I never knew him. The only way I'm going to solve this whole mess is by learning even more about him. More about the things he hid from me. You knew so much about Esau." The words came out quickly, and yet he was afraid of learning the truth.

"Yes, I suppose I did."

"You knew that Esau was gay and you never told me."

Raquel was already in a negligee in front of a mirror combing her hair. Jacob stared at her reflection.

"I thought that was common knowledge. I assumed you knew."

"I didn't know."

"So you are angry that Esau was gay and a suicide?"

"I don't know what I think."

"Are you angry with me?"

He hesitated.

"Yes, you are. Darling, I never had influence on his behavior. Why are you angry with me?"

"Well, I'm angry that you never mentioned ... this whole group of people who seemed to be a major part of his life here in Buenos Aires. Like Smith and De Solis. You and Bertha. And who else? I don't know who else there might be. I was his brother. His twin brother. What do I know of him?"

She got up and embraced him as he slid his pants off. "I loved Esau. Your brother was gay, and I knew I could never be intimate with him. I saw Esau in you. Yes, when I held you, in my head I embraced him. The way you talk and the way you move, everything reminded me of him. So I thought of you as a straight version of him. I'm sorry for saying this.

Jacob, that's how I felt, at first. I know how I feel about you now. I am with you because of who you are. I love you, Jacob."

He pulled her toward him. She kissed back stiffly and clutched the hair on the back of his head as if to prop herself up. A steady rain outside made thumping noises on the ledge outside their window. Water appeared to be seeping in under the window, forming little drops on the sill. Suddenly, a blue flash shattered the blackened sky into lighter shades of gray. A crashing boom followed.

"My heart jumps in a storm like this." She rested her head on his shoulder. They moved quietly to the large bed as if afraid to wake a sleeping guest. They lay down together, and Raquel leaned over him. He sat on the edge of the brass bed, slipping his shirt and shorts off. He hugged her in a tight embrace. She rolled her tongue over his lips. For a moment, he watched her hands as they moved over his legs, then up his arms and to his face. Then he grabbed her supple thighs, pulled her onto his lap, and buried his head in her full breasts.

"I'm falling into a deep abyss, Jacob," she said. "I feel frightened on the inside. You know, like a spooky little cat. Please give me room."

"I won't let a little thunder threaten you." He settled against the headboard, allowing her to spread out in the middle of the bed, where she opened her luscious thighs and began to masturbate, facing him.

"No, no, please don't interrupt," she whispered when he moved toward her. "Please. Permit me, darling. Permit me to delight in the curves of my own body, in my breasts, in my hardened nipples, in my flesh, and in my thighs. Jacob, pinch my nipples. Yes, pinch them. Yes, this feels so good. Do you wish to lose yourself in the depths of my flesh, my bones, my belly, my smells? Look how you sit, so erect, sweating, stirring in your cravings. Touch yourself, too. Yes. Do it." She fingered herself with repeated movements, writhing in ecstasy. "I have endless passions, Jacob." Her thighs shook violently and, finally she moaned, breathless, just as her head dropped, and her hair cascaded across his belly. He stroked himself more and quickly, until he could no longer hold back. He closed his eyes, then opened them to watch himself erupt spasmodically across his hairy stomach.

CHAPTER SIXTEEN

It was Friday morning, their second day in Buenos Aires, and the Trumball celebration was forty-eight hours away. When Jacob arrived at her gallery, Alice ushered him in with barely a greeting. She kept her head down and motioned him to the same chair on which Jacob had last sat, upset over Bertha's casual revelations about his brother.

"What an unexpected pleasure," Bertha called out, bursting through the beaded curtain and the back room. She had watched his entrance and steeled herself to face him.

He gave her a fake smile. He was here on business—again, the business of Esau. He couldn't help noticing that even on a bright sunny morning, Lavazzo Fine Arts was disagreeably damp with a kind of gloominess that seemed impenetrable to the colorful ensembles that Bertha called a wardrobe, including this morning's orange and lime green caftan that she'd accented with turquoise jewelry.

"Are you interested in some of my other artists? You're not here to discuss Esau's sexuality, I hope?"

"No. What do you know of the forged painting from Esau, the one that was passed on to De Solis?"

"I wasn't aware of anything until last night, when General De Solis cautioned us to be silent about this matter."

"I don't believe you," he said, staring her down.

"I don't care what you believe." She looked over at Alice, who got up from her appointed spot at the rolltop desk and stood by her.

"I think you will, when I tell you that I've spoken to the FBI." His poker face didn't reveal his lie; he felt it was a necessary deception to get at the truth.

"Really? And what ever for?"

"About forgeries."

"I'm not sure I follow you, Jacob."

"Where my late brother was concerned, that is."

"So what does this have to do with me?"

"They know all about Esau's handiwork with Trumball's canvases."

"You didn't answer my previous question," Bertha replied.

"There were two other paintings Esau took to Buenos Aires and returned to my gallery in New York."

"Yes, *The Swan's Crossing* and *Inimitable Transgressions*. What of them?"

"Was a sale made of these two Trumball works?" Alice moved closer to Bertha. "Who were these sold to, Bertha?"

"I looked them up this morning," Alice interjected. "I suspected that Señor Rose might ask after them. Both pictures are on General De Solis' yacht." Just then, Bertha shot a furious glance at Alice.

"You understand, there's a black market here for many things," said Bertha, suddenly changing her tune, warming to Jacob with a kindness that did little to disguise her alarm. "Art and money and drugs and automobile parts...."

"If both pictures are on De Solis' yacht, how do you explain my having them in storage, back at my gallery in New York?"

"I'm afraid the explanation is all too obvious," she said.

"I sent the paintings with Esau, maybe five months ago, for De Solis' inspection. The two paintings were returned to me unsold," he said, resisting a chance to yell at her until he could find the underlying cause of this unscrupulousness. "Where were the fakes made for De Solis' yacht? Were they painted here?"

Bertha turned to sit down. Alice stood above her, sullen but not defeated. Quietly, Bertha began recounting her role in their operation. "Smith had arrived to pick up the paintings, which came by diplomatic courier. De Solis held the two pieces for a few days, or maybe a week, until Esau arrived, then he returned the paintings." She paused; now her expression was tense. Alice held her hand.

"Tell me more," he said.

"I permitted Esau and Alice to paint these forgeries in the back, behind my gallery. I took a fee for each of them from the general. Trumball wasn't the only artist copied, mind you. Esau then brought the real paintings back to you. No harm was done. This last time, with the *Lea* painting, the canvas arrived but Esau did not. When General De Solis discovered he had a fake, he offered you $9 million for purchase of the real painting."

"And you and De Solis thought you could sell those early Trumballs on the black market for exaggerated sums without being exposed?" Jacob was in awe of their brazen hubris, and the idea that they thought they could get away with such a swindle.

"I'm sorry." Her admission toughened his determination to do something. She had been a trusted go-between, a recommendation from Esau. It appeared now to Jacob that, like his late brother, her only allegiance was to cash.

"Did you ever suspect that there were more reasons for the forgeries?" He headed to poke his head in the back room, but stopped short when her phone rang.

"I'll just be a minute," Bertha said. He stood there, furious but victorious. The puzzle was coming together.

"It is Smith on the telephone, and he wants to meet with you this morning, at the racetrack. He said you would understand."

"He said I would understand?" Jacob repeated, still in an angered daze. "And how would he know I'm here?"

"I let him know, last night, after you stormed out of the casino. I had called to check on Alice, and, well, your message demanding to meet with me was on the service."

"Which racetrack"

"Hipódromo Argentino, at the corner of Libertador and Dorrego. Smith said he'd be waiting for you at the finish line at precisely 12 noon."

"We're not finished," he warned, pointing a finger and opening the door to depart.

Jacob jumped into the car and ordered Ortiz to drive to the racetrack. "The Hipódromo Argentino."

"Sí, señor. The Hipódromo. It is in San Isidro. There is no racing now. It is too early in the day."

"Just do as I say, Señor Ortiz. Please." He had no reason to take his anger out on the chauffeur, yet he needed a punching bag. Jacob was more furious with Esau than ever before. His brother's duplicity added to the worry he'd given their family—his unknown whereabouts and confidential professional posts. How his brother could betray him and use the gallery as a base for fraud, was beyond his comprehension. Had Esau hated him? For all those years? Why was this the time for payback? How else could Jacob understand the depths to which Esau's swindles had potentially jeopardized his reputation and everything else that Jacob had ever worked for?

Now he knew the answer to Raquel's question from the night before: "Do you hate your brother for killing himself?" No. He could not feel hatred for him. Disappointment for the fact that he killed himself. Betrayal for lying and cheating, for violating their sibling bond. Is that what all those years of covert work had taught him? To turn on your own flesh and blood?

More and more it became apparent to Jacob that he was in a nightmare of a situation. In order to crack the code and to get the hell out of this place, Jacob had to start figuring out the brother he thought he knew.

Back at the gallery, Bertha sat crying audibly and awaiting an inevitable fate that her dance with avarice never tempted her to consider. She could hardly blame Alice, but she could barely speak to her. Not just yet. They were accomplices and could help each other only if they remained united. Still, each ignored the other and kept to her own space within the ruined rooms of Lavazzo Fine Arts, a business that just moments ago had begun to resemble its appearance.

CHAPTER SEVENTEEN

He found the famed Hipódromo Argentino empty, an undisturbed oasis of trees and blooming flowers that hugged a two-story clubhouse made of clapboard, and which was for the most part only occasionally canopied—as if the notion of rain and racing were simply incompatible. Not a soul was around, not even a groundskeeper, as he surveyed the property. Assuming most racetracks to be the same the world over, Jacob walked around easily and found the finish line, where a slow-moving van was raking and turning the track's soil. *Finally, the sight of another living being,* he thought. He stood behind the track's gate, waving to the van and waiting expectantly, but the van and its driver ignored him as it drove away in the opposite direction toward a shed that held a wooden scoreboard atop its roofline. Again, he heard the purr of an engine.

The van reappeared. It was moving in Jacob's direction. As the vehicle drew closer, he could see the passenger's white jacket, a contrast to the dark figure behind the steering wheel. At once, the vehicle accelerated as it approached the finish line, with a velocity that left Jacob covered in dirt.

Dusting off, he gathered himself as the van whizzed past again. This time, he thought he'd seen Smith in that front seat. He didn't have another chance to draw that conclusion. The vehicle turned off into a distant paddock and disappeared. If he were its intended target, he cared little to prove it. He was going to get the hell out of there and find his way back to the entrance, where Ortiz sat comfortably in the Mercedes, awaiting him while he conducted his business. He leapt over the fence, just as he'd entered, cursing loudly, angry at each day's laundry list of offenses toward him.

As he made his way around the track, past the initial furlong, Smith suddenly appeared, wearing a white jacket.

"Thanks for showing up." Smith extended his hand.

"What the hell was that all about?" Jacob demanded, still dusting off.

"What are you taking about?"

"That business with the van!"

"I asked you here to discuss the general's story."

"He just wants to steal the painting. Isn't that right? And you're mixed up with De Solis."

Smith stared at Jacob and then nodded. "Your brother Esau and De Solis and myself were partners of a sort."

"I'm beginning to understand that."

"Business between us was good. This is not bullshit."

"I'm not happy about that. I'm not feeling too good about my brother now."

"We were making lots of cash, salting it away, living the good life."

"Yeah. Terrific. The good life." Jacob looked directly at Smith, filling himself with indignation and skepticism about Esau's values. "Where are your ethics, Mr. Smith? Esau was a good man. Why this?"

"Esau got greedy, somehow," Smith ignored Jacob's outburst, "and started skimming off the top, putting away more of De Solis' profits each month into secret accounts."

"I know now that my brother was a crook."

"When De Solis got wind of Esau's swindle…." Smith fell silent.

A horrible void hit Jacob. He looked to the ground, biting his lower lip. "Go on…. Don't stop."

"I suspect that he had your brother killed."

"You're full of shit. Do you hear me?"

"No. You listen to me, you stubborn son of a bitch. I call the shots."

"My brother killed himself, you bastard."

"They never proved the suicide."

"How do you know?"

"I just know," Smith said.

"And what were you doing with all this money?"

"We were involved in a racket to buy arms, which we smuggled off to third-world countries and sold for some pretty remarkable prices."

"Oh my God. Where was Esau's head? His heart? How could he have done this? Why would I ever believe a word you say?"

"Because I … was Esau's friend."

"He never mentioned you."

"I was his Esau's buddy. Damn you." Smith restrained himself from grabbing Jacob by the throat.

"Raquel doesn't know you either. She was Esau's friend. So, Smith, just who are you?

Calming down, Smith paused and spoke softly. "We were buddies in Nam, and in Cambodia."

"What does that do for me?"

"Then Esau left for South America."

"Give me straight stuff. Real insight into my brother. Then maybe I'll believe you."

"What would you like to know? Like when we worked for army intelligence in Cambodia? Or what kind of covert operatives we were for the U.S. government when we worked in South America? Look, I can't tell you more than that, but I'll cut to the chase and warn you. If you don't produce the money, over $80 million, pal, De Solis will see to it that you return home in a body bag."

Jacob eyed him. "What the hell are you talking about? Sounds to me like your story is bullshit."

"I told you enough. Do you understand the importance of Esau's role in our organization? The three of us were a partnership. De Solis dealt in arms. I negotiated the transactions. Esau was our treasurer."

"You're losing me Smith. I expected more from you."

"Why?"

"You were Esau's good buddy. You said that a few times. I believed you."

"Shut up. Do you hear me? Shut up! Esau deposited our earnings into an account that could only be accessed by code. Which only he knew, at first. Afterwards he transmitted information to us. Like this time on the back of your painting."

Jacobs' heartbeat pounded. He broke out into a sweat with bits of dust still on his face. Suddenly, Jacob realized he was the target now. Smith fixed a dark stare on Jacob's eyes. The art dealer stood muddled, trying to figure it all out, and struggled to determine the consequences to his next reply.

"I want to believe you. For the sake of my brother's honor." Jacob's panic subsided, slowly letting him breath more easily. He watched Smith, but couldn't tell if he told the truth.

"Hey, you're a bright man," Smith finally said.

"How do you know?"

"Because your brother was a clever bastard. Set in his ways. Like you. At times, shooting from the hip. You know, acting impulsively. Other times, immovable like a boulder. I had a way to reason with him."

Jacob studied Smith carefully, though not realizing that Smith studied Jacob's every facial gesture, every body movement, every word, even his reasoning. "Give me a day and you'll have what you need."

"Okay. You're my pal."

"I hope that I am."

"You can trust me."

"I will."

"Together we'll succeed."

"Yes."

"But divided?"

"Divided, we fail," Jacob filled in.

"No, divided you are screwed."

"You got it."

"Don't patronize me. I don't like that."

"I'm not patronizing you, Smith."

"Good."

"I'm working damn hard to accept your terms."

"Trust me, not De Solis. And don't mention this talk to anyone. Not even the actress. We understand each other, don't we?"

"We do." Jacob was bluffing, buying time for himself and certain that the only way he could stay alive was to make them believe he could lead them to the money. His poker face added to this foil. He accepted that they would eventually kill him. The thought sent shivers through his body. He knew that they wouldn't do a damn thing, though, not until he disclosed, uncovered the information that they believed he had. *Now it all fit together. Esau was communicating a code with his letter, for sure.*

Suddenly, Jacob glanced across the track up to the tote board. He thought he saw a man atop it waving furiously at him. When he looked again, he saw another man, this one on the other end, signaling with his hands for Jacob to drop down, to hit the ground.

Seconds later, loud shots rang out.

"Get down!" said Smith, pulling Jacob to the ground.

"What the hell is this?" Smith said nothing. Jacob's stomach was churning. Yet again on this trip he considered his own mortality.

He looked around, but his quick scanning of the track and clubhouse revealed nothing. The men on the tote board clutched the boards with the surfaces of their bodies. Smith darted across the flat track. Jacob quickly realized, he'd be a target if he remained pinned to the ground. He raised himself up to follow Smith. After at least a two-minute pause between bullets, another round of gunfire erupted in a riveting spray of ammunition. Jacob ran faster, not more than ten feet behind Smith, and cleverly darting in the winding fashion that Smith instructed him to follow. Jacob, even in his dazed apprehension and breathless fatigue, could understand the purpose of snaking along the track as their only hope for eluding the shots.

Without warning, he saw the galloping hoofs of a large horse chasing them down just as they reached the other side of the track.

"Don't look back!" shouted Smith. "Just keep moving."

Jacob noticed the rider's ominous face mask in black. Thinking it was De Solis, he took a few more glances back than necessary, slowing the pace he'd set between Smith and himself. As Jacob faced forward once more, trying to build as much speed as he could to catch up to Smith, he heard a loud blast. Whatever the harsh sound, it was meant to take Smith's life.

Smith crashed to the ground right before Jacob's eyes. The sound of the horse's hoofs pounding the turf were nearly at his back. He stopped running and stooped down to Smith's body, searching as best he could for the bullet wound, when he felt the thunder of that horse almost on top of him. Jacob dropped to the ground again, slithering on his stomach to find some outlet for escape. He could see the horse and rider speed around the turn. He continued his belly crawl, not knowing if it were safe to get up. Then another volley of shots rang out, but none of the bullets hit the turf around him. And, again, the horse and driver approached swiftly.

"Up, up, damn it!" the rider snapped as he tried to hoist Jacob onto the saddle with one hand. Even in Jacob's distressed state, he noted the rider's mask had only slits for the eyes.

"What the hell is going on?" Jacob roared back as he rolled away from the horse.

"Stay down," the rider said. Jacob looked up to see him fire the contents of a smoke canister, filling the air with the dense, smoky fog, enough to obscure the track for Jacob to make his escape.

"Stay down until I return." Jacob tried to get up and run, but the rider yelled, "Stay down, stay down!" and galloped around the next turn. Another battery of shots flew over the patch of smoke and fog, as Jacob staggered onto the grassy field.

"Up, now! Up! Now!" the rider shouted again as he emerged out of nowhere and swiftly hoisted Jacob onto the saddle. The man said nothing to Jacob until they reached a rear exit. "I want you to leave immediately. Do you understand?" Jacob was so alarmed he could barely speak. "Don't look back. Your car is outside this gate."

Jacob did look back, and he saw a couple of men drag Smith's limp body and place it in the van. The horseman rode off. Ortiz was waiting, and Jacob slid into the Mercedes as Ortiz, sensing danger from Jacob's perspired, torn condition, floored the accelerator, screeching out of the Hipódromo's parking lot.

Jacob's phone rang as they rounded the corner to the hotel.

"FBI agent Sullivan calling Jacob Rose."

"You got him," the art dealer exclaimed, hardly catching his breath. "Where are you calling from?"

"I'm in Buenos Aires, trying to save your ass."

"Thank God, you're here." Jacob breathed a sigh of relief. "Get me out of Buenos Aires. Okay?"

"Get back to that hotel. Continue with your weekend plans. That's all you need to do. That's the reason you're here, right? And don't mention anything I say out loud," Sullivan warned.

"I don't know what the hell's going on. I've almost been killed twice now, and Smith … is dead."

"I know."

"How would you know?"

"Who do you think rescued you at the racetrack and brought you to your car?"

"You? Was it you? Damn!"

"You'll get Raquel killed, too, if you don't stop messing around. So work with us."

"You know the painting you found in Esau's apartment? De Solis thinks I am looking for money, encrypted in a code back of that canvas. Like I was a partner with my dead brother."

"Are you?"

"I'm not."

"Why would De Solis expect you to find the money, if he didn't have a pretty good idea that you know something?"

"Because I was Esau's brother. His twin. Does he realize that Esau and I hadn't a shred of contact for nearly thirty years?" he said, beginning to panic.

"Well, keep your cool."

"Cool? I could be killed like Smith. I'm next."

"What makes you so sure?"

"Smith was shot, killed, murdered right in front of my eyes."

"They won't kill you. Yet."

Jacob didn't hear Sullivan's last word. "I'm getting out of here. Out of Argentina. I'll get the old man, the painting, Raquel, and we're leaving. See you, Sullivan."

"Try to get your passport back. If you can pull rabbits from a hat, you'll be able to pull that one off, too. You're dealing with a total nut job."

"No shit!"

"Now play along with us and in forty-eight hours, you can resume your normal life. That's all. By Sunday you're out of here. We need you to pretend we never had this conversation"

"And what do I do in the meantime?"

"Stop playing detective," Sullivan offered, barely pausing between each directive.

"What's my reward?"

"Your ass, your painting, your life. Do you need more incentive?"

The car turned into the hotel driveway. "Yes, goddamn it! I want any files you have on my brother's involvement in art forgeries. Immediately. I also want you to arrange a flight to get us out of this country, safely, with no ramifications whatsoever. If you can fulfill this, then I'll play along."

Jacob knew exactly what he was going to do: he would pretend to crack the code—maybe he actually would—and let De Solis somehow find out. That's the only way he would gain time to save himself.

"Don't go to the police, or the American Embassy. Because nothing ever happened at the Hipóodromo. Do you understand? Everything will be taken care of."

"I understand."

"You're on."

"Just as long as you understand me."

"I told you, you're on.

"Is it a deal?" Jacob asked. He guessed that the FBI never negotiated when they wanted something. They just took it. If there were any validity to Smith's story, the prospect of over $80 million without a paper trail could be the first great heist of the twenty-first century.

"What's the matter? Are you listening to me?"

"Yes."

"Okay. You've got a deal," Sullivan replied, and hung up immediately.

Just then, a series of sharp clicking sounds came though his phone and some quick utterances in Spanish. He suspected that they had tapped his phone. *But who?* He had no idea, but could imagine De Solis' goons watching his every move. "Thank goodness for Sullivan," he repeated to himself.

CHAPTER EIGHTEEN

Jacob returned to the hotel, marched to the desk, and requested his passport. Although he had cut a deal with Sullivan, he decided that he wanted out now, out of Buenos Aires. He tapped the desk bell fiercely, when a tall clerk in black tie greeted him. The man showed a smug bearing that was unresponsive to demanding American clientele. The lobby had turned into a beehive of activity as the president's visit loomed closer. Secret Service personnel at each corner of the grand lobby looked forceful, but always looked ahead. It seemed as if this was a convention for the hard of hearing. Jacob had never seen as many earpieces in one place and at one time. He felt similarly about the dark aviator glasses across so many faces in one room. The thick hotel carpeting muted the sounds of feet scurrying back and forth.

"Our apologies, señor," the clerk replied to Jacob's request to obtain his passport, which he'd left with the hotel for safekeeping when he first registered. "There will be a slight delay."

Jacob returned this news with a sour expression that hardened the clerk's intolerance. "Explain, señor."

"It appears that government officials are making routine inspections," he said without the slightest concern.

"I demand my passport. I want it now."

"We will have your passport returned to you shortly. I am sure of that."

"Routine inspections?" Jacob repeated.

"Sí, Señor Rose. I'll ring up when it's ready."

"I will expect that."

"It will be just short delay. A little inconvenience."

"No, señor. You don't understand. It's a grave inconvenience."

The clerk remained expressionless. Jacob walked off. He wasn't about to make a scene in the lobby and draw further attention to what he'd begun to think was a conspiracy. Sullivan's words now seemed anything but hollow.

He returned to the suite, shaken and angry. He pushed through the double doors and startled Raquel. She was sitting up on the bed, comfortably immersed in the September issue of *Vogue,* reading the profile they had written about her. She wore the hotel terrycloth robe as if she'd just emerged from a bath, which indeed she had as Jacob was witnessing Smith's cold-blooded assassination.

Jacob had never felt so grimy and disheveled. He looked as if he'd been shaken down by a gang of thugs.

"Darling, what happened to you?"

"Smith is dead. I saw him killed. Shot right in front of me."

She didn't say anything at first. She simply stared into his eyes, then, taking a deep breath, as if to prepare for whatever seemed to be the next crisis, she pushed his hair off his forehead and took the rumpled tissue she'd had kept in her robe pocket and wiped the sweat and dirt from his brow.

"Sullivan, the FBI guy. I told you about him. He's the one who found Esau's body. Do you remember? Well, he's here now. In Buenos Aires. Thank God, I got somebody I can trust. I know he's on my side. He saved my life, Raquel. They were shooting wildly."

She hung on his every word. "Who, darling? Who?"

Jacob looked around the room as if others could hear him. Raquel's glance followed his. He got up abruptly, tearing himself from her embrace, and turned the TV on full blast. He motioned her to join him by the window, which he opened so that the noise of the city, its populace shouting political chants and making general mayhem, would commingle with the rushing breezes that blew the curtains back. He now saw himself as a man on the run, suspicious that every location might be bugged.

"I don't know who 'they' are," Jacob said, breathing laboriously.

"Jacob, relax. Please. Take some deep breaths. This is all too chaotic."

"Sullivan assured me that everything would be taken care of. I shouldn't do anything. I shouldn't even go to the police."

Raquel drew her breath. "Where did this happen, Jacob?"

"At the Hipóodromo."

"The racetrack?" She shook her head quizzically.

"Smith called Bertha while I was visiting her this morning. He asked me to meet him at the racetrack. He said it would be private, a place we could talk without any one listening in."

Raquel hesitated. "Yes, and so you went to the racetrack."

"I don't want to relive everything just now." His heartbeat slowed.

"I'm trying to understand you."

"I realize, but bear with me."

"Of course, darling."

He poured a glass of white wine. "They shot from the tote boards and the grandstand. Smith went down. Murdered. I dropped to my belly...."

"What are you saying?"

"A rider on a horse scooped me up. I couldn't figure out who it was."

Raquel studied him. "My God. You've been through hell. This trip has become a nightmare. Please, tell me everything. I want to know." She paused, watching him shake his head. "You're frightened, aren't you?"

"When I got back to the car ... Ortiz was waiting for me ... Sullivan was calling on the cell phone."

"How did the FBI know ... in advance ... that this shooting would take place today?"

"I don't know. It's like my moves are known in advance." He glanced around the room. "I don't see any surveillance gadgets here. I've looked, believe me. I'm sure they got us covered."

He stared at her for a moment and motioned to flick on the remote and to raise the sound level of the TV. They walked through the open terrace door. "Sullivan told me not to say anything to anyone. And not to go to the police."

Raquel gazed down at the street below. "You must go to the police. You must report this."

He knew that she was right, but for the moment he'd become suspicious of everyone, and at the same time tried hard to believe that

Esau was blameless in these events. "Sullivan said he'd take care of everything."

"I will go with you. I have some influence in this city, after all."

"I'm not sure." Jacob turned away from the terrace door and refilled his wine glass.

"What did Smith talk about before he was shot? What was so important to him?" Raquel asked.

"He told me ... that De Solis' story," he hesitated for a moment. "De Solis' story on the assassination ... is pure shit. Which I knew was true."

"What are you telling me?" she asked slowly.

"None of you would believe me!"

"What else did Smith say?"

"That code ... that De Solis told us, would give him information on an assassination plot...."

"Yes, the code. I know."

"You don't know. It's a code to a secret bank account with eighty million tucked away somewhere."

"That's preposterous, darling. Do you really believe JD made up that story to get his hands on money?" She hesitated, wondering if her outburst was justified.

"I believe a man was killed for telling me the truth."

"I can hardly believe this at all." She left and poured herself a glass of wine, took a sip, brought the bottle, and refilled Jacob's glass.

"Believe me."

"Why, darling. Why?"

"That phony general has been forging Trumball's works and keeping them on his yacht."

"What are you talking about?

"I'm talking about a scheme to extort large sums of money on the black market. That, I suppose, is small potatoes when you see a man shot dead in front of you."

"I can't believe what I'm hearing."

"Bertha confessed it all."

"Then she masterminded this hell?"

"No. I told you she's merely a hostage in these art frauds."

Raquel looked down at her glass in total frustration. "I don't know what to believe."

Jacob thought about his brother's and De Solis' partnership. *One day before, just one day before,* he repeated to himself, *I was headed to Buenos Aires for a long festive weekend. A sale of a famous painting and a gala honoring Trumball. Now it's turned into an inferno.*

He spoke as precisely to Raquel as he would in informing a buyer about the authenticity of a particular painting. "Bertha was a willing hostage. Esau brokered these paintings with De Solis for sale. Which Esau, with the help of Bertha's partner, or whatever ... that Alice...." Jacob cut himself off, he could barely finish his story.

"Explain this to me slowly," pleaded Raquel, who asked him to sit on a terrace chair and recount what he was trying to tell her in exasperated breaths.

"These paintings of Trumball's, and some others, too ... Esau and Alice copied them, right down to the last brushstroke. You want to talk to me about noble motives?"

"How do you know that you can believe a word Bertha says?"

"Because she admitted to her role. De Solis was kicking back cash her way just to keep her quiet. You don't think she's running a legitimate business out of that shithole gallery, do you? On top of that, De Solis has two of Trumball's paintings on his boat."

"You're certain of this?"

"Yes, that little Nazi Alice confessed that they copied those paintings, returned them to me, and held the forgeries for De Solis' yacht!"

"No!"

"Yes, Raquel. That son of a bitch could have sent me the copies! Do I have forgeries in my inventory? Imagine! Fakes, that I could have sold … and that any serious buyer would take to have authenticated. Trumball himself admired the workmanship of the copy."

"I understand the ramifications, I do…."

"Do you? Are you aware that if De Solis' fakes find their way into the art market, any attempt I make to sell the true paintings could cast doubt on the legitimacy of my whole inventory?"

"Of course."

"And what art buyer or artist, wouldn't believe that I wasn't somehow involved in this scheme? With my twin brother at the center of it all?"

Jacob paced nervously, desperate for a solution. He'd have to go to the police, despite Sullivan's admonitions. A man was killed in front of his own eyes. He might have been their next target. He hadn't told Sullivan of Bertha's admission. There hadn't been time in all the turmoil of the shots fired at the racetrack.

"Jacob, you must go to the police. You must report the shooting, at the very least."

"And what about the fraudulent art?"

"We don't really know whether it's true or not. I mean, until you return to New York and authenticate the Trumball canvases, you might be opening ... what do you call it ... a can of worms? And all for nothing."

"No, not for nothing...." Jacob was positive that Bertha's confession was the only truth.

"Seriously, Jacob."

He paced some more. "I know what I should do. And you're right."

"Report this to the police," she said softly. "You must report what you've seen, what you know to be true."

"This nightmare is turning worse by the minute."

"Please, darling. Tell them everything that is related to Smith's murder."

A thousand questions flooded his brain. He needed to retain good sense, his sanity. "I'd be better off if I went to the American Embassy."

"The embassy will probably say that it's a local matter."

Jacob glared at the neighboring buildings and the sharpshooters already in place. A dress rehearsal, he supposed. Two more days, forty-eight hours, he calculated, for the presidential motorcade to pass through and for him to come up with a way out of the pile of dung he'd stepped in. He turned to look at Raquel, whose face was drained of color.

He grabbed Raquel and kissed her violently. "Esau placed the number of a secret bank account back on the back of that canvas. He was in partnership with De Solis on this scheme." He remained fixed on her for a moment. "You knew Esau."

"Yes. We were often together ... at events."

"Was my brother a crook?" He waited for what amounted to a few beats. "You'd know if he was a crook."

"Esau was not a crook. Not when I knew him, certainly."

"Why did he want to screw me? I feel like I haven't made good on a promise to him. Why is this turmoil happening? What was my promise?"

"I don't know, Jacob. Perhaps it was not that premeditated."

She pressed herself against him, and he discovered that her eyes were swollen with tears. She began kissing him. "I'm sorry. I don't know what to say. I'm at a loss. Is it my fault for trusting JD? Am I so blind not to see what's going on?"

"You're not blind, darling."

"Am I an insensitive bitch?"

He managed a smile. "Is that what that magazine article said about you?" Jacob changed moods instantly, traveling away from anxiety. That's what had separated his personality from Esau's, he'd realized: his brother was a single-minded hunter after his prey. Esau could never switch emotional gears.

Jacob took her hand, slowly caressing it. "Get dressed. We're going to the American Embassy. It's my only corner of the States here."

"That's the correct move, I suppose," an exasperated Raquel replied.

"Even with your celebrity, I'm not sure the police are going to want to tangle with De Solis."

"As you wish, darling," she said, offering a small smile to show him hope as well as her allegiance to him, above all.

He took his shirt off and began to undress, and showered quickly.

What a monstrous day, he thought, as he dried himself off after the hot shower. In the bedroom, he fixed his eyes on at Raquel's legs as they made their way into silken stockings that fastened to a garter. *If life could be more like a moment of her kind of sheer beauty.* He watched her in silence. He didn't tell her that his passport was held up in a bureaucratic snafu, which he also believed to be De Solis' doing. No, if there was any genesis to this mess, it was because of Esau.

Damn that Esau. He turned away from Raquel, returning to the bathroom, to slick back his hair. He could see Esau on that Cornell soccer field now. Esau the big jock all covered with hair. A masculine mascot. A man's man, as they say. A man's man. That moniker had another meaning now. Damn that Esau, who'd taken off for parts unknown without little if any communication with his family. Esau had dug a crater in their father's heart ... their mother's, too, with his cruelty and coldness to them.

"I'm ready, darling," Raquel said.

She wore a simple, black skirt and a tight-fitting, tan jacket over a beige silk blouse. She looked gorgeous and happy, just as if she'd never had a day in which she doubted herself. That was the actor in her, ready for the next scene and always looking her best. With her brand of savoir-faire and the confident reserve he had as part of his arsenal, he felt a little less anxious about whatever unknowns lay ahead for him during the next forty-eight hours.

CHAPTER NINETEEN

The obelisk, sitting smack in the center of Nueve de Julio like a spike pricking the vista that stretched to the nearby sea, was the scene of local unrest. Molotov cocktails were set off around the landmark, though Buenos Aires locals dispersed leisurely among the row of outdoor cafés, oblivious to the mayhem, to talk politics. Jacob focused on the sounds of rioting pedestrians a few blocks away, which hardly made the city any more appealing at this time of its history. In fact, it only reinforced his sense that he was walking in hell's corner of the world. Argentine police stopped the limousine at every corner to let protesters by.

"Jacob, my country is in trouble." Raquel held Jacob's hand in hers. "We don't want a push from the right. Do you understand how difficult it is to live within a veiled threat from military oppressors? This is our history."

"I am trying to understand."

"There is much trouble in Argentina. Economic trouble. People without jobs. All this is mixed in with concerns for security."

"Is that what is happening out there?"

"When this happens the military becomes bold and we could have a repeat of the 'dirty wars.' Period," she said.

Ortiz pulled up to the U.S. Embassy on Avenida Colombia.

"I hope this puts an end to my craziness," Jacob said, as he opened the heavy oak door to the two-story Italianate building. They strode into the well-lit foyer, where subdued gray walls mingled with the black-and-white portraits of American emissaries who'd served the U.S. in Argentina.

After about a three-minute wait, a receptionist appeared. She was a slender woman, as starched as the pinstripe blouse she wore with a simple skirt.

"I'm afraid our ambassador is busy with preparations for the presidential visit on Sunday," she announced, enunciating each word. "His assistant, Mr. Miller, will gladly see you. Won't you come this way?"

They followed her down a hallway and into a back office, which it seemed to Jacob had been at one time the kitchen of a grand mansion. Miller's demeanor reeked of the good-old-boy network, once a requisite for State Department employment. "Miller here, Joshua Miller. Please, please, have a seat," the robust man said, pointing to the wingback chairs in front of his mahogany desk. Miller rubbed his pointed nose as he noticed Jacob admire a photograph of him with two former presidents, dressed in black-tie, at some state dinner. He held back an exploding sneeze from his thinly spaced nostrils until he could pull a tissue from a box in his drawer. "Forgive me!" Miller attacked his hanky vigorously. Nose wiped, he turned toward them again, his back erect in his chair. "Now then, what can I do for you?"

Before Jacob could answer, Miller turned toward Raquel. "I must tell you, I've enjoyed your movie performances a lot, Ms. Gingold," he said slowly, in a dry and elegant Southern accent. "I am a fan of Argentine films."

Raquel smiled and thanked him.

"I want to report a murder," Jacob said grimly.

"A murder," Miller repeated slowly.

"A man was shot in front of my eyes. It took place at the Hipódromo Argentina. Earlier today."

"Doesn't horse racing begin later in the day?" Miller said, discomfited, and surprised to hear of the murder's locale.

"True, but I was asked to meet a man there."

"A member of the racing commission?"

"No."

"A horse trainer?"

"No. I'm sorry, let me begin again," Jacob said, merely for the sake of being polite. "The racetrack was chosen because it was a place for a confidential meeting between me and a man named Smith."

"All right. Please elaborate," Miller replied, adjusting his seat to focus on Jacob, whose earlier insecurity in the face of an arrogant gentile seemed to affect his ability to explain his story.

"A man named Smith met me there. He spoke with me for a few minutes and then gunfire, out of nowhere, erupted in a steady stream of bullets. We tried to run for cover, but he was shot. Luckily for me, a rider on a horse came by, grabbed me, and brought me to safety outside of the racetrack's entrance. That's where my chauffer was waiting in our limousine."

"I see," said Miller, barely concealing a grin.

Jacob cleared his throat. "I'm sorry. Do you think I'd make this shit up?"

"Let's not resort to using foul language," Miller admonished. "That's not our style here. Particularly in the presence of a lady." Raquel averted her eyes from the sight of Jacob's encroaching anger.

"Look, are you going to help me or not?" Jacob replied testily.

"Don't be pushy. I agreed to meet you, so please, carry on."

"Where was I, now?" Jacob reflected.

"Let's back up a minute," Miller requested. "Why did you meet this Smith at the racetrack in the first place?"

"He requested that I meet him there."

"You must first tell Mr. Miller about General De Solis," Raquel interrupted.

"The former General De Solis," Jacob corrected.

"First, who is Smith, and again, why did you meet him at the racetrack?" Miller asked, still very much confused.

"Smith is De Solis' right hand. He is an American. He wanted to meet there because he felt our conversation wouldn't be overheard. I've already told you that."

"So you have, but why the need for secrecy?"

"Well, Smith told me to be careful. You see it involves my twin brother, who killed himself ... just a few months back, in New York City."

"I'd figured you hailed from there," Miller confessed. Jacob ignored the comment. "Excuse me a moment, please," Miller said and abruptly left his office. Jacob's eyes roamed the walls of the room, glancing again at the photos. Miller returned almost immediately. "I'm having our people check the racetrack, and the hospital emergency rooms and the morgue. Go on. What does General De Solis or former General De Solis have to do with all of this?"

An aide entered the office, interrupting them. She was a pale-skinned young woman, with a long, oval face, her hair hanging straight, her clothing conservatively frilly in the manner of a Southern belle. The young woman introduced herself as Agent Reinhart and said she was from South Carolina. "What part of the States are y'all from?"

"I'm from New York," said Jacob, standing.

"Oh, I would have guessed that you're a Yankee."

Jacob nodded yes, and cleared his throat. "Yes, I'm a New Yorker. And an enthusiastic New York Yankees fan."

"Yes, of course. I'd like to tape y'all's conversation from another room, but I must ask your permission first."

Raquel looked up at Jacob, who walked over to a wall dotted with photos. "Okay with me," he said.

"Yes, that's fine," Raquel replied.

"I feel better that that's out of the way," Reinhart said awkwardly, before leaving the office.

Jacob continued. "I'm an art dealer. He bought a painting from me. He arranged a reception and gala at the Museum of the Moderns for the artist, Laban Trumball, here in Buenos Aires. I represent Trumball. What I didn't know was that De Solis already had a copy of the painting. A forgery. You see, the original was found in my brother's apartment in New York, after he killed himself. He brokered the sales of paintings for me, in Buenos Aires. When I learned that General De Solis was interested in purchasing the work *Lea with Two Love-Apples,* I immediately asked the FBI to have its Stolen Arts Division authenticate the painting that they found in my brother's apartment. This isn't unusual. Art dealers often use the division. Since I knew of the prospective sale, but not of the fake, I felt it was necessary to get the painting authenticated before a transfer of title."

"Now I'm trying to follow you," Miller said. "So you had the painting authenticated…."

"I brought the real painting with me the other day. I had no knowledge there was also an existing fake…."

"I'm with you…."

"When we arrived, De Solis invited us that afternoon for wine and cheese in the hotel dining room."

"General De Solis then told us that he had a fake, sent to him by Jacob's brother," Raquel added, realizing that Jacob was withholding information. "And the artist and I convinced Jacob to make the exchange. General De Solis also told us that there is coded information on the back of each canvas, outlines of a plot to assassinate the president of the United States."

"How could a code exist on the back side? Wouldn't the FBI have noticed?"

"No. The artist, in the days when he was painting furiously, would jot down notes to himself. The code was ingeniously woven in as part of Trumball's scribbles."

"Does anyone else know about this?" Miller inquired, leaning over his desk, showing concern.

"Only U.S. Special Agent Sullivan from the New York City field office of the bureau."

Miller leaned back in his chair, placing his clasped, opened palms around the back of his head. Just then, an aide entered the room to serve the tea. Miller excused himself again.

Miller returned after a moment, holding a file of papers in his hand. "We're trying to get hold of this Agent Sullivan for his report. As soon as we do, we'll inform you of our findings. We're taking what you've said very seriously, I assure you." He remained standing.

"Are you dismissing us?" asked Jacob with a sense of disdain.

"For now, yes. I would report the incident to the local police. Maybe they have something. There is no need to tell them anything else. Keep the other parts of the story to yourself, as Agent Sullivan had cautioned."

"Thanks," Jacob offered, curtly, dissatisfied that he was left without any real guarantees. "Thank you, for your attention to this matter."

"Thank you, Señor Miller," Raquel said, with a quick wink.

"The pleasure is mine," said Miller, discreetly fawning over her courtesy.

"We'll be in touch. Good day, Mr. Rose, Ms. Gingold," Miller said, standing at his desk.

Jacob left Miller's office quickly, as he headed with Raquel down the long corridor back to the reception area. He whizzed passed the receptionist, without any good-bye. It was 2:45 that afternoon. Jacob told Ortiz to drive to the police station. He realized they needed to return to the hotel to wash up and proceed to Raquel parents' house in San Isidro for that evening's dinner to celebrate Trumball and his painting. He was in a hell-bent mood, restless, shaking his leg in the rear seat, furious that he had been deceived into thinking his painting ever had a legitimate buyer in De Solis. He closed the glass partition. "Did you believe Miller when he said he had no knowledge of the racetrack events?"

"I don't know what to believe," Raquel answered.

The police station looked like a movie set from 1940s New York. An officer sat out front in a white uniform, mustache smoothed flat above his lip, with a slightly balding head that reminded Jacob of the owner of the coffee shop just down the block from where Jacob and Esau grew up on New York's Upper East Side. Jacob asked the man if he spoke English. Raquel translated and then told him in Spanish that Señor Rose wished to file a report.

"What does he wish to file?" the man requested in Spanish.

"He saw a man shot. A man is dead," Raquel replied.

"Just a moment," the officer said. He had a pleasant manner of speaking, Jacob thought, although he only spoke Spanish and Jacob didn't understand a word. Perhaps Buenos Aires police were on their best behavior with tourists. He wondered whether the cop had recognized Raquel. The officer raised his hand indicating to Jacob to wait, and then picked up a phone to call inside. A detective emerged from a back room. "Señorita Gingold and Señor, what is your name?" he asked in English.

"Rose. Jacob Rose."

"Please, come with me." The stout detective led the way to a little cubicle toward the back of the station. The walls were painted a pale green. The chairs were solid mahogany. The air was stagnant. "Sit, please. Now, what do you have to report?"

"I saw a man shot dead. Ambushed."

"Where?"

"At the Hipódromo. It happened today at 12 noon."

"Señor, I have already been apprised of the shooting."

"Then why are you asking me these questions?" a perplexed Jacob asked.

"Formality," he shrugged. "Precaution. Indeed, we have been informed of this by your embassy. They told us you would be coming here. We have investigated the racetrack and we have found no bullets and no body. An attendant at the racetrack said he saw a man running wildly. The man jumped over the fence to his limousine, parked at the gate. Was that you, señor?"

"Yes, sir," Jacob said angrily. "I witnessed a murder. And yes, I did jump over a fence."

"Señor Rose, we won't charge you with trespassing at the racetrack. Americans sometimes do strange things." He reached over to Jacob and shook his hand. "If we receive other news, we'll inform you at once," he said as a farewell gesture. "Señorita, we are honored by your presence." He bowed slightly, and she extended her hand, which he shook as they hurried out of the station.

Back in the Mercedes and returning to the hotel, Jacob asked, "What do you think? De Solis got to the police quickly, didn't he? That detective didn't say one word that was true. Not one word."

"Jacob, I wouldn't know." Raquel paused. "I should call JD, shouldn't I?"

"Don't you believe that I saw Smith shot?"

"I said I wanted to call JD to get his understanding of what happened to Smith. After all, Smith was his trusted ... how would you say ... lieutenant."

"Smith was murdered in broad daylight. Honey, don't you see what the implications are now?"

"I don't know what you're referring to."

"If I don't find the money, I'm cooked, too. Like Smith. American Embassy or not. The embassy people were of no help."

"Jacob, Argentina is a country of laws."

"Yeah." He was nodding his head. "A country of laws. And Jews also believed that Germany was a country of laws when the Nazis took over."

"Don't be disrespectful. Please."

"You're right. I'm sorry. I'm normally not insensitive," he sighed. "My apologies. I've just got to find this money somehow, and find out if Smith's story is true. I didn't get a good feeling from the police or that clown Miller. At least, Sullivan seems to know what's going on. Of course, he'll be pissed that I went to the embassy."

The day was far from over. Jacob knew that he wasn't chasing phantoms, here. He was determined to break the code and find the money. That's what De Solis expected of him. Nothing less. The prospects hung above him like a noose, one he feared, with his monogram engraved on the knot. Jacob tapped his jacket pocket making sure his brother's letter was there.

When they returned to their suite, Raquel told Jacob that she would make a quick trip to the general's villa and confront him face to face. "No, I won't call him. I think it is better for me to visit with him."

"I don't think that's smart," Jacob replied wearily. He knew that once Raquel had made up her mind to do something, there was no way of stopping her.

"This man was once my lover. I know what I'm doing."

"Perhaps you do," he said, his thoughts preoccupied now with Esau's letter. "Promise me that you'll be careful. Okay?"

She managed a smile. "I'll return by five. Then we must rush off to visit with my parents. I want you to meet them, darling, so very much."

CHAPTER TWENTY

Raquel phoned De Solis from the car. "I'm on my way to see you. It is important."

"What is important that you must see me this very moment?"

"When I get there I will tell you."

"I await your arrival."

In less than twenty-five minutes, Ortiz swung the car to a checkpoint at De Solis' compound in Palermo Chico. A servant waited and led her quietly to the general's study, which looked out onto a vast garden, lush with thick, tall, green hedges surrounding several fields of wild orchids. The garden was the size of an American football field. The study's French doors were opened, and a light breeze blew the room's sheer lace curtains with a lazy rhythm.

"Welcome, my love," said De Solis in a way that suggested he was still smitten.

"JD," she said, embracing him with a soft hug and a kiss on each cheek.

A man dressed in military attire brought Raquel a glass of champagne and De Solis a scotch. She decided to deal openly with De Solis, believing he would tell her the truth. Weren't they lovers in the past? During the horrifying period of the "disappeared ones"? Her parents had been appalled that she could have an intimate relationship with a rogue who was responsible for the deaths and disappearances of Argentines who opposed him. She had never seen JD in that light, and truly believed that he was a man of the people. He had pleaded innocent to charges of crimes against humanity brought by a tribunal of the newly formed civilian government. When he had fallen from power after the Falkland Islands war with England in the 1980s, he had remained in prison, where Raquel visited him, although infrequently.

She believed he had loved her, and that what little spark of that love remained in him, she could ignite. When they had all been much younger, Esau, Raquel, and JD, she had had a way of teasing him. She remembered how De Solis had responded whimsically to jesting, and when they were alone, making love, how hard he had penetrated her again and again, until his triumphant moment.

De Solis became excited looking at Raquel. She was sexy and seductive without ever trying. Her moist lips and beautiful eyes seemed to undress him, encouraging him to flirt. He smiled endearingly, trying to control his stirring passion for her.

"Circumstances have placed us in a strange alignment. You agree?" he said.

"This has nothing to do with the rotation of the planets," she snapped.

"A woman's fury!" he said. "You are gorgeous. You still excite me as no other woman ever has." He leaned toward her.

"Speak honestly to me," she continued.

"I always have."

Raquel rose from her chair and walked, as if on a stage, to the fireplace.

"I have always loved you, JD," she began. "I loved you then, and in a different way from how I love you now." Her eyes avoided direct contact with him. He approached her, held her hands in his, and embraced her tightly. They knelt together in front of the fireplace and kissed fiercely. They remained in their embrace, and she kissed him again, though not without a sense that she was wronging Jacob. She'd begun to feel good with Jacob in a way she hadn't felt with anybody else in a long time. Not since her romance with General De Solis.

Raquel pulled away quickly from him. "If you were planning to regain power, would you begin by eliminating your perceived enemies?"

He snapped his fingers loud. The lieutenant entered with champagne in two long-stemmed glasses on a silver tray, served, and quickly left the room.

"My dearest, are you talking about Smith."

"Yes."

"He was a good man. Very good."

"Smith told Jacob that you lied when you said the painting had a coded message about killing the president. Smith said that Esau inscribed a code, and that it represents a secret bank account with millions of American dollars."

"And you believe Jacob?"

"I believe him." Raquel was taken aback by De Solis' accusation. "Of course, I believe Jacob. He would never deceive me."

"Esau deceived him. Were they not brothers? Twin brothers?"

"I will not believe Jacob is lying, not when Smith gave him this information."

"Let me explain about Smith."

"I'm here for your explanation."

"Smith was a trusted aide. What happens in this cloak-and-dagger business is that one makes a great many enemies."

"Did you kill Smith, JD?"

"No." He waited a moment. "You realize that he was arrogant. A man of his talents must remain in the shadows. I warned Smith about this to his face many times."

"Why is that?"

"If he shows himself off, his enemies will get to him first."

"Are you saying that Smith was a rogue?" She asked in disbelief, troubled now with the brutal reality that was enveloping her. And Jacob, yes, dear Jacob, she forced herself to admit, was onto figuring out some kind of liaison between JD and Esau.

"I'm saying that Smith came out of the shadows when he shouldn't have."

She sipped more champagne. She was beginning to feel lightheaded. "Why did he make up that assassination story for Jacob?"

"To feed Jacob disinformation." De Solis walked to the door leading to the garden. He seemed eager to give her a moment to ponder his words.

"When I first fell in love with you, at eighteen, that was years ago; you were larger than life." She followed him to the open door. The sun covered the garden in bright white light. "I'm not interested in deceptions. I want you to talk to me as lovers do."

De Solis looked ready to make love to her. His eyes were on fire. Raquel recognized what was happening.

She replied angrily. "I'm not going to have sex with you, JD. I've done that before."

"And I never heard you complain."

"That's not why I'm here."

"So what is it you want?" His face turned red. Without warning, he shouted and smashed his glass against the doorpost. "I'm a busy man. I've work to do."

"I, too, have work to do," she said, showing no signs of being intimidated. "Why was Smith feeding Jacob lies?"

"My dear, in the art of diplomacy, it's not called lies. It's called disinformation." De Solis emphasized.

"Why?" She glared at him. "I want to understand."

"To discover if your opponent is withholding information from you. In this case, vital information."

Raquel looked dissatisfied. "I don't know whether to believe you."

"Information about money. Lots of money, as you mentioned before," De Solis added, to emphasize his viewpoint.

"Then Smith was telling the truth?"

"Yes. Jacob is the thief. Do you understand? That's why he is in Buenos Aires."

"No. Jacob's here to celebrate Trumball."

De Solis frowned. "Have you been taken in by his falsehoods? Have you become so easy to fool? Has living in New York done that to you? Don't be naïve, my dearest. It doesn't become you."

"Jacob thought that you invited him here to purchase a painting from his gallery for a very large sum of money."

"So?"

"He also tells me you've made forgeries of other art works, too."

"Jacob is the thief. He is attired in the clothes of an art dealer."

Raquel was stunned. "And the shooting? And Smith's body?"

"The police tell me there was no evidence of a shooting at the racetrack. What do you make of that?"

Raquel came there to clarify her thinking; now she was disappointed and confused by JD's repeated accusation that Jacob was the offender. "I want to hear the truth."

"Don't ask anything more just now," he whispered.

He took her hand and they walked in the garden. Birds chirped in the cool air. Wisps of clouds floated under the pale blue sky. Long shadows fell from tall trees as the sun lowered to the west. De Solis snapped his fingers once more, and the lieutenant came running with more glasses of champagne on a silver tray and a blanket that the aide spread out on the lawn.

They sat under a white tent. Within an instant, the aide returned with a picnic basket of fruits, cheeses, and crackers and white damask napkins. The lieutenant left the garden after placing a red rose on top of the straw basket. They ate pieces of cheese and sipped champagne.

"This is like old times, yes?" De Solis asked.

"Yes, like old times," she replied. A faint smile forced itself on her lips. "Juan Domingo, there's more happening here. More than Smith's murder by a group of unknown thugs, or Jacob being lured to Buenos Aires in order to extract huge sums of hidden money that he knows nothing about."

"You are sure of your conclusions?" De Solis asked.

"I am certain there's more here than meets the eye."

"Then share it with me."

"You can no longer tell me the truth, I see. I've always been captivated by your charm and your desire to do justice."

De Solis ignored her remark. "I'm holding a memorial service for Smith. His burial will be private. His remains have already been flown to his family in the United States."

"That is touching, JD," Raquel said, unsure of whether to be sarcastic or sympathetic.

"Do you think I would honor a man I've killed?"

She said nothing as she continued to search his eyes.

"You and Señor Rose must attend. This memorial is by special invitation only. Please understand, I've arranged the memorial for tomorrow, Saturday night at eight o'clock, so that nothing will interfere with Señor Trumball's gala at the museum on Sunday afternoon, or your parents' cocktail reception, this evening. The memorial will be at the Basilica."

"In Recoleta? Next to the cemetery?"

"Yes. I thought it would be fitting for an American

"How very beautiful."

"Will you participate in the memorial ceremonies?"

I barely knew the man."

"You know me. He was close to me."

"I don't know."

"It would mean a lot to me to have you extend yourself this way."

"How so?"

"You can convey the pathos in poetry, and that would be a most magnificent gift to me at this time."

"What is it you that would like me to read?" Raquel took a breath.

"I'll leave the choice to you. I trust your sense of propriety."

"A poem?"

"Yes. Choose a poignant poem by an American poet. Read it to the mourners, with feeling. Please."

"I will oblige you, JD."

"Well, then, until tomorrow. I must take my leave, as there is much to do," he said as he helped her up, escorting her into the study. A cherub-faced maid dressed in a gray uniform with an overlapping lace apron around her waist walked Raquel back to her limousine. Ortiz was permitted to drive up to the house, where he waited. When he saw the front door open, he jumped to attention.

It was a brand-new scenario, Raquel thought on the ride back. Jacob a crook? Smith a killer? JD the righteous one? JD had hardened his heart to her, she realized. He listened to her, but told only his side. At least a side he was willing to show her. This afternoon, he seemed ready to assault Jacob's character, to expose Jacob's own deception. De Solis was always serious, Raquel remembered.

CHAPTER TWENTY-ONE

Jacob was immersed in his laptop, checking the gallery's sales and conferring with an associate about an upcoming Rothko show, when Raquel walked in.

"So he called me a crook?" Jacob said. He knew there was little love lost between him and De Solis. "And Esau, too?" That accusation seemed less plausible. Why insult Esau's memory? After all Esau made tons of money for De Solis, Jacob thought.

"Darling, Smith told you that story for disinformation purposes."

"Smith was giving me disinformation? What the hell for? To test my response?"

"He wanted to know what you knew. Disinformation is their way of finding out if you're withholding something important," she explained. "Are you, Jacob? I don't want to see you hurt, darling."

Jacob flicked the remote on and pushed the volume on the TV on high. He wasn't taking any chances of them listening in. This routine was becoming all too commonplace. He also turned on a bedside radio to a classical music station that Raquel had preset for him. "I'm coming to believe that Bertha was on to something. Am I being tested?" He spoke softly, and with the ruckus of noise at full blast, Raquel strained to hear what he said.

She moved closer to him. "Smith was killed by his enemies. JD doesn't know yet who these people are. Are you playing a game?"

"I'm not playing at anything. Sullivan knows every move I make."

"Then hand your clues over to JD," she pleaded. "If it is money he wants and you can find it, give it to him."

"What clues? That I know there's no assassination plot?"

"Is it really money they are looking for?" she asked trying to figure out the threads of truth.

"Of course it is. I have to uncover Esau's role in all of this." He sat her down on the bed. "I can't even form the words. What I am about to say is so horrifying."

She looked at him, startled for the moment. "What is it?"

"I don't believe anymore ... that Esau killed himself."

Stunned, as if stung by a wasp, she grabbed on to her right arm with her left hand. Raquel spoke slowly. "How can you say that or even think that?"

"I can say that. And I'm becoming more and more certain."

"But the government autopsies...."

"I took their word on their findings. We had no way of determining what may have happened. Who thinks clearly when you're told that your brother committed suicide? My parents, even now, can't and won't acknowledge how Esau died. Do you understand their grief?"

"Yes, I understand. Though the FBI said outright that it was a suicide."

"Maybe disinformation started back then."

"Are secret bank accounts listed back on of the painting, Jacob?"

"I think so. There is some code. I can't say for what. Smith was murdered for telling me about this puzzle."

"And that's all you know?" she asked softly.

"Yes. Why are you doubting me?"

"I'm not doubting you, darling."

"Then why do you think I have something to give De Solis, something other than what he already has?"

"I just don't want you getting more involved in this than you already are," Raquel said, as if to warn him. "Whatever you know, just hand the information to JD and let us get on with our lives."

"You're scared, aren't you? You know what he's capable of."

"I don't want to see you start something you cannot finish." She was shaking her head. "I'm ready for this weekend to end, darling. I really am."

"Nobody's more eager to leave than I am."

"Well, steel yourself a little bit longer," she added quickly.

"What for?"

"De Solis set a memorial service for Smith at the Basilica tomorrow evening. This is a beautiful space next to the Recoleta Cemetery."

"What has he cooked up now?" Some new pitch was coming, Jacob thought.

"I've been asked to read a poem for Smith."

"A memorial for Smith?"

"At eight o'clock. Tell Maestro Trumball, too. JD pulled the memorial together quickly, so nothing would interfere with the Maestro's day of glory, Sunday, or this evening's reception at my parents' house."

"And you expect me to attend?" he asked calmly.

"Yes, it's the only way. You must show De Solis that you are not backing down."

"I've got to let Sullivan know."

"Do as you wish."

He decided to play along. "What will you read at the memorial?"

"It might be nice to cause a little controversy," she replied, regaining her sense of humor.

"Are you reading in English or Spanish? Smith was an American, you know. Maybe he was also Esau's buddy, as he kept saying."

"I thought about that. I'd like to read from Allen Ginsberg's 'Howl.' He is the American poet so often identified with the left." Jacob nodded, but waited to hear her reasons. "It will make De Solis' stomach turn, since he has always been identified with the right." She giggled like an adolescent making a faux pas. "People here take left and right very seriously."

She quickly telephoned the concierge and in Spanish told him that she needed a collection of poems by Allen Ginsberg in the original English, not a Spanish translation.

"What time tomorrow tonight?" Jacob asked.

"Eight o'clock."

"I've got to get back to my work," he said with a determination not to give up until he succeeded in breaking the presumed code.

"I'll leave you with your computer. I want to sink into a hot bath. But we must get ready soon to leave for my parents' home. Darling, I can't wait for you to meet them."

Jacob flicked off the TV sound, but left the radio playing.

From the bathtub, Raquel watched him closely through the mirrored door, revealing his backside as he punched in different sites on the Web, engrossed in a plan now to crack the code. This trip was rough on Jacob. Raquel looked pale. Was Esau murdered? Was Jacob next if he couldn't find where Esau had hidden the money? she thought as she soaked herself in the tub.

She emerged from her bath, redolent of fresh lavender. Jacob greeted her outside the bathroom. A Cheshire cat smile across his face. He led her playfully to the bed.

"Open the terrace doors, darling. A breeze would be nice." He did what she asked and returned to the king-sized bed. "Now then, are you planning to make love to me in broad daylight?"

"I most certainly am." He decided that penetrating her womanhood, absorbing the scent of her flesh, and tasting every square inch of her skin, feasting on her breasts and crotch, would give him the release he yearned for. He never could have imagined that cameras were focused on the large bed, broadcasting the event through secret channels to the general's bunker

"Give General De Solis what he wants, or he'll turn on you," she whispered, nibbling his ear.

"When I get the correct information, I'll give it to Sullivan."

"JD will stop at nothing until he gets what he wants."

"I'll give him his due, too."

Soon enough, they lay together on the satin sheets. Raquel gently played with his fingers and stroked his hair. "I know how difficult this trip has been for you."

"It's been tough," he allowed. He held her hand tightly against his chest. "Before this madness, the only hardship I could anticipate was Trumball's drunken remarks."

Raquel stretched out on the bed. His lips met hers. After a while, he moved to her neck, his tongue moving in circles down to her breasts. He licked her nipples until they were hard with desire, and kissed her stomach slowly, hungrily. Slowly, he savored her crotch and soft thighs, lifted her legs up on his shoulders and thrust in and out of her in a relentless rhythm. When he made her moan, then scream in ecstasy, he came in a series of volcanic shudders.

And so did she.

They shared the quiet that swept over them, and lay in each other's arms. He was exuberant and for the time being even a bit giddy. Raquel arched her back, stretched, and walked into the bathroom to douche. She showered with a luxurious soap and smiled as she thought about reading the Ginsberg poem.

Jacob showered after her, and prepared for this evening's event with her parents. He shaved slowly, naked in front of the bathroom mirror, cursing the day, and wishing very hard that the Argentine government would arrest De Solis for being the thug that he was. By the time he was ready to leave for the cocktail reception, his heart warmed as he wondered about Raquel's parents. He sighed with relief. All the same, his obsession with Esau's note penetrated his thoughts once more.

CHAPTER TWENTY-TWO

A tall, thin valet helped Trumball step out from the backseat of the limousine. Dozens of cars were parked in and around the driveway of the Gingold's large, Georgian-style brick home. Raquel's father, Albert, eagerly awaiting his only child, welcomed her with his customary wide embrace and placed a paternal kiss on her forehead. He was a stocky, gentle man, with wisps of gray hair combed to the right side of his head. Her mother, Emma, a very thin lady, waited inside and peered through the door, evaluating Jacob. Few of Raquel's beaus had ever passed her mother's muster. Jacob Rose would be no exception.

"My little child," Emma called out in Spanish, kissing her daughter on her lips. "I have missed you, precious angel." Jacob and Trumball trailed behind Raquel.

Then suddenly turning, "Is that him?" Emma gestured ambiguously. "He's too old for you," she whispered.

"Mama, that is Señor Trumball, the artist."

Trumball chatted with Señor Gingold, while Jacob broke away to join Raquel and her mother. "Emma, nice to meet you," he said.

"The pleasure is mine, Jacob," she replied through a broad smile.

Trumball marched toward then and interrupted, "Where are you hanging my painting?"

"And you must be Señor Trumball," said Emma, who approved of artists and enjoyed their quirks. It was no secret she had problems with Raquel's chosen career. She felt sometimes uncomfortable with her daughter's success because of the actress' fame and lack of privacy, which, to Emma's mind, modest people looked down on. Her daughter was a rebel, almost from the start, to her father's delight and her mother's lukewarm response.

Raquel knew exactly how her mother felt and wished Emma could open up lots more. Surviving the camps at Dachau and the murders of Emma's parents had made opening up impossible.

Once inside the large foyer, Fernando, the butler, stood by to greet them. He carried a large tray that held flutes of champagne. Jacob took one and handed it to Raquel.

"Beware. My parents' friends are the Argentine version of the New York crowd," Raquel said.

"You serve vodka, don't you?" asked a worried Trumball.

"Yes, of course we serve vodka. I already warned the staff about you, Maestro," Emma replied with a wink and a smile.

The family waltzed past a number of old friends before moving toward the marble fireplace, atop which Fernando was about to hang the Trumball painting. An early Chagall canvas was removed for the octogenarian's work. "Center it over the mantle, Fernando," Albert instructed the butler, while Trumball disrupted the preparations, bowing slightly to the various guests who had begun to encircle them.

They applauded loudly, ceasing their enthusiasm only when Albert took Trumball by the hand, nodding appreciatively to all around, and asked the group to join him in a toast. "To the United States of America's greatest living artist, Señor Laban Trumball. L'chaim. Salud."

Jacob knew that like Raquel's parents, their guests were among city's major art collectors. But could they tell that the painting was a forgery, which his brother painted as a piece of a larger deception? Jacob hoped not and paced for a moment before he tasted his second glass of champagne.

"How's this for high esteem?" Trumball yelled at Jacob, jostling his dealer from his ruminations to bring him back to the celebration at hand.

"Very nice," Jacob responded.

Trumball already moved to two svelte, blonde sisters, daughters of one of Emma's friends. The sisters fawned over the old man, and after, Trumball whispered, "Celebrate later with me in my hotel suite. We'll drink and toast, 'Salud,'" they whispered back, "Salud," and moved quickly away giggling.

Trumball walked to the painting and asked his audience for complete silence as he finished his vodka and placed it on the fireplace mantle. Then he waited for every guest to file in from the adjacent rooms. "I feel privileged to be in B.A.," he announced, referring to Buenos Aires by the colloquial initials used among the natives. "I am honored that the Gingolds have given me this special cocktail reception."

"Bravo, señor," a short man with a Van Dyke beard called out from the crowd.

"Gracias, señor," the old man said robustly. He picked up his glass of vodka, sipped, and bowed his head. "I must confess tonight." The room went silent. Jacob began to cringe. "All is not what it appears to be." Trumball's voice went soft for the moment, almost inaudibly so, as Raquel moved closer to Jacob. They could only anticipate what Trumball might say next.

"He isn't out of his mind, is he, darling?" Jacob didn't respond. "I hope I am just being a little paranoid."

"He's a lunatic, Raquel, and you know it."

"Shouldn't you stand closer to him, Jacob?"

"What the hell for?"

"What if he calls the painting a forgery, or talks about JD?" she whispered.

"What you see here isn't really what you see," Trumball continued, as if lecturing to a crowded room filled with eager college students.

"Bravo," the same voice bellowed from the back.

The old man reached over again to the mantle piece grabbed the vodka and took a final sip from the shot glass. "I want you all to come closer, to stand near me so we can look at the painting together."

"Oh, he wouldn't," Raquel said with a sigh. "My God."

"Shit, I think he just might." Jacob realized he had to divert the artist before he went too far. "Maestro, allow me to toast to you on Argentine soil," Jacob called out, and stepped forward, raising his glass of champagne. "To Laban … Trumball," he began clumsily, "whom we … celebrate tonight … for … his remarkable … lifetime … achievements…." Trumball stared at Jacob incredulously. The art dealer smiled, searching for a way to wrap it up. "With the best of his work yet to come, I salute you, Laban Trumball."

The crowd cheered, and Jacob felt triumphant, even as Trumball continued his declaration. "I want you all to stand near me so we can look at this painting together."

"Señor Trumball," Emma interjected, "please tell us the history of *Lea with Two Love-Apples*."

"Saved by your dear mother," Jacob said to Raquel.

Trumball nodded vigorously and lifted an hors d'oeuvre from a passing tray before he washed it down with another glass of vodka that Fernando had just brought him. And so Trumball began. The room was hushed.

"Paris in the 1930s. Europe was in turmoil, as we all know. I was a young artist painting in Montparnasse. I painted *Lea with Two Love-Apples* and nineteen other paintings in the series as an homage to the Bible." He explained that Lea was one of the biblical Jacob's wives, who was barren, but conceived after eating love-apples. "Several of these paintings are now in private collections, a couple of them in the Pompidou Centre, and one is in the Prado, I think." He stopped and scratched his head. "There's another in Cologne, and two are here in Buenos Aires," he continued, unaware that his paintings hanging in their current homes were perhaps more impressive to him than the polite patrons who stood and subtly rocked back and forth as they listened patiently.

"Most of the others are in my own collection," Trumball rambled, and paced back and forth in front of the canvas. Jacob caught his eye and shot him a piercing stare that melded with a slender smile. "I suppose one day this big shot art dealer of mine will try and sell them for me."

"God he's drunk," Jacob murmured. Raquel nodded and smiled.

"Enough about me," was nearly the last of Trumball's utterances until, after considerable pause, he concluded: "Sunday afternoon, at the museum reception, I will tell you all my entire life story." Jacob let out an audible sigh; Raquel rolled her eyes. "Until then … drink, talk, and be cheerful."

"Salud, dinero, y amor," another voice boomed from the back of the room.

"A toast," Raquel translated for Jacob. "Health, wealth, and love."

"Una persona muy famosa," a man brushed up to say to Jacob. An old chum of Albert's, he was interested in seeing more of Trumball's art. "A very famous personae," the man explained to Jacob. He badgered Jacob for a business card, mentioning he would be in New York next month. Jacob could only hope that he would be there, too, but the sight of this man, whose full crop of blond hair bore a slight resemblance to De Solis, only reinforced his focus on the chaos he found himself in. Jacob handed the man his card and turned away.

"Darling, are you with us?" Raquel nudged, noting Jacob's solitary state in the corner of the room.

Emma stood right behind them. "And how are you both enjoying yourselves?"

"This is a lovely gathering," Jacob said hurriedly. "I can't thank you enough."

"Tell me Jacob, what is it that led you to your profession? Was it scholarship?" Emma asked, disregarding her daughter's angry look.

"I've never studied art. No," he responded, almost curtly.

"Really?" And to what do you attribute your success?"

"Well," he started, turning first to Raquel for an approval to strike, "the rush I get, when I make a substantial sale."

"A rush?"

"Yes. A rush of adrenaline that grabs hold of me."

"I appreciate your honesty." Emma excused herself. "Oh, darling, I see that Señor Mendoza the director of the museum has finally arrived."

They all made their way over to greet Mendoza, who stood next to Trumball, listening to a story the artist was telling the two blonde sisters who once again flanked his side.

"Jackson Pollock drank like a fish," the artist continued, nurturing the impressions of these bubble-headed swans, both of whom had stylishly dressed in vintage Courrèges. Perhaps they had prodded him for gossip of the art world, mused Jacob.

"We knocked back a few in the old days," the old man offered. The blondes simply smiled, unfamiliar as they were with colloquial English, while a courtly Mendoza pretended Trumball entertained him with insider knowledge of the late artist, who had died in 1956 in a car accident in East Hampton.

"You must excuse me, señor y señoritas," said Mendoza, backing away from the conversation, bowing, almost relieved. "I must speak with an old acquaintance." Trumball cordially waved him off. Jacob, who had been eavesdropping, approached Mendoza with a handshake.

"You're not sticking around for the rest of Trumball's story?" he joked to the museum director, who returned only a hesitant smile. He was clearly amused by Jacob's humor, to which he also offered a quick, nervous acknowledgment before fleeing to other parts of the large drawing rooms that at least a hundred more guests had now filled.

Jacob watched Raquel work a room and found great solace in the party's festive rhythm, one that found most of the guests engrossed in, though oblivious to, the hanging forgery he feared would expose him.

"I'm so pleased for Señor Trumball," Mendoza said, as he returned, reinvigorated since their last conversation. All Mendoza had needed was a stiff drink to loosen him up, Jacob sensed. "What a triumph Sunday afternoon will be for him," Mendoza went on. "Señor Trumball will feel like, how do you say in America, 'a million bucks,' no?"

Jacob nodded. "His career has been brought back to life, there's no doubt about that."

"Señor, I have asked my associate to snap some photos of the painting while we are here. For the museum's archives."

"Won't there be an opportunity to do that at the museum?" Jacob asked, hesitantly.

"Sunday will be frantic," Mendoza insisted.

"I see."

"And as long as we have this opportunity right now, why should we wait?"

"No, I don't think we should encourage the guests to take pictures."

"It will take only a minute," Mendoza said, perplexed at Jacob's resistance. "Besides, I see no other cameras here."

"Not until I speak to Trumball," Jacob continued with some alarm. "You must understand how fussy he is."

"Of course."

Jacob waved to Trumball, who was flirting shamelessly with the two young blondes again, inattentive to anything else in the room. When he finally trotted over, aggravated by Jacob's disruption, he yelled at Jacob, who pulled him quickly aside.

"Where's the fire?" asked Trumball.

"Listen to me carefully," Jacob began, as he whispered to the artist about not drawing any more attention to this version of his work, specifically dissuading the artist from allowing any photographs before Sunday's swap with the real canvas. Mendoza remained standing near, straining inconspicuously to pick up their conversation. He was left on edge by the odd theatrics that had followed his simple request.

Jacob asked Trumball to sit down by the entrance hall and rejoined Mendoza. "I'm sorry, he says no photographs," he told the museum director.

"I understand," said a disappointed Mendoza.

Jacob spotted Raquel, and Mendoza followed him. She had been standing by a small circle of her parents and their friends, listening to them discuss, ironically, the subject of economic depression. Argentina was struggling to achieve political stability and had just seen its latest minister of economics resign.

"Our situation is a symptom of a global economic breakdown," Albert said with an earnest concern for his nation's less privileged.

"I don't think we'll ever see the kind of depression that overwhelmed us before the Second World War," Jacob interrupted, while tugging at Raquel's side to pull her away.

"History will repeat itself, I assure you," Alberto replied, taking a sip of his drink. The others only half listened, distracted now by the sonorous melody that Trumball's snoring performed.

Jacob wandered off with Raquel to be with Emma for a while.

Emma chatted with an informally dressed man in his forties. "Jacob, this is my cousin Saúl. He prepares the new Internet sites for some of our art galleries. I don't know a thing about that. He asked to meet you. Now I will leave you two."

The men exchanged handshakes. Saúl was a plump fellow with bushy eyebrows.

"I'm not familiar with Argentine websites. I have a damn good one in New York."

"You should check our sites, even if only to register one in Spanish."

"Yes, sure thing."

"The Lavazzo Gallery represents you here. Yes?"

"For the time being."

"May I propose a site for your artists who are readily available in Argentina? Maybe with the young artists in your group? At least register a domain name. And get your number."

Saúl seemed energetic, Jacob thought. And why not keep this project in the family he chuckled to himself. "And you would localize the website with an Argentine name?"

"Yes, I would do that so you will have a registered domain name here.

Jacob was shaking his head. "Sounds good."

"I'm certain you'll be pleased, Señor Rose."

Jacob spoke heartily. "Register a name for me. Okay?"

"Okay. I am happy to do that for you. Maybe you'll be my client, too."

"Jacob Rose Galleries, S.A. Get the number for me." Jacob reflected for a moment. "By the way, what do you mean by a number?"

"When the site comes up on the screen, the ... the ... how do say in English, IP address ... the number. These show up on the bottom of the computer screen."

"Ah, yes," Jacob said. "Send me a bill for the registration and for your work. We'll talk more when I return to New York. I promise. A pleasure, Saúl." Jacob shook the cousin's hand warmly and moved toward Raquel. "We really ought to go," he suggested firmly to Raquel. "If I may," he turned to Albert, "I'd like Fernando to help me with the painting."

Mendoza interrupted, suggesting that he take the painting back with him. Another idea that Jacob briskly declined. The museum director didn't give up. "You will have the painting to us well before the afternoon gala, no?"

"Yes, of course," Jacob assured the director, thankful the evening had ended without further stress. Mendoza smiled, but said nothing. He just stared, as Jacob accepted the velvet cover from Fernando and slipped it back over the forged canvas, handed it to Raquel, and went to collect Trumball.

While at the other end of the room, Emma told her daughter, "He's a fine gentleman. I'm happy now that you are with Jacob."

"I am happy, too, mama.

"Let me escort you to your limousine," Albert offered graciously as Jacob approached. "I noticed you met my cousin. He's a fine boy."

"Indeed, he is. He's registering a website for me here in Buenos Aires."

"Good," Albert said, shaking Jacob's hand warmly. "You won't be disappointed."

"Go, darling," Emma announced. "Señor Trumball looks tired."

CHAPTER TWENTY-THREE

They returned to the hotel at 11:45 and bid good night to Trumball. Once in their suite, they quickly undressed, both feeling worn-out from the days' activities. Jacob surfed the TV channels, desperate to fall asleep, but he was restless. Even a hot shower didn't relieve his weariness, or calm his nerves.

At 3:30 a.m., Jacob was resigned to the fact that sleep was not to be his. What he needed was to determine where Esau had hidden the clues to the very code that would now save his life. He showered again and shaved, careful not to rouse Raquel from her slumber. Less than thirty-six hours remained until Trumball's gala, a countdown that had disturbed his thoughts most of the night. He thought about the conversation he'd had with Albert's cousin, the website designer, the one who'd told him that every site has a numerical correlative. Were those the kinds of numbers on the back of Trumball's canvas: relational symbols to an Internet destination? Or were those numbers in the letter a clue to the code? He looked around the room. He was certain the letter was the only thing he'd had left of Esau. And he knew its contents by heart. Then he saw the keys to that brand-new Lincoln that had sat in that garage before he saw it destroyed and ran for his life.

Now the car was gone; it was history, probably sandwiched in some distant junkyard. Only the car keys remained. He'd almost forgotten he'd had them. What use were they now? he asked himself. He picked them up and jingled them, manipulated them, as he sat hunched at the edge of the bed. They were regulation Lincoln keys, by all accounts, each of them encased in a black plastic coating. As he spun them in his palm, he felt the relief of some kind of lettering on one of the three keys: Sanders & Co., Buenos Aires.

"The car keys," he mumbled, weighing their worth, stirring Raquel as he spoke to himself aloud. He grabbed the phonebook from the drawer in the nightstand. Sanders & Co. was a locksmith, a local locksmith. "I've got something."

He ordered coffee from room service. An attendant arrived within minutes with a carafe of steaming coffee and a basket of croissants. Raquel stirred as Jacob thanked the bellboy. He returned the bedroom, when she asked, "Were you having bad dreams?" her eyes still glazed with a sleepy frost.

"No. You need to sleep in order to dream."

"You haven't slept?"

"Not much, I'm afraid," he said. "Listen, I've got a hunch I want to play."

"A hunch? Don't be so cryptic before I've had a chance to sip some coffee. Please." He poured her a cup.

"We've got to get to this locksmith today. Sanders & Co."

"I can't say I see your logic any clearer," she yawned, in between small sips of coffee.

"These keys, 9 July—don't you see? Sanders & Co.? It all fits together … somehow," he said, staring off into space, trying to think like a detective.

"What in heaven's name are you talking about?"

"I've got to show this third key to the locksmith who issued it." She sat up attentively and placed her cup on the nightstand.

"The keys? From your brother's car, the one parked at the 9 de Julio garage?"

"Exactly."

By 10:15, they were dressed and en route to the locksmith, having left Trumball behind at the hotel to sleep off his hangover.

Ortiz parked outside of the pedestrian thoroughfare at Av. Florida, while Raquel and Jacob hurried to a small, street-level locksmith on the 300 block that bore the name Sanders & Co. They thought it odd that the shop would bear an Anglo name, so Raquel inquired in Spanish for the proprietor. Ronald Sanders was a short, muscular man in his middle sixties, sporting a shaggy red beard. And he had a British accent. "How can I help you?"

"I need you to tell me anything about this key," Jacob demanded, relieved at the same time to be speaking English. He placed the car keys on the counter and undid the third key from its ring. He handed it to the locksmith, hoping against all hell that it would mean something that it would offer up a clue, perhaps, to save the day—hell, to save his life.

The locksmith took the key and turned it over a few times. "Lovely day, isn't it, sir?" Jacob nodded in response, while Raquel stood by staring from behind her dark sunglasses.

"You're an American chap, aren't you?" the locksmith added, by way of small talk.

"Yes," said Jacob, breathlessly.

"Now, sir, may I inquire why are you so intrigued by this particular key?"

"It was attached with these car keys," he said displaying the others in his palm. "These belonged to a car my brother owned. It was parked in a garage on 9 de Julio."

"Shouldn't I be talking with your brother?"

"My brother is dead."

"Oh, well, I'm terribly sorry, sir. May I ask your brother's name?" Jacob stood before him, saying nothing. "So that I might check my records for his purchase?"

"Esau Rose."

Sanders punched in the name on his computer. "Rose," he repeated. Raquel looked up at Jacob, who remained silent, pensive, determined that this key was the puzzle piece he'd prayed for. "Here we are," said the locksmith, buoyantly. "Indeed. I duplicated this key for him for an airport locker." Jacob breathed the first sigh of relief he could recall since he'd arrived, and suddenly felt twenty pounds shed from his shoulders. "But ... but ... let ... me qualify that this is a dummy key," said Sanders to Jacob, still dumbfounded despite Raquel squeezing his arm. "We aren't permitted to duplicate airport locker keys. All that your brother wanted me to do was to imprint certain numbers on this one. Here, notice the numbers, 4427." Jacob shook his head: could this finally be the end of the road? "I suppose that it might pertain to the locker's number. I'm not certain."

Jacob faced Raquel and grinned widely, a delicious first. He could actually feel his facial muscles relax. "You've been very helpful," he told Ronald Sanders, before grabbing Raquel's hand and dashing out of the shop and onto the street.

They arrived at the airport in twenty minutes, jumped out of the limousine, and ran toward security. "Ask him if there is a special place for airport lockers," Jacob said.

The man responded with a stiff demeanor. "Sí, señorita. You can go downstairs, to the left," he answered in Spanish.

Jacob convinced himself that vital information was in that locker, maybe the money itself, though he couldn't conceive of $80 million packed firmly and securely and stored in a shoebox in an airport locker. Perhaps this was only one piece of the puzzle, or perhaps it was the whole puzzle, which would tell him if Smith was correct in warning him that De Solis was after the money. Perhaps there also existed information that would shed light on Esau's apparent dark side. Was there some kind of calculated deception around a core detail of his life, one that he'd wanted to maintain as a mystery? Something ghastly he'd never wished his brother and parents to know about? His being gay seemed trivial to Jacob's mind. No, it had to be something else, something sinister. There was only one way to find out: Jacob would have to break into that locker and get at its contents. He had to know who his twin brother really was and why he'd traveled so far from his origins, his character, his integrity.

No sooner had they got to the lower level than Jacob stopped in his tracks, stunned at what he saw before him. An entire section of lockers had been ripped from the wall and smashed wide open. Any contents within these metal scraps were trashed, littered about in a chaotic pile of rubble. He could barely catch his breath as he treaded lightly toward the area that would have contained number 4427. There, strewn about, opened and empty, a mangled locker yielded its contents of nothing.

"I'm dead," he said stoically. This felt like his last chance. A good hunch gone sour, and the time bomb attached firmly to his body, such as it was, ticking louder than ever.

"What are you saying?" She saw how his face quickly turned white.

"You heard me. I'm now on their most-wanted list. I'm a dead man," he uttered as he stared at the locker. "They got here first!" he shouted.

"You are not a dead man," she assured urgently, grabbing his arm to embrace him. "Nothing like that can happen here."

"Criminals have their own laws," he said, resigned to continued despair. Raquel did not answer immediately. "Look, they got to the locker before I did. De Solis' men have what they wanted. They don't need me."

"Darling, please, I will call JD."

"Why do you insist on speaking to him? He's a murderer. Can't you accept that?" She could not. Raquel believed that JD was forced to use criminal methods for honest ends; at least that's what she knew he did in the past.

"Jacob, please. I know JD. His methods are not always clean, but he cares deeply for this country."

"What was my brother doing with these people? Murderers, con artists, criminals," he said, shaking his head.

"Don't jump to unnecessary conclusions."

"My own flesh and blood, my twin brother. How can one family member be so corrupt, so diseased?"

"Let's get back to the hotel," Raquel insisted. "I'll call JD."

"Are you insane, woman?" Jacob felt cornered, to be sure. Was there anybody he could trust?

"Please understand, at one time, he loved me. I know he still feels affection for me. I still see it in his eyes."

"What are you talking about?"

"I mean that JD would never harm you, knowing, as he does, how much you mean to me." Her words offered little comfort.

Jacob glared. "Why do you defend his actions?" He no longer thought he believed in the human capacity for decency. Not here. Not now. Raquel didn't answer.

Jacob called Sullivan on the limousine cell phone. If he had a lifeboat in Argentina, it was Sullivan.

"Didn't I tell you to stop playing Sherlock Holmes?" Sullivan screamed.

"I had to follow this lead."

"I had to follow this lead," Sullivan mimicked. "Right. And you won't be satisfied till you get yourself and Raquel killed, will you?"

"Look, I chased down a key. It was on the ring that Esau left behind, the one that held his car keys. The extra key belonged to an airport locker. They got there first." Jacob could see no error of judgment in what he'd done; just the error of underestimating what he was up against.

"Who is 'they'?"

"I don't know, but they sure as hell know every move I make."

"Well, let me tell you, they found nothing."

"How do you know this?"

"I know how cat and mouse is played. Anyway, I just received a call from my sources. So count yourself goddamn lucky."

"Lucky? I'm stranded here without a passport, tormented by a madman who thinks I've got access to $80 million left by my shit-heel brother and who's ready to kill me if I don't come up with it! How's that for lucky?"

"You'll be okay, if you goddamn stay away from trouble!"

"Trouble? As if I invited all the shit that's been happening to me?"

"Listen, I want you to meet me at the hotel lounge."

"What for?"

"We'll have a drink."

"What the hell are we toasting, my funeral?"

"Relax, pal. I just want to tell you a few things."

"Like what?"

"Like I want you to concentrate on your social rounds with the artist, take in some sights, perhaps. And that's all. You read me?"

"I'll be at the hotel in half an hour," said Jacob, frustrated at Sullivan's dressing him down, yet grateful he had someone to watch over him.

"At 12:30, my friend."

"I'll see you at 12:30."

When they arrived at the hotel, Raquel fled to their suite, while Jacob waited in the lounge for Sullivan. Jacob felt more than a bit indebted to the FBI agent. In retrospect, it was Sullivan who'd found Esau's body.

Because of a required government autopsy, the family could not bury him as promptly as Jewish tradition dictated, but Sullivan arranged the return of the body as fast as regulations would permit. Sullivan had also found the painting and had the canvas authenticated. And again, it was Sullivan who had saved Jacob's life at the racetrack after Smith was killed.

Jacob was trying to keep his chin up. He had faith in Sullivan's methods, and he believed that De Solis had probably bought the idea that Jacob held the contents of the locker. If this bit of deception gave Jacob the upper hand, it was transitory, and he knew it. This extra bit of time was merely a temporary reprieve that would allow him some breathing space while he made his next decision, one that could very well keep himself alive.

CHAPTER TWENTY-FOUR

Waiting in the hotel bar lounge, Jacob began to assess whatever hopes he had for uncovering Esau's doings in Buenos Aires and whatever chances he had of finding the money, especially now that his key theory had left him no wiser or safer. This was a life-and-death chess match, and De Solis would have to make the next move if he thought Jacob had gotten to those airport lockers first. Jacob had only the note that Esau had left him. He still refused to let anybody see what he'd received from his twin just two days after his death. Jacob cherished that yellow sheet of paper. It was all he had left of his brother.

Special Agent Sullivan suddenly appeared. Jacob couldn't help noting to himself how little he paid to his personal appearance. His suit was gray, but rumpled, and threadbare at the cuffs. A salesman had clearly selected his tie, too, Jacob concluded.

"Let's order some drinks." Sullivan settled into the leather chair opposite Jacob, who sat cross-legged, looking reflective and vulnerable. "You'll be glad to know that our boys are covering every square inch of this place."

"I don't feel any safer," Jacob replied.

"They're protecting POTUS. I don't think you've got too much to worry about."

"I now know where I fall in that pecking order."

"What do I have to do to convince you to stay out of trouble and just have a nice dinner tonight with your friends, go to your celebration at the museum tomorrow afternoon, and then go home on Monday or Tuesday?"

"How about a miracle?" Jacob cast his eyes around the room, noting the hustle and bustle that could easily camouflage his murder, when the waiter approached to take their order. "Scotch and water, Agent Sullivan?" The agent nodded. "Two scotches and water. Two please," he repeated for emphasis.

"Answer my question, Jacob. What do I need to do to keep you away from trouble? Bop you over the head?" Sullivan smiled.

"You know," Jacob began, suddenly shifting the subject, "I don't know if I ever thanked you. I mean for getting the painting authenticated for me."

"The boys and girls of the Stolen Arts Division were doing their job. Now I asked you—"

"Also, I'm not sure if I thanked you enough for getting Esau's body back to us so that we could arrange a proper funeral for him."

"Look, that's the tough part of my job, but we do what we can when the surviving family is left to cope with the loss of their loved ones."

"My parents were especially grateful."

Sullivan gave a twisted smile at the abundance of all this gratitude. He was a tough man who performed a tough job. There wasn't time for sensitivity in his line of business. "We don't get many thanks for what we do. But we do it anyway."

Jacob accepted his drink from the waiter and stirred his glass. He leaned back against the chair, his one arm outstretched in a casual mode. "You've saved my ass several times in the last forty-eight hours." Sullivan waved it off. "I know that Esau was up to something. Smith told me so, just before the fatal shot. And there's loads of money involved."

"You've told me this already, Jacob."

"But I've come to believe that Smith was killed for giving me that information."

"And what if Smith was setting you up?"

"Why would he?"

"Maybe he wanted the money for himself. There's your answer."

"Well, what if…?" Jacob was nonplussed.

"You're an art dealer, and I'm sure you're a hell of a good one…."

"There's a pile of money out there in some secret account," Jacob interrupted, "and it's probably a trail to an even bigger viper's den." Jacob paused a moment to gather his thoughts. Sullivan just stared at him. "I've got to find out why Esau had turned to crime. Call it a matter of family honor, if you will."

"No, I won't … 'cause it's bullshit. You're pissed because you thought your brother was some upstanding guy."

"I think I know where the bank accounts are. If you try to tie my hands, I may never know the truth about my brother, and De Solis will get what he wants."

Sullivan leaned forward and lowered his voice.

"If you give me that information and stay the hell away from everything else, I promise you, Jacob, our government can proceed against these slime bags, and you'll be home free."

Jacob listened cautiously, then decided the Feds would have to go one better in their commitment to him; they would have to secure his safe departure from Argentina. It was nonnegotiable, and he demanded it from Sullivan.

"Remember what I asked from you at the track? I want everything now, passport, airline tickets, removal of any file on my brother relating to forgeries."

"I just need a little more time with that, Jacob. I'm convinced that later in the day, I'll have everything in place," Sullivan said reassuringly. "How do you think you can get at that bank account? If you can deliver that info without sticking your neck out, I can deliver it to my bosses and put a stop to this craziness, once and for all."

Jacob was intrigued by the prospect of this kind of federal assistance, as well as the guaranteed protection of his government from De Solis' potential atrocities. "An account with that kind of money will expose them to an investigation, and then we'll have the goods on them." Jacob nodded. He knew it was the right thing to do. "I'll need your full cooperation in providing us this access before any of this can come to light."

"And I'll need your solemn assurance that I'll get out of here safely."

"I just told you that I'll have everything set by tomorrow morning. Come on, now. You just finished telling me how thankful you are for all I've done for you and your family. What? Now you don't trust me?"

"No, no, of course I do," Jacob said, looking at the floor. His head was spinning. "I just need to make sure that I get those three airline tickets, my passport, and a safe return to New York."

"I hear you. I give you that promise. Look, I'm speaking on behalf of the United States government here. What more do you want?"

"You'll have that bank information in a few hours," Jacob said, refusing to believe he'd just offered Sullivan a complete lie. But this was something more gargantuan than staying one step ahead of De Solis and his minions. The U.S. government was bending over backwards to protect him. His obligation was now a matter of duty. And all he had to do was crack that damn code.

CHAPTER TWENTY-FIVE

At 3:45 on the barroom clock, and after drinking a few more scotch and sodas by himself, Jacob returned to the suite, buzzed but determined. Raquel was already in the bathtub, preparing herself for this evening's memorial for Smith.

Convinced that Esau's letter was the key to untwisting the current noose around his neck, he made his way to his laptop. He quickly checked his e-mail for messages, and, before he could read all of these, a thought flashed across his mind. "Wait a minute," he whispered. "That's it! Damn! Damn! Saúl, the cousin. That's it. Thank you, Saúl. Thank you for offering to set up an Internet site for my gallery in Argentina."

Jacob recalled the explanation of Señor Gingold's cousin: "Each domain has its own corresponding numbers…." At least that's what he thought he'd heard this man say. So he checked 555637455, which was written on back of the fake *Lea*.

The website for Schweizer Treue Bank/Swiss Trust Bank came up brightly on his laptop screen. "Damn it," he exclaimed with glee, though Raquel was in the bath, unaware of her boyfriend's success. She'd remain in there, as she did every day, for more than an hour; the price she paid for being ravishing. He pounded his fist on the table with excitement, then walked to the refrigerator and pulled out a bottle of 1998 Joseph Drouhin's Chassagne Montrachet. He poured a glass and looked out the window. His feeling elated turned quickly to bewilderment. The soldiers on the rooftops were even more prominently placed than they had been before. Suddenly it dawned on him that when he'd made love to Raquel, the terrace doors might have been open. He quickly closed the doors and pulled the curtains shut. "This is ridiculous," he thought, as he opened the doors and returned to the laptop with a full glass of chilled white wine. He wouldn't let paranoia get the best of him.

The bank site asked for a user name and password. "Shit," he mumbled, "what now?"

"The letter, the letter," he reflected. *Where the Obelisk meets the sky, 9 July 1970.* These are key words. He figured he'd try 09071970, which was Nueve de Julio 1970 in numerical terms, the garage where Esau had parked that Lincoln.

Nothing, nada. He reversed them; still nothing.

He stood up quickly, pacing the room with his hands in his pockets. He jingled his keys in his pocket as he crossed back and forth. "Of course, the key." Jacob removed the keys to Esau's Lincoln from his pocket and examined them again. He tried the locker number as a user ID. Nothing. If the keys were a clue to anything specific from Esau, Jacob believed that he had arrived at those lockers too late. And now he'd exhausted the various combinations of numerical clues that Esau had left, both from the canvases and from the date on that letter. *That damn letter.* That's all he'd had left of his brother. He pulled it out again, if only to reinforce what he already knew, which, thanks to Esau, was next to nothing. How was he supposed to find clues that Esau had left behind when there weren't any? And after he told Sullivan he had the code, too! He took a deep breath and stared at the letter once more. He'd have to find something. He knew his life depended on it.

"You used to remember mine, I remembered yours."

What did Esau mean when he wrote that in this letter? How am I supposed to know what that means?

He sat there, searching his mind for any shred of possible rationale to all of this. Jacob was worried about the place being bugged. Even though he was not doing a lot of this aloud, he turned the TV on. Unexpectedly, he remembered a game they used to play as kids on those long drives to Martha's Vineyard for summer vacation. *Esau, Jacob. Translate those words to numbers,* he told himself. Those numbers had been wild cards which could be combined with the numbers on license plates of passing cars in a game of poker. He wrote their Hebrew names on a piece of paper. *Esav and Yaakov.* All letters in the Hebrew alphabet have a numerical equivalent. *Eyin, sin, vav is Esav.* For the moment, Jacob could not recall the order of the letters. He pulled out a sheet of paper and began writing, *aleph, bet, gimmel, dalet, hay, vav.* "What's next?" After a few tries, his memory finally came to his aid. *Ayin* is the sixteenth letter. Jacob wrote sixteen. *Shin* is the twenty-first letter. *Vav,* the sixth letter of the alphabet. His name, Yaakov. The Hebrew letters for his name were *yod, aleph, kuf, bet.* Once he discovered each correlative letter and number, he entered these as the user name, one that would, with any luck, correspond to a user name or password. But which one? *C'mon, c'mon, damn it.* He punched in 1-6-21 for Esav, then 6-10-1-11-2 for Yaakov. And then the sorry result: "Error. Not Found. Check user name or password." *Shit. Nothing again. Nada.* He reversed their names, Jacob, Esau, and tried punching those numbers into the user name and password in the same fashion. Again nothing. He felt doomed. What he'd remembered as a quirky play on numbers they had once upon a time enjoyed as kids had turned up nothing.

Then, suddenly, it dawned on him, smacking him like a swift kick to his gut. *These are key words.* Key words. The key was the password. *You used to remember.* USED. User ID. Those numbers are the user ID. So he first keyed in the 16216101112, the user name. If ever he'd felt like he'd hit the jackpot, it was just then, at that moment! He backed off shortly, took a sip of his wine, and told himself to calm down. You've gotten nowhere so far. Just go easy, he told himself. He pressed 4427, from the airport locker as the password. His heart pounded as another long pause began. The damn Web is so slow. So slow. Endless waiting and wondering. Hoping against all odds. When it opened, after so many anxious minutes, he could hardly believe what he saw. The site gradually unlocked to some kind of elaborate Flash introduction. Then it began blinking before it morphed into its next advisement: "Waiting for Access." And so he waited, too, before another round of blinking letters made their striking revelation: "Mr. Esau Rose, New York, New York, United States." And on the next line: "Press for Account Balance." "Holy Moses!" He leaped up from the chair giving a high five against the air.

This was almost too good to be true and not a moment too soon. He never experienced this sort of luck, he reminded himself. Still, he felt the noose around his neck suddenly loosened, removed. If the protection of the FBI had been like an insurance policy, here was the opportunity to cash it in without having to die first. He pressed for account balance, just as instructed, and he started to feel that same surge of positive adrenaline that he'd long ago felt at Cornell when he'd flip hurriedly to the back page of a term paper to find the A for which he'd hoped. This moment held the same feeling of accomplishment. When the amount appeared, he was startled: the account balance read only $8,000,000. *There's supposed to be eighty-eight million! That son of a bitch. Now what?*

Jacob was exhausted and seemingly scared all over again, when he stopped himself from another fit of anxiety. At the very least, he had something to give to Sullivan and maybe to De Solis, if he were forced. That's what mattered. Relief. He tore up his little pieces of paper. He knew he'd remember what he'd done, and he certainly didn't want anybody getting hold of the information before he was ready to deliver it. He had the ace up his sleeve. But would that be enough to get him out of the country safely?

After ten minutes of further self-absorption, while Raquel continued her bath, he received a call from Trumball. "Yes, a memorial to Smith," he found himself yelling into the phone. "Raquel will read a poem by Allen Ginsberg."

"In Spanish?" Trumball asked.

"No, in English."

"Allen Ginsberg? Why not the twenty-third Psalm?" inquired the artist.

"Because De Solis wanted something American. Smith was from Boston, apparently."

"So, why not one of the Lowells, or what about Robert Frost?" the old man pressed.

"Just be here at seven."

Raquel emerged from her bath and beauty treatment and began searching through her wardrobe.

"I did not expect to attend this event, much less have to read at it. What on earth shall I wear?" she seemed to ask no one in particular, as she continued towel-drying her hair.

"How about something to die for?" Jacob returned with a wink. He stripped naked and jumped onto the bed, hard and ready, inviting her to return to their sheets to dishevel them once again.

CHAPTER TWENTY-SIX

At 7:25 that Saturday evening—less than nineteen hours before Trumball's gala at the museum—Jacob felt less the prey of De Solis' machinations. Jacob had cracked the code for $8 million of what was supposed to be a bigger pot of gold. He knew he could count on Agent Sullivan to make good on his promise to return him safely to the U.S., where, among other things, he would get to the bottom of any other existing forgeries in his gallery's inventory. Funny, he'd nearly forgotten about his anxieties over his reputation, especially in the face of what had seemed to be a loaded gun aimed directly toward him.

Sullivan was a good man, he reminded himself as he sat with Raquel and Trumball in the hotel lounge over coffee, waiting for Ortiz to drive them to the Smith memorial. He thanked God the FBI had their best team in Buenos Aires, if only for POTUS, perhaps, but he swore he could already feel the payoff himself. The nightmare would be over within twenty-four hours, and he couldn't wait to return home.

Still, Jacob knew he had to produce the remaining $80 million, or convince De Solis that he knew next to nothing about the whereabouts of the money. He had another scheme already burrowing its way through his thoughts: he would get the general to believe he was on the verge of figuring out where the balance of the money was. He was sure he could buy enough time with this ruse to obtain his safe return.

He smiled at Raquel, who sat with an open book, *Allen Ginsberg: Selected Poems 1947-1995*, in her lap like a movie script; she was wearing a simple black dress, unadorned. Jacob wore a black suit, white shirt, and Hermes tie. Trumball, on the other hand, shifted restlessly on the banquette, sporting his usual oversized, chocolate brown corduroy jacket with its worn elbow patches, and a gray turtleneck sweater. A couple of hotel lounge waiters stood by attentively, adjacent to the Secret Service agents, who sat idly drinking coffee.

In the distance, Jacob noticed a familiar-looking figure, though at first he couldn't place him. "There's that card dealer from our dinner with De Solis and Smith," Jacob recalled. "The man I said was cheating in my favor," he said, staring coldly. For Jacob, the dealer was just one more reminder of De Solis' treachery.

"I wouldn't have turned on him," interrupted Trumball. "I would have walked away with my winnings. Pride is for stupid people." The artist was now on his second glass of vodka, but Jacob was left to wonder how many shots the old man had drunk upstairs in his suite. He'd told Trumball earlier that it would be okay to stay behind, but the old man had insisted on attending the memorial.

Raquel looked at the dark-complexioned and square-built man, who standing with a group of two other men. "He is handsome in a brooding sort of way," she said, as she observed the dealer.

Eduardo the dealer recognized their stares and nodded to them. Jacob waved flamboyantly, mockingly, though he was certain the dealer wouldn't detect the difference. "I'll bet he's spying on us. That whole group over there looks like thugs."

"You didn't tell me what you found on your computer," Raquel said.

Jacob held his hand over his lips and told Raquel to do the same.

"Why would I do that?" she asked.

"For one, I don't thing anybody needs to know what we're talking about."

She gave Jacob a skewed look, but then shook her head in agreement. "Yes, darling, I'll cooperate."

"I found an account my brother stashed away in a Swiss bank to the tune of eight million dollars."

"That money is rightfully yours, sonny," Trumball interjected. "Don't be stupid. Your parents and you are his heirs." The old man, who seemed to be oblivious, obviously was listening, yet resisted Jacob's instructions for secrecy.

"I have to check when the deposit was made," said Jacob to Raquel, ignoring Trumball.

"If the deposits were made over a period of time, it is most likely is yours, no?" she asked keeping her head down as she flipped her hair.

"If the money were deposited in a lump sum and recently, then I don't have a right to it."

"Why not?"

"Dirty money. That's what it is."

"That could be checked," Raquel offered, stroking Jacob's arm in reassurance.

He shook his head. "This might surprise you. I'm hoping a deposit was made just the day before Esau's death."

"Then you're saying it's JD's money?"

"Well, it's money he was paid by crooks or crooked governments. Who knows?" Jacob was already plotting how he would find out for sure, but he wasn't going to share this with a soul, not even Raquel. "Excuse me," he said to each of them. "I forgot to call Agent Sullivan."

"Use your cell phone, darling."

"I'm going to use a public phone." Jacob looked behind him to see if the card dealer was following, but the dealer seemed intensely involved in conversation with another man who'd just joined him.

Jacob got Sullivan on the second ring. "I think I found the money."

"You think? Well that's good news."

"I've got to check if the account is Esau's private bank account or if it's tied up with the general."

"We can check that for you. Understand, of course, that if it's Esau's rightful money, then you and your parents are his likely heirs."

"Anyway, we're heading for Smith's memorial," Jacob said.

"I'm on my way. You know, he used to be one of our people, until he left the agency some years ago."

"Really?"

"You know what surprises me, Jacob, is that your brother never mentioned Smith to you."

"Esau never mentioned much of anything, it turns out. Except that he wanted my list of art patrons to solicit funds for the president's re-election. Look, I called to rendezvous with you secretly, to give you some information I have. A bank account. I won't give you any information over the phone." Jacob spoke determinedly.

"I understand. Here's what we'll do. Let's synchronize our watches first. During the memorial, at 8:15 sharp, you'll excuse yourself to Raquel and tell her to cover for you if asked. Say that you're going to the men's room. Then you'll slip out and meet me at the Recoleta Cemetery. It's right next to the Cultural Center.

"Yeah, I know that it's next to the cemetery."

Sullivan gave Jacob directions to the Duarte family tomb. "Meet me in front of Evita Perón's crypt."

"What if the cemetery gates are locked?"

"They're not," Sullivan said.

"Do you have the airline tickets and my passport?"

"Assure me that you will bring the codes to the money at the cemetery and my bosses will authorize that I bring your tickets and passport with me."

"I assure you, but with one qualification."

"Which is?"

"Smith had said they were looking for an account with $80 million. That might not be true. I've only found $8 million."

"Let me talk to my bosses. I'm sure we still have a deal. This is just what I've needed to expose these people for good," Sullivan said, and hung up.

As Jacob approached Raquel, she asked, "Did you reach Sullivan?"

"Yes."

"And?"

"He'll check when the deposits were made," he told her, leaving out the part of negotiating for airline tickets for their exit. "Shall we go?" he said, an arm extended to the door. "I want to arrive on time."

As the two men stood, Raquel proudly placed her arms in theirs and exited the lobby with the same kind of self-satisfied smile she wore to collect film awards.

CHAPTER TWENTY-SEVEN

The garish, pink Centro Cultural Recoleta was lit up with its necklace of multicolored lights. To Jacob's eye, the effect looked like a giant brothel. Sitting next door to Recoleta Cemetery, the Centro Cultural was housed in a former convent, with small auditoriums for music, theater, and dance, and a multitude of galleries for art. A grassy plaza at its rear sloped down toward the river fills. Limousines arrived at the front entrance, one at a time, as elegantly dressed women and men alighted and entered a now-lengthy queue.

The three, Trumball, Raquel, and Jacob, arrived promptly at eight, as the orchestra inside began playing Samuel Barber's solemn "Adagio." At 8:10, waiters emerged with trays of canapés, while attendants walked about with bottles of champagne. There was a festive aura throughout the place. Chattering couples and clinking glasses mixed with the music.

Jacob was puzzled.

"Is this is a memorial to a dead man?" he asked Raquel. He assumed it would be more somber. Quieter. Less crowded.

Jacob lifted two glasses of champagne from a tray, while Trumball asked for a shot of Stolichnaya. De Solis was deep in conversation with some military men, but nodded to the three across the room, glancing at them every ten or fifteen seconds.

A few minutes later, Jacob excused himself. "Don't wander off; stay here so that I can find you," he told the old man. "I'll be back shortly," he said to Raquel. As he looked about, he saw no one he knew and quickly made a ninety- degree turn toward a side exit to find his way to the gate at Recoleta Cemetery. He had to locate Evita Perón's tomb, at night, no less. Talk about bizarre. He'd taken down every direction Sullivan had given him about the Duarte family tomb and Evita's crypt. Yet, he wouldn't be hurried. He held the cards, and they would play by his rules.

Waiting in the middle of the night in a desolate cemetery with the moon shining brightly on numerous rows of marble gravesites was unnerving. Jacob wasn't superstitious, but as a kid he'd seen many horror movies. He looked behind him, stared at the moon, looked all around, and then checked his watch. 8:20 p.m. Sullivan was late. Jacob was never late. Always on time, or a just little early for an appointment, but never late. On the rare occasion that he was, he never excused himself. He heard his father's voice from almost thirty years ago. "When you excuse yourself, you accuse yourself," he told his boys.

Thoughts of death and burial raced through his mind. The decision to bury Esau aboveground had been his own. He frowned on belowground burials, and knew that Esau believed in the same. In a bizarre conversation as college freshman, they had laid out plans for their eventual demise. Lying deep within the earth with their bodies decomposed spooked him. Death had seemed so far off then; immortality had seemed more likely to grip their senses. He stared out at the many tombstones lighted eerily by what seemed to be a harvest moon. At college, the boys' conversations mostly involved Esau's success at sporting events, he remembered. Esau needed to prove that he was better at sports. More agile. More gifted. Esau had made the wrestling team at Cornell and he had been on the fencing team. Esau was also the first of the brothers selected for the soccer team. Jacob, however, had tried out for the campus theatre group. In their senior year, his big moment was playing Lopahin in a production of Anton Chekhov's *The Cherry Orchard*. His parents had driven up to see him perform. A naïve time in their lives. The old thoughts melded with the darkness and wraithlike silence that cloaked the cemetery in the night.

"Over here. Follow the light." He saw a white beam of light bouncing off the black granite crypts, and heard Sullivan's voice in a loud whisper.

"What a place to rendezvous."

"Keep your voice down."

"Where's Evita?"

"She's here. Airtight and thirty feet under. Right in front of you." Sullivan pointed to a stately tomb marked *Familia Duarte*.

"Do you have my plane tickets and passport?"

"First, a history lesson," Sullivan said, as he turned off his flashlight. "General De Solis comes from a family of body snatchers. Did you know that?"

"I'm not that interested."

Sullivan wasn't deterred. "His father and uncle snatched Evita's body and hightailed it to Italy. Did you know that?" Jacob shook his head no.

He realized he was going to get a history lesson, despite his protestations. "Juan Perón himself brought the corpse back from Italy in the middle of the night. Two decades after she died. Two decades." Sullivan held up two fingers of his right hand in Jacob's face. "Your General Juan Domingo comes from a long line of body snatchers."

"He's not my general."

"He might be your girlfriend's, then."

"I don't know what you're talking about. Do you have what I want?" Jacob asked anxiously.

"Hell, yes. You got what I want?"

"Yeah. Show me yours."

"Here's your passport. Airline tickets for three. All yours, my good man. Once you show me the code, and you better not be bluffing or faking."

"Here's what you need. All neatly written on this little sheet of paper and placed in a nice, self-sticking envelope."

"You are a classy guy, Jacob. You did well. Now we have the goods on these clowns. The higher-ups will really be happy."

There was an odd silence as each studied their respective treasures and expressed satisfaction.

"Well, you've got work to do. And I've got what I came for," Jacob said with relief.

"You've got one more day in Buenos Aires, so don't blow it."

"I won't."

"Then you're off to New York."

"Yeah, I can hardly wait."

"I'll leave first, so give me a few minutes. Don't walk through the cemetery. Go toward the field behind the center and enter from there. If you're spotted, you have an excuse, like you needed air or something."

Jacob left the cemetery and walked over to the sloping field behind the Cultural Center. He didn't tell Sullivan that the bank responded to his e-mail querying the differences in the amounts of the account. He took a shot that Smith might have told the truth. The instant he thought of how comfortable he'd become, the moment abruptly ended and he became anxious. Jacob surveyed his options. He had to find the $80 million as an insurance policy.

Lights from the Cultural Center cast oval shadows, illuminating patches of grass and spotlighting a few trees. He looked at the river below, reflecting the moonlight above. The days here had taken a toll on him: he was exhausted. He stood looking at the sky, impatient and eager to return to the hall, but he decided to wait at least five minutes.

Out from the shadows of the grassy surround, a figure emerged very suddenly and dealt him several fierce blows to the gut.

"Who are you? What are you doing?" Jacob sputtered, clenching his stomach to his face and daring to stand. Instead of gaining his balance, he sank to his knees, coughing up blood. The figure kicked him in the head. Jacob was writhing in pain, but he gathered enough strength, what little was available to him in agony, to pull at the man's legs, tripping him to the ground. Staggering to his feet, Jacob kicked the assailant hard in the kidneys. As he folded in pain, Jacob wrestled him to the ground and then mashed the attacker's face, which lay buried in the grass. Despite all the commotion, he felt for his pockets, making sure that his airline tickets and passport were still in place. Was this Sullivan? He thought, reneging on the deal? When he bent down to get a good look, a light popped on in one of the halls of the Center. This distraction allowed the man a moment to struggle to his feet.

"You, the card dealer," Jacob shouted. "You son of a bitch. De Solis put you up to this."

"Work with us," Eduardo said, with a distinctly Latin accent, gulping air by the mouthful and still twisting on the ground in pain.

"You attack me and now you want my cooperation?" Jacob asked, still exhaling heavily himself.

"I want to know what you know."

"Who wants to know what I know?"

"General De Solis," the card dealer confessed, having underestimated Jacob's ability to fight.

"Then let him ask me himself," he shouted, dusting his trousers of grass. "Why does he need to send a thug to beat me up? Huh?" Jacob's adrenaline was pumping; he was ready for another round, obvious to him that he could take the card dealer handily.

"The general is a man of great consequence. Don't screw around with him"

The man handed Jacob a white handkerchief, which he tore from the dealer's hand to mop the blood still shooting from his nose in slow spurts. "So, he doesn't do his own dirty work, is that it?"

"General De Solis is on your side."

"Sending you to beat me up is being on my side?"

"I was attempting to scare you."

"Then why did he tell me some bullshit story about an assassination plot against the U.S. president?"

"I don't know."

"He was always after the money, that's why. Well, you can tell him I have the code to the money and that I've shared it with the proper authorities. You tell him that, okay?"

The dealer barely nodded.

"He can check with the United States FBI, because now they have the code," Jacob continued.

"I will tell him, señor."

Jacob brushed himself off and walked into the hall. He stood in the rear and listened to Raquel beginning to read from Allen Ginsberg's poem "Howl."

The card dealer inched his way toward De Solis, who was surrounded by aides. Jacob watched them huddle.

Raquel loved an audience. He had never seen her in a live performance. Her face was somber as she looked over the heads of individuals and caught people's eyes.

She began to read. The guests were silent.

What sphinx of cement and aluminum bashed open their skulls and ate up their brains and imagination?

Moloch! Solitude! Filth! Ugliness....

Raquel read further. She paused at key lines, as if to give the guests a chance to digest Ginsberg's word.

Ashcans and unobtainable dollars!

She looked her audience, aware that she had their rapt attention, smiled faintly, and went on reading.

Jacob had trumped De Solis. He had his evidence. Sullivan needed to finish the job. The art dealer felt the pain from his confrontation. His hip ached; he began to limp lightly yet he wouldn't complaint. He got what he wanted from Sullivan. Soon he would be ready for the final assault, Jacob assured himself.

Applause for Raquel's reading broke out, and Jacob hurried to the podium and saw several aides from De Solis' circle quickly usher her out of the hall. Jacob followed quickly, calling after her. She wouldn't turn around. She kept moving forward, without so much as a word. Then Raquel entered the general's Bentley, guarded now by two soldiers.

"What the hell is going on here?" Not a word in return. The car sped off. "Hey, Sullivan. Over here. Fast." Jacob stood motionless on the curbside outside the Centro Cultural. "What the hell just happened?" All at once the woman he loved, the one who shared his bed, his confidence, had simply walked out on him. "Why the hell did she race off in his car?" he yelled as Sullivan approached. "They kidnapped Raquel. Right in front of my eyes."

"How do you know she was kidnapped?"

"What do you call it?" Actually, Jacob wasn't sure if she was really kidnapped, but this was no time to speculate on alternative scenarios. "Why would she ignore me and rush into De Solis' car?"

"I ask you. What makes you so sure they took her against her will?"

"Damn it Sullivan, don't play games. I called after her a few times and she didn't even look my way." This was getting to be too much for him, but he had the code and so did Sullivan.

"Take the old man and go back to the hotel. Look, you've had a rough night. I see that you were punched pretty badly, too. What happened?"

"By De Solis' thug. A card dealer. I have to get Raquel. This is madness."

"My guys will check it out."

"You're always saying your guys will check it out. Damn it!" There was little Jacob could do. Raquel was gone, and until Sullivan could look into it, he had little choice but to collect Trumball.

Sullivan led the art dealer back into the hall to look for the artist. Jacob clung to an assumption that there had to be a rational explanation for Raquel's actions. Yet a woman fearing for her life would not go quietly into the night, especially when her public surrounded her. What might they have threatened her with? He tried desperately to see her face in his mind's eye. Nothing. Why did he think that she might have turned against him? Anger distorted his trust in her. He reprimanded himself for the grandiose plans that he'd come up with for buying his way out of Argentina. It was his own stupid fault to have believed that there was any resolution to pure evil.

Ortiz was running toward him, somewhat wobbly, a cell phone in his hand. "It is the señorita. She must talk to you."

"Where are you, Raquel? Why did you run off? You're okay, aren't you?" he asked all in one breath. "Are you unharmed? Answer me!"

"I'm fine, really, darling, don't worry about me. I'm at JD's villa. Don't worry."

The feeling of relief was only momentary as the gruff voice of the card dealer came on the phone. "We are holding Raquel as, shall we say, insurance. She will stay here overnight."

"Let her go! Unharmed. Immediately!"

"She wishes to be with us. You produce the code for us and all will be well."

"Put her back on the phone!"

"I'm afraid that's not possible. She is resting now."

"Put her back on the damn phone!" he demanded.

"Contact us with the information of your brother's accounts and we'll talk." With that, Jacob heard the dial tone.

Ortiz followed Jacob, who briskly walked back into the hall to find Trumball.

"I drove him to the hotel half an hour ago," interrupted Ortiz. "He was tired."

"Well, I'm ready to return myself."

"Sí, señor. My pleasure."

Jacob got in the limousine and immediately called Trumball.

"Go to sleep, old man," he intoned. "I was checking to see that you're all right."

They drove slowly past the cemetery. A little city of the dead, Jacob considered, looking at the many tombs and family vaults of Argentine politicians.

Soon he heard himself say good night to Ortiz as he entered the unusually busy hotel lobby. It was only hours away from the presidential visit. He strode to the bar. He needed a drink, and only a martini would do, he thought. It was just after midnight.

CHAPTER TWENTY-EIGHT

Raquel rested in a comfortable guest bedroom at General De Solis' villa, down the hall from his private office. The room was furnished with a woman in mind. This was often a way station, of sorts for the women De Solis brought to the compound. Raquel had slept here only one other time. For De Solis, Raquel was his ideal, his Evita, against whom every other woman had to compete in feminine glamour and raw sex appeal. So much so, De Solis kept the mahogany armoires stocked with a full wardrobe in Raquel's size.

"See that I have bottles of mineral water," she demanded.

Eduardo the card dealer picked up the phone in room. "Bottled mineral water for our guest, please. You understand that General De Solis has asked me to look after you," he told her.

"Yes. So?"

"He wants you to contact the art dealer once more."

"Why does he want me to contact the art dealer?"

"To convince him to cooperate. Smith's murderers haven't been caught. They are after the money. It is not safe for your friend."

"Yes, thank you. You can leave now," she told Eduardo. She suspected that, despite his sudden interest in Jacob, he masked his own greed for whatever it was De Solis and company felt Jacob was keeping from them.

It was her meeting with the general at the memorial for Smith that convinced her. De Solis, in an aside to her, blamed himself for not taking the events of the last couple of days very seriously. "The car chase in the garage. The blown-up lockers at the airport. Smith's murder. I should have known that trouble was following," he said. "I didn't. I was too involved with my own agenda. He was my guest. I was not a good host. I failed Jacob. Will you forgive me? I assure you that I will get to the bottom of his troubles."

She decided immediately to go back to JD's compound, even if it caused Jacob to wonder whether she was or was not kidnapped. She had to learn the truth. She owed it to herself. She owed it to Jacob.

By this time, Jacob was on his second martini. He removed his jacket, loosened his tie, and moved to one of the nearby sofas, stretching his legs. It must have been past 1:00 a.m., less than twelve hours before the gala at the museum. Nursing his drink, Jacob remembered the first time he had telephoned Raquel, just days before Esau had committed suicide.

"Esau told me you are free to date," he had recalled saying.

"Date?" was her reply.

"Yes."

"I don't care to date," she had said firmly. "No, I don't even know what the word means. You North Americans want to 'date,' whatever that is."

"Raquel, it doesn't have to lead anywhere," he'd told her. "My calling you was Esau's suggestion anyway. He said that you wanted to meet me." Jacob was surprised by her reaction.

"Yes, that's true. I wish to meet you. I'm busy now, with my work and my friends and my film. I told you that I would be making a movie about the 'disappeared people' in my country during the junta period. Didn't I? I am working with a General Juan Domingo De Solis. He's consulting. We'll talk more at a later time," she had said.

What a bitch, he had thought. He had never known he could be so stung by her rejection. After hanging up, he had done his best not to think of her. The following evening, she had sent an e-mail.

"Jacob, I gave you a hard time yesterday," he had read. "Please accept my apologies. Will you meet me Friday evening at the Film Forum for a showing of one of my favorite films? The show starts at seven."

That event had been three months ago. Three months and a breathtaking romance later, and he was now drinking his second martini in a lounge far from New York, still trying to figure out who there was left to trust in this world. Then his cell phone rang.

"Raquel?"

"Darling, I want you to know I'm all right. Really."

"Why did you leave me and go off with De Solis? Why didn't you respond when I called you?"

"I am sorry, Jacob. It was a moment of madness. I'm okay, now. JD is off somewhere. I don't know. There's a lot of activity in this house now. I couldn't stop thinking of you, darling."

"Why are you there?"

There was silence for a moment. "Please don't ask that question. Just know that I'm acting in your best interests."

"Why are you there? I have a right to know," he asked indignantly, despite knowing that she was famously stubborn.

"I am safe. The real painting is here with me. In a garment bag. JD wants to escort me to the gala."

"So he kidnaps you? Raquel, come to your senses."

"Two young soldiers are guarding the painting."

"I hate to say it to you this way. If you love me, you'd come back to the hotel. We'll leave from here this afternoon, with Trumball."

"I love you, Jacob. You must trust me. Do you?"

"Of course, I trust you." He ordered a third martini and sipped slowly.

"Then accept that I wish to be here. I'll arrive with the garment bag. We'll switch the paintings at the museum, and the Maestro will have his triumphant day in the sun. Trust me, darling. Get some rest. It's time that we both got some sleep."

"Aren't you concerned that Smith was killed? You're staying with the murderer. Can I be more explicit?" He began to slur his words. Finishing his second martini often did that to him. He had become skillful at slowing down his speech, hoping nobody noticed when he was somewhat smashed. "Go to the mirror, Raquel, and look at yourself," he said angrily.

"Don't play Hamlet." She hung up. Jacob was stunned. First, she shunned him and went off with De Solis, now she slammed the phone down.

After the third martini, he was ready to doze. He returned to their suite and quickly threw his clothes off. Raquel was all right, he supposed. Just stubborn. She had to do things her way. He had his passport and their flight tickets. The FBI had his brother's secret account. And the painting—yes, Trumball's exquisite art, that was the reason for the trip to Buenos Aires after all—was safe and ready to be returned and switched in time for the museum reception.

All the assurances he made to himself didn't stop him from obsessing over Raquel. He had his papers and the FBI on his side, so he told himself to relax. No luck. He couldn't. Thinking of her made him realize that he had to find the remaining money. He would leave that task for the morning.

CHAPTER TWENTY-NINE

Raquel was still awake at 2:15 a.m., waiting for De Solis, pacing about in a furious state of impatience, when he finally knocked on her door.

"I've been here almost four hours," she said in Spanish, as she glanced at her watch and took a seat.

"Please don't be upset with me. I was detained by any number of details...." De Solis said with a sincere voice, but she was still displeased.

"It's always the same old story, JD."

"My darling, I cannot help it if some of my lieutenants cannot follow a simple set of instructions," he pleaded. He was exhausted, but seeing Raquel had animated him.

"I don't like having to wait for anyone, especially when I'm doing you a favor."

"I understand. I had instructed my aides to make certain that you received every courtesy. Did they comply?"

"Every courtesy but haste!"

He waited for her to calm herself before he poured them each a glass of scotch from the same crystal decanter that she'd already visited while she'd waited for the last several hours. He sat down to join her on the plump loveseat, but she was restless and began pacing again.

"Your aides have informed me that Smith's murderer has not been caught and that they fear for Jacob's life."

"That is true."

"Which part? You assured me that no harm would come to Jacob!"

His shoulders lifted. "That is what I ordered. I wish no harm to your friend. Let him lead us to the money. That's all we are after. And then this whole ordeal will be finished." Raquel took a seat at the other end of the room. She was still brooding.

"Jacob thinks I've betrayed him," she said after a moment's pause, turning away in anguish. "I didn't respond to his calling me when I entered your car. I ignored him! Do you realize how difficult that was for me?"

"Then you really love him?"

"Of course, I do! But deep down, I'm afraid what we are doing will backfire."

"You are doing this for his safety."

"He doesn't know that. He must think that that I have betrayed him. And I'm not sure that he has any awareness of the money, despite what he has said to me."

"I am sure that he does. Twins have a way of knowing or guessing what the other is thinking," De Solis told her.

"And that is a perfectly foolish rationale," she argued. "They had not seen each other in years, and now one twin is dead."

"Esau was alive when he arranged to hide the funds."

"Jacob must think I've turned against him," she said. "Don't you understand?"

"No, I'm not sure that I do."

"Jacob and I haven't known each other long enough. On one level of his mind, he thinks I am always acting." She paced in front of the bed. "What is the line between fiction and truth?"

"My dear, don't be philosophical." He started to laugh at her. Raquel was usually straightforward, despite her occasional fondness for melodrama.

"Sometimes even I can't distinguish between truth and lies," she said.

"Telephone Señor Jacob again. Explain your position here, that you are under a sort of house arrest. Beg him to believe that you have not betrayed him, as you say."

"Why should he believe me?"

"Because he wants to believe you; it's all he has left."

"He's been an unknowing victim from the moment that we arrived. You forget that this whole trip here has turned sour for him."

"What are his alternatives? Tell him to cooperate." De Solis filled another glass of scotch for himself. "And that you are worried for his safety."

"I am worried for his safety. The sale of the painting has not occurred as he expected. He learns that his brother painted forgeries of his artist's work. He sees Smith murdered. I turn my back on him.... No, he would never believe me now."

"My darling, there is a great deal of money somewhere that belongs to me. Señor Esau had arranged a transfer to my account, then took his own life."

"It doesn't make sense. Why would Esau have arranged the money for you, JD, and then kill himself, leaving you to wonder where the funds are? Leaving money to sit abandoned? Why would Esau have betrayed you?"

"These are details that do not concern you. I ask only that you deal with Esau's partner in crime to all of this. Señor Esau is dead. I believe that Jacob was a partner with his brother."

"How can you be certain?"

"Because Señor Esau was his brother's representative here in Buenos Aires. Surely they shared a good deal of each other's business plans." Raquel shook her head, unconvinced that Jacob knew anything about his brother's outside dealings. "Señor Jacob must share the information he has from his brother, if he knows what is good for him," De Solis demanded. "They were in this together. I am sure of that, my dear. Was there anything Señor Jacob has said that you have not told me?"

"There are many things I have not told you about us."

"I am referring to anything about the money and Señor Esau."

"I have told you … he has said nothing."

"Think, my love."

"You have asked me that already. Your only hope is if Jacob figures out where the money might be hidden, but I am certain he has not the vaguest clue."

"Unless we figure that out before him."

"I hope you do just that. Then this nightmare will be over," she said sharply. She looked less certain of herself than at that moment at the memorial when she quickly agreed to go off with De Solis.

"Do you ever think of the old times?" he asked suddenly.

"We went over that the other day."

"Yes, but before you left Buenos Aires for the States, you were more like your old self."

"You mean I still loved you," she said defiantly.

De Solis stared past her, unprepared for Raquel's refusal to rekindle old desires. For De Solis, who considered himself the ladies' man, her iron will was irritating. As she sat opposite him in a spectacular silk nightgown with hand-painted feathers in a dizzying design; all he saw were her splendid breasts and her dark hair twisted in a braid down her neck like an innocent schoolgirl. He reached out to stroke her face.

"No, JD. No, you cannot do this to me, or even think this way," she said matter-of-factly. "There is no meaning to your desires for me."

"Not even for old times' sake?" He was used to grabbing his woman and seeking his pleasures; most would yield in his arms. He shared too much history with Raquel, so he hesitated and he began to plead. "It is important to me now. You must understand," he said raising his voice. He needed to feel that she was still vulnerable to the pleasures of their former passions, even if he had to stir her memory with his touch for her to recall that scalding desire they once shared. Even if he had to insist on it.

"No!" she said emphatically, reflecting back to just one year ago, how when she, Esau, and De Solis had drunk champagne and danced through the night in the tango clubs of Buenos Aires. How Esau would always excuse himself before daybreak, leaving her to ride home with De Solis. They would spend the day together, making love, vowing they would one day lift Argentina's morale and bring power back to the people. How JD had told her to wait for him when she left for New York to pursue her film studies. How she'd told him he needn't worry, because their love could never be rivaled. He'd had ambitious plans for them that he could not share with her then. She had vowed fidelity. Much had changed in the past year. She'd met Jacob, and while she'd never planned it, she now realized she'd fallen deeply in love with him. "You have what you need from me. I'm helping you put pressure on Jacob. Isn't that enough?"

"I want to love you. Again. Tonight." He knelt in front of her and placed his head on her lap.

She stroked his hair, distractedly, not without some degree of guilt for having abandoned their love for what she'd discovered in New York. "No, JD, the love we had is no longer meant to be," she said softly, her eyes moistened with nostalgia.

"Enough of your patronizing," De Solis blurted, angered by her platonic attentions. He rose to his feet. "Continue the pressure on Señor Jacob. I shall return this afternoon, when we will go off to the gala at the museum together."

Raquel looked away from him. De Solis was not a man who could accept any amicable compromise. A pity. She'd enjoyed his friendship.

He strode out briskly and slammed the door, which, unknown to Raquel, could only be locked from the outside.

The phone rang in Jacob's room ten times with ear-shattering volume before he picked up. He cleared his throat.

"Yes."

"Jacob, please hear me out."

"Are you okay?"

"Yes, I am being treated very well."

"Why don't they release you?"

"I am not in harm's way and I shall see you at Trumball's celebration at the museum. The painting is here with me. I promise you, Jacob, all will be well. But now I must go."

The phone clicked off, and Jacob was left with a panicky feeling in his stomach.

Raquel's bedroom door opened, rather unexpectedly. It was De Solis again.

"Any new information?" he asked, pointedly.

Raquel shook her head no, surprised and a little shaken by his silent, sudden entrance. She considered putting a chair in front of her door, though she knew De Solis still loved her and would never hurt her. His interest now was in retrieving his money. She was merely another one of his aides.

"Try again when the sun is up and it is morning," De Solis demanded and slammed the door shut.

CHAPTER THIRTY

Two hours passed, and at 4:00 a.m., raised voices and crashing sounds awakened her out of a deep sleep. She threw on a robe and tried to open her door. It was locked. She panicked a bit, captive amid violence somewhere in the villa. As she looked around the room, the noises seemed to come from above, where she noticed a small, square duct covered by an ornate grate at one corner of the ceiling. She grabbed a side chair and brought it to the corner of the room, stood upon it, and looked through the duct grill as if trying to peer at the noises. The voices grew louder. "I want an equal share of that money," she heard a voice bellow to another man, who responded by saying the money wasn't found. Raquel pushed up at the grill and loosened it. She placed it inside and to the side of the crawl space. The area was wide enough for her to push her head through. Could she enter the space entirely? She quickly got off the chair and slipped out of her silk ensemble and into a pair of pants, a T-shirt, and flat shoes. She turned off all the lights off except for the small lamp that sat on a nearby table and wondered if they would come in to check on her. After setting several pillows under her blanket, shaping them to resemble her sleeping body, she returned to the chair, hoisted herself up to the crawl space, slithered inside, crouched, and moved slowly toward the fracas. She could recognize one of the voices as that of the card dealer: Eduardo's booming monotone was made even more grating by its amplification.

"You think that all the money is yours now?" Eduardo shouted.

"You think that I'm planning to cut you out, don't you?" another man shouted back. Raquel ignored the discomfort of the crawl space to get closer. This other voice was faintly familiar, and she strained to recall where she'd heard it.

"Nobody else knows about the money!" Eduardo yelled back. "I want a one-third share; don't tell me you haven't found the money!"

Raquel crawled closer to the light. It was becoming brighter as she approached what was surely De Solis' office. She was frightened for her life. She knew she couldn't make a sound as she reached the duct over the office.

Through its own ornate grate, she peered into the room. She held her breath and tried not to move. Her assumption was correct. Yes, she'd recognized Eduardo the card dealer's voice. But she was not prepared to see who belonged to that other voice. "No, it can't be," she repeated. "He faked his own death at the racetrack?"

It was Smith. De Solis had lied.

Suddenly Smith removed a gun from a desk drawer. Eduardo was startled and lunged for the Smith, struggling to get the gun from him. Raquel started to crawl backwards to her room when she heard the muzzled sound of a shot. Slowly, she moved forward again, lifted herself slightly, and saw Smith standing over the card dealer's body. Eduardo wasn't moving. His head was twisted at a grotesque angle and wriggled like jelly in Smith's arms. Smith dropped Eduardo's limp body to the floor, took a white handkerchief from his pocket, wiped the gun clean, and placed it back in a desk drawer.

Three guards entered. Two men lifted the body and left the office. "Clean this room and then lock the door. Nobody is to go in the room," she heard Smith order. "Nobody!" They turned out the lights and left the office. One of them jiggled the doorknob to ensure the office was locked. She could hear their footsteps fade away.

Raquel waited only a minute before she felt it was safe to jump down. She pushed the grate in front of her, descended quickly, and moved to the only illumination left in the room: the computer screen atop the desk that contained the gun that killed Eduardo. She was tempted to take the gun for her own safety, but time was of the essence. She moved to the monitor and booted up the computer on De Solis' desk. She sent Jacob an e-mail. She typed quickly.

I AM IN JD'S OFFICE. NO TIME TO WASTE. NO TIME TO TELL YOU HOW. CARD DEALER IS DEAD. SMITH IS ALIVE!!! DEATH WAS FAKED. YES!!! I BELIEVE YOU. WATCH OUT FOR YOUR LIFE!!! I LOVE YOU, JACOB. DON'T WORRY ABOUT ME I CAN TAKE CARE OF MYSELF AND I AM ALL RIGHT.

She signed off and hurriedly got back up into the crawl space, carefully closed the grill, and crept quietly back to her room. No one seemed to have entered it while she was in the duct above. The garment bag was still there, she noted, trying to catch her breath as she tiptoed back to her bed. She pulled the covers close around her. De Solis had probably locked the door from the outside to protect Trumball's painting, she reasoned, thankful that it wasn't just the canvas. Her life had been spared.

CHAPTER THIRTY-ONE

Smith pretended to return to his small house on the grounds of the general's estate, but instead, he hurried off to his waiting Lincoln that he'd left idling outside the complex of garages.

Eduardo, that pig! He had it coming to him. He wasn't satisfied with what he would get. Smith moved behind the wheel and sped off, shaking his head, fuming at the idea of this underling demanding to be paid off when they still hadn't found the money. Smith's only regret was that he hadn't killed that bastard earlier. A five-percent cut for doing nothing but keeping his mouth shut! He hated anyone who didn't subscribe to his standards of dedication to an agreed-upon game plan—a way of thinking he'd honed during his career as a mercenary.

His thoughts quickly turned to Esau, who was to have received a share equal to Smith's and the general's, but who would never get to collect now that he was gone. Murdered. Smith felt certain that De Solis had been behind it and had Esau killed once he knew that the painting was on its way. Smith believed with all his heart that De Solis had Esau eliminated, once he felt he didn't need him any longer.

Smith gritted his teeth in frustration. He zipped along at 95 mph on barren dirt roads in the quiet of night through Palermo Chico, the sleeping suburb of Buenos Aires. Driving eased his tensions; he took his anxieties out on the accelerator of the Lincoln Town Car. He headed for the open road to Cordoba, some 700 kilometers away. De Solis ordered the meeting for 5:00 a.m., and Smith knew he would have to arrive precisely on time, neither early nor late. No matter what was going through Smith's head, he would stick to the game plan, as agreed.

Since Jacob had arrived, the emotional upheaval of Esau's loss was particularly tormenting for him, especially these last forty-eight hours. He had grappled with the idea that Esau had screwed him, certain that he'd hidden the funds for himself alone, or for himself and Jacob, though he knew in his heart that Esau would never have betrayed him. Besides, wouldn't Jacob have found the money by now? It seemed obvious that Jacob had been scared into doing his damnedest to solve the puzzle, but still nothing had been yielded to De Solis or him. Clearly, Jacob didn't know much. Smith did not know that Jacob had already solved the riddle of the coded $8 million, or that he had given this information to Sullivan and the FBI. Still he believed that because Jacob and Esau had been twins, they had to know each other's business.

For a man faithful to a game plan, nothing was working according to one. He thought back on the original strategy that he and Esau had devised to hide all the money—and screw De Solis and his gang while they disappeared together forever. The two were to have changed their identities. They had even found an excellent plastic surgeon in Germany who would have transformed them physically. Smith managed a smile as he reflected on those times, even as he wanted his sorrow to crush him. He would never have let himself cry. Crying was for sissies, and he knew it offered no solution. The only vindication of Esau's death would be to grab all the cash for himself. How many nights had they had spent together, in the seediest bar imaginable, just outside of Buenos Aires, scheming? Too many to recall, but all too memorable, to say the least. *The best of times were at the Palacio,* he laughed to himself. Quickly, the Lincoln made a sharp U-turn, and instead of an aimless destination to kill both time and tension, he decided to pay a visit to this freak show passing as a nightspot.

There, in addition to hatching their plot, they had spent many a night laughing, drinking, and exploring different looks for each other. Yes, there, at the Palacio, among a smorgasbord of vagrant types known as patrons, they had shared the secret known only to them. In that den of depravity the customers would never notice, or even care to notice, these two super macho men knocking back one whiskey after another as they whispered to one another their most heartfelt promises.

There at the Palacio, no one had ever given a damn that these two *uber- masculine* mercenaries, in frumpy dresses and long, blonde wigs, were a couple of part-time transvestites, each wearing more rouge than an aging hooker while they gesticulated with rough-hewn, oversized hands. Certainly no one there, or at anyplace else for that matter, ever knew that these two men were deeply in love.

As he began to approach the Palacio, his determination was startled by the sight of De Solis' black Bentley shining under the light of a half moon, in a nearby field just a hundred yards or so from the bar, and on the other side of the dirt road. He pulled into the field, got out of his

Lincoln, and walked toward the gleaming machine, its headlights having flashed to order him inside.

"Out for a nightcap, are you?" De Solis asked, amused but angry.

"Why have you followed me here?"

"Do you have the code or not?" De Solis demanded.

"No."

"Is the art dealer still under surveillance?"

"Of course."

"And the actress?"

"Your former mistress is locked in her room, just as I left her," Smith said, defiantly. "What is the point of this interrogation, out here, at this hour?"

"How dare you address me like this!" the general shouted. "Suppose the art dealer discovers the code this morning."

"The room is covered with hidden video cameras and microphones. Have you forgotten? We will know the moment he does."

"Threaten him with killing the actress. If he doesn't come through, kill the two of them."

"Are you crazy? Then we'll never find the money."

"We? You will find the money. That's your job! Then eliminate them both. She crossed a line with me," De Solis yelled, emphasizing each word.

"My share was one-third—now it's one-half. Isn't that right?"

"Eliminate Jacob Rose."

"Again, what would that prove?"

"Are you going soft?"

"No."

"Then kill him. And kill her. Then no evidence will exist. Nobody else is aware of the code."

"Or the money."

"I've told you, within hours I will take over the military, and we will have many chances to get at those funds."

"How?" Smith asked, refusing to be put off.

"I will discuss this we when meet at dawn for our strategy session."

He stared at De Solis, "I know you eliminated Esau."

"No!"

"Then who did?"

"He killed himself"

"You ordered him killed." De Solis leaned over to pull up a phone. Smith watched him, staring coldly. "You expect everyone to follow your orders. You ordered Esau killed once you knew the painting was on its way to Buenos Aires."

"You're a fool," said De Solis. "Why would I have killed him before we got the code from him? We have been over this many times already." Smith bit his lip and ceased his accusations. He knew more now than he needed to hear from the general. It was clear that De Solis was a madman. Suddenly, as the sound of a helicopter roared from above, they heard shots fired.

"What's going on?" De Solis bellowed to his driver.

Before he could look out the Bentley's darkened windows, a mortar shell blasted the vehicle. The doors flung open. The driver was hit and slumped over the steering wheel; blood squirted from his neck and splattered the windshield. The Bentley's hood was on fire. Two government soldiers pulled up out of nowhere in a dark green Hummer and ran toward the vehicle, firing with drawn weapons. Smith rolled out of the Bentley, and hit the ground for cover, the dim neon of the Palacio's sign a blurry vision in the distance.

"I'm shot!" screamed De Solis. "Get me out of here!" he called to Smith, who quickly pulled him away from the seat of the car and onto the ground.

The soldiers spotted Smith and began firing more blasts in his direction. Bullets sprayed Smith and De Solis just as another mortar shell rained down on its target, the Lincoln. Smith and the general watched as it missed and blew the soldiers to pieces.

"To hell with the coup," snapped Smith, who sprang to his feet. He took his black gloves out of his coat pocket and placed them on his hands. De Solis looked up at him in agony. Then Smith yanked his Glock from the holster.

"You killed Esau!" he yelled again, pointing his gun at the general.

"What if I did?" De Solis said, barely able to speak as he moaned in pain. "I had that big maricon blown away. Now," the general gasped, "there is more for us." He tried to get up, but he could only manage to crawl slowly toward the Lincoln. "Get your vehicle," he pleaded to Smith, who stood with his gun raised, as the helicopter whirled in departure, certain that they'd hit their last mark. "We'll return to my villa at once," De Solis ordered, bleeding heavily from his arm, but watching Smith in disbelief. "We must return. I need help!"

"I'll help you," said Smith, moving closer to De Solis, as he aimed his gun at the general's neck. He was sweating heavily as he contemplated his next move, while De Solis writhed in pain, still pleading, now more desperately, as he continued to lose more blood. Smith put the gun back in his holster. De Solis' eyes were tightly closed as he held his wounded arm close to him.

Smith staggered over to where one of the dead government soldiers laid in a pool of blood, his torso just a shredded cavity of internal organs, exposed. The other soldier's body was severed from the waist down. Smith pulled a gun that hadn't fired from the remains of the two soldiers.

"I'll help you, you son of a bitch," he yelled to De Solis, as he knelt over the general's battered body. "Open your damn mouth," Smith demanded. De Solis did not move. Smith aimed the soldier's gun at him. De Solis could only look up in horror.

"Buenos noches, puta," said Smith, as he felt a sudden rush surge through him and he fired into De Solis' throat, then into his skull. Blood and vomit spewed from the terrified face of his victim as Smith fired one more shot through the general's open mouth. He cleared his throat and spit on the corpse of the man that killed his beloved Esau.

"That's for cutting out my heart, you crazy bastard!" With that, Smith dropped the gun on the ground and walked back to the Lincoln. He blasted the music of the Doors on his CD player. Then he turned his lights on, pulled out onto the road from the battlefield behind him, and started back for Buenos Aires. He halted the car, screeching to a stop.

Love me two times, baby.

Love me twice today.

He drove in reverse gear a couple of miles, targeting the parking lot behind the Palacio. He had vindicated Esau and needed a drink. De Solis lay dead ahead, obliterated and abandoned, a maggot's breakfast the next day, if the authorities didn't discover him first.

Smith entered a barely lit dark room. A pool table sat in the middle, and the bar stood at the far end. Straight ahead were the bathrooms, barely visible, assigned to male and female, though it was clear that both were used by either, including some of the visitors to this place who fit into neither classification. The bathrooms were mostly drug dens anyway, where some junkie was usually face down in the last stall, or somebody else could be found doing a bump of cocaine off a urinal. The entire Palacio was one big toilet.

Some of the patrons were outfitted as gauchos, though Smith knew the real ones would never enter this pit without a disguise. The jukebox pounded Blondie from its speakers, as a dwarf woman, topless, offered her pathetically huge titties to Smith's darting eyes. He shook his head, and she moved along. Boys not much older than fifteen, and other young men, wore tight, black jeans. They all looked alike: penetrating, dark eyes, spiked black hair, or slicked back from all the grease that a few days without a bath will produce. They sported their bulges like badges of pride, rubbing their crotches at least once every other minute, as if anyone there needed a reminder of what they wanted. In another part of the room, the sixty-year-old madam of at least one well-known Buenos Aires brothel held court in a corner booth, which, every once in a while, found her slipping below to fill her mouth with the cock of some young sailor who'd paid his ten dollars in advance.

Smith found his usual stool at the bar. He hadn't been here since Esau had left Buenos Aires six months ago. Here they had found a place where they could dance the tango and no one would lift an eyebrow. When they danced, they spoke little, preferring to look deep into the other's eyes, just holding each other close. Smith yearned for these shared moments now that Esau was gone: their searching conversations; their dogged determination to raise hell; and the quiet moments of sipping their whiskey slowly, jabbing the other in the shoulder and shouting, "I love you, bonehead," to one another. Smith became wistful now that he thought back on the twenty five-year love affair that began in a foxhole along the Mekong Delta, just before the fall of Saigon. For so long, they had had only the Palacio at which they could openly celebrate their bond.

"The usual?" whispered Antonio, a husky youth with bulging biceps, black hair, and a throbbing crotch. Smith nodded, but barely looked up.

No sooner was the drink placed before him than he found one young man sitting next to him. He nodded hello, and the young man asked for a light for his Marlboro, which Smith offered, grudgingly, his Zippo extended without giving the kid a glance. The young man inhaled deeply.

"Can I refill your glass," he asked Smith, who stared straight ahead.

"Does it look like it needs refilling? Take a hike," he snapped, as the young man slid away faster than a cockroach in bright light.

He wasn't looking for chitchat. He wanted to ruminate. Though De Solis was history, Smith was still astonished by his boss' final commands: he had ordered him to kill Jacob and Raquel. How could he do that to the memory of his only lover, Esau, the one human being who had ever shared his principles, to say nothing of rescuing him from isolation and loneliness? He sat sipping whiskey, unable to block the Doors' song from his mind. It had been Esau's favorite. And it had become their song.

He remembered Esau saying, "That song is from the heart of a poet."

"It's bullshit," Smith recalled himself saying, but he'd grown to love it anyway. *Love me two times, baby, love me twice today....* It reverberated in his head, like an endlessly repeated mantra; for now, he heard nothing else.

CHAPTER THIRTY-TWO

Jacob woke shortly before 9 a.m. to a barrage of telephone rings. He hoped it was Raquel, assuring him that she was safe and explaining why she would be going directly to the Trumball luncheon without him at her side. No matter, he knew she'd promised to be at the museum and to bring the painting. The gruff tone of voice on the line, however, was Sullivan's.

"Can you be here in thirty minutes?" Sullivan demanded, matter-of-factly, without so much as a how are you.

"Could we say 10: 30, if you don't mind? I've had a rough night," Jacob said. He rubbed his eyes, picking up the travel clock on his nightstand to check the actual time.

"What now? You weren't out playing cops and robbers again?"

"No, I didn't sleep too well last night." Jacob emitted an audible yawn, still trying to shake his desire to hit the snooze button and roll over. "Have you forgotten that Raquel was ... abducted?"

"I told you we'd look into that. Seems everything's on the up-and-up," said Sullivan.

"Well, she called a couple times last night to say she was all right."

"So what's the problem?"

"I'll see you at 10:30," Jacob replied.

"Ten thirty it is," Sullivan barked. "At the U.S. Embassy on Columbia Av.," he added. "We'll be teaching you how to look like you've been hit by a bullet and take a fall."

Jacob's final yawn shook his entire face. When he hung up, he laid his head back down on the pillow and belched a hearty laugh.

"What a damn trip! A lousy jaunt to Buenos Aires in Trumball's honor at some prissy museum lunch turns into an episode of *The A-Team*," he yelled at no one.

"Argentina is on the brink of economic collapse. The middle class have taken to the streets with tear gas and grenades in hand. And on top of everything else, the president of the United States is arriving at any minute. Yeah, welcome to Buenos Aires."

If there were a bright side to be considered, however, Jacob was relieved that he'd tracked down the money, even if he was still short $80 million. Still, he had nothing left of Esau with which to track this cash. He'd been given a set of keys and a cryptic letter, and he'd exhausted both. It was out of his hands, as far as he was concerned. He'd already turned over the code for the eight million to Sullivan. He'd done his good deed. The rest was their job, he reasoned.

Slipping a robe over his naked body, he focused on the plan he'd hatched with Sullivan to undo De Solis' plotting. It was an ingenious scheme for safeguarding his exit from Argentina. Sullivan had assured him that the museum would be heavily staffed with FBI agents and additional security. Jacob was worried that De Solis and his thugs had received word that he was planning to leave the country after Trumball's luncheon. Sullivan tried to convince him that there was no way De Solis could know anything about this plan. Jacob was still insecure. They might try to stop him, he'd insisted. *Or they just might try to kill me*, he pondered.

Besides, as Jacob saw it, the museum would be a perfect place to stage a phony code-breaking, in Mendoza's office, so that De Solis would get wind of this longed-for event just as Jacob would actually be fleeing the country. He had already made a promise to Sullivan that he would verify how he'd arrived at Esau's $8 million account by cracking the IP number, and demonstrating this for him at the embassy was part of the plan he'd negotiated in exchange for his return home.

The best, however, was yet to come. The luncheon theatrics that would render his embassy visit a mere dress rehearsal would take an even juicier turn, according to Jacob's plan—this was the part that he relished most: Sullivan was to pretend to shoot him, using fake bullets, of course, just as he was hacking away at Mendoza's computer to locate the cash. And just as Jacob would announce he found the money, he'd get shot. At that point, De Solis' goons, who presumably would have been casing him throughout the party, would race to inform the general of the money's discovery and Jacob's sudden-death playoff. By the time they'd reached the office, Jacob strategized, he would be out the back door—with Raquel, Trumball, and the $9 million painting he wasn't selling—and the emergency service people would place them in an ambulance and whisk them away to the airport.

It was perfect, he thought, as he ambled toward the shower, where he washed off a night's sleep and shaved quickly.

Jacob couldn't care less about the Trumball luncheon. He was eager to stage his charade and get back to New York. Thank goodness for Sullivan, who had already delivered on his promise when he handed him the tickets and his new passport. Even though he had been repeatedly threatened, there was one aspect of this whole disaster that almost made it all worthwhile: it had brought him and Raquel closer together. He had hoped for that to happen, this being her native country, where, he suspected, these lovers would be able to commit themselves to each other. Strangely enough, the tension-filled events of the last couple of days had created a sense of ease between them, a feeling he hadn't experienced in a long time.

He pulled out his tuxedo, shirt, and the pearl studs and matching cuff links that Raquel had persuaded him to splurge on at Mikimoto in New York. He still snickered at having to wear a dinner jacket to an afternoon luncheon, just because his eccentric artist demanded black-tie as a dress code and the museum was too gracious to alert the old man to such an obvious faux pas. He put his shoes down and glanced at his laptop. He was due at the embassy in a half hour, he realized, but he really wouldn't have another opportunity to check his e-mail after he'd packed what was left to pack and take with him to see the Feds.

Surely the gallery would be inundating him with any number of inquiries and updates. He wondered how he ever managed to leave for a weekend in the Hamptons given how dependent his staff was on him. He pulled up his e-mail account. One Rose Gallery entry after another scrolled past his eyes. Then, an e-mail from Raquel. "What the…? Must be dated incorrectly," he said to himself before noting that, in fact, it was dated as new! How's that possible?

He wasted no time opening it.

Jacob felt a shiver across him. SMITH IS ALIVE! His life, his sense of hope and reason, his entire MO for getting the hell out of Buenos Aires was now suddenly thrown into question. Paralyzed. He suddenly felt mute, nauseated, so fearful was he that Smith was lurking outside the door.

Was Smith operating independently of the general? How had he staged his death? Yes, of course! This was all just another by-product of De Solis' evil machinations. Smith was just another pawn, he told himself, his face brightening. He breathed deeply, but his heart was racing.

He'd have to call Sullivan.

Wait! How did Raquel manage to send an e-mail?

He paused.

No.... Unless.... No.... But, then again.... No.... Still, somehow Raquel had gotten to a computer. The note was hastily written. That had to attest to its legitimacy. Yeah, right.

He quickly phoned Sullivan.

"Look, I've just learned that Smith is alive," Jacob said, still panic-stricken.

"What are you talking about?" Sullivan asked.

"Just what I said, God damn it! I received an e-mail from Raquel sometime during the night."

"Was this before or after she called you?"

"What difference does it make? She e-mailed to warn me!"

"Look ... what can I tell you?... Maybe they've drugged her."

"Screw you, Sullivan."

"Jacob, listen to me: that guy's a corpse!"

"Well, what if he's not?" Jacob asked in a stutter. "Why would Raquel send this to me if it weren't true?"

"Will you relax, already? Get your ass down here, and we'll deal with it." Sullivan hung up abruptly. If Jacob could have seen the frightened expression on Sullivan's face, he might have felt a sense of solidarity.

Or he might have felt totally screwed.

CHAPTER THIRTY-THREE

Jacob left the hotel with pain in his gut.

As usual, Ortiz was out front.

"The United States Embassy."

"Sí, señor," Ortiz replied as he pulled away from the hotel's driveway.

Twenty minutes later, the Mercedes pulled up to the embassy.

Jacob entered the front door of this now-familiar old limestone mansion, its plush surroundings quietly disguising the din of activity in the back offices, where much of the activity was focused on the American president's arrival from Uruguay. He felt a pang of sadness: Raquel had been with him that day when they came to report Smith's murder at the racetrack; now she was confined to a compound where Smith, apparently, roamed free.

As he stood looking about, a woman, easily in her mid-forties, approached him with an extended hand. She wore a crisp, pink, Oxford shirt, and a double-strand set of good pearls. Her navy skirt was knee length, and a bright pink, patent leather belt hugged her waistline.

"I'm Cornelia Middlemarch, for the bureau," she said, barely smiling through clenched teeth. "You must be Mr. Rose."

"I am."

"Agent Sullivan is waiting for you." Jacob nodded silently, as he gave her the once-over. "This way, please." He followed, noting her rigid gait and perfect posture.

She took him into a conference room, past Mr. Miller's office, where Sullivan sat with his briefcase open and numerous papers strewn about. "Thank you, Corny," Sullivan said. She gave nary a glance at either of them as she left. "Heck of a lady," Sullivan said admiringly. Jacob said nothing and sat down at one of the mismatched office chairs adjacent to Sullivan's seat at the head of the table.

"You want a glass of water or something?" Sullivan asked, but Jacob shook his head. The air-conditioning was going full blast and Jacob felt cold. He pulled his jacket close around him and looked around the room, which was bare of any decorative trappings. "Strictly utilitarian," Sullivan said. Jacob was in no mood for pleasantries, as he thought about Smith on the loose. "We've got to head downstairs," said Sullivan, gathering his papers.

"Show me the way," Jacob said, following him out to a nearby elevator. "If Smith's alive, what do I do?" he asked, getting right to the point.

"You're supposed to leave everything to me," Sullivan said, pressing the elevator's basement button.

"And what about Raquel? How safe can she be?" Jacob sighed, depressed to find himself in another situation over which he had no control. "I've got to get a hold of her."

The elevator opened on to a room that reminded Jacob of his high school gymnasium. The walls were painted a light green. An indoor track encircled the perimeters of the ceiling as a balcony, though the room was without any other athletic references. A fresh-faced agent waved hello as they approached. Beside him was a table with several Smith & Wesson handguns and rifles. He appeared to have been awaiting their arrival.

"She's fine," Sullivan finally replied.

"How do you know?"

"Because De Solis isn't about to kill this country's greatest actress, that's how," said Sullivan, who was growing impatient with Jacob's apparent distrust of the FBI's efforts at keeping the situation under control.

"Everything's ready, sir."

"Thank you, Dumont. That'll be all." Sullivan waited until the young man had left. "Good kid. A little too eager. Still a little wet behind the ears. I wanted you to meet him now; he'll be driving the ambulance to the airport."

"Are you ready for the demonstration, Mr. Rose?"

"I suppose so," Jacob said.

"What I'm about to show you, Jacob, is how this whole thing works. I'm going to shoot you two or three times, you drop to the floor, and I'll tell you what I think."

"Hold on. How about I shoot you first?"

"What, you don't trust me?" Sullivan laughed. "You think I'm going to kill you?"

"No ... just oblige me."

"All right. You'll shoot me, I'll show you how to fall, and then you try it. Ever shot a gun before?"

"Well, I've done skeet shooting. Does that count?"

"It'll have to do. All right, this is the rifle I'll be using. Go down to the far end and shoot me two or three times."

"You're planning to shoot me two or three times?" Jacob asked.

"Yes, and you'll fall to the ground, just as I will show you, only in your scenario an EMS will run in, place you on a stretcher, and rush you outside the museum. An ambulance driven by our friend Dumont will be taking you to the airport."

"Good," said Jacob, suddenly more cheerful.

"This way, De Solis' idiots will think you're off to the hospital."

"I'll be off to the airport with my passport and tickets!"

"That is correct," said Sullivan, returning his enthusiasm.

"What about Raquel and the old man?"

"We'll get them into the ambulance well before you're shot."

"Damn good," Jacob said, nodding, with a sigh of relief.

He walked about thirty feet from where they. He somewhat awkwardly aimed the rifle at Sullivan's heart. "These bullets are fakes, just blanks, right?"

"Yeah, yeah, just fire. And watch how I fall."

"You're the boss." Jacob aimed and fired twice.

Sullivan collapsed backwards, letting out a short moan.

"Are you okay," Jacob asked. No answer. "Sullivan. Are you okay?"

He still wasn't moving. Jacob rushed over toward Sullivan, who was splayed out across the floor, his head cocked to the side and his eyes wide open in shock. Panicking, Jacob put his hand on the man's neck, searching for his pulse. He couldn't feel anything. He got to his feet and ran toward the elevator. Frantically pushing the button, he suddenly felt the mouth of a gun in his ribs.

"Gotcha," Sullivan laughed.

"What the…? Why on earth would you do something like this? That's not funny; you had me scared shitless."

"I did it to stress a point to you. Once you hit the floor, you got to be completely still until we get everybody out. If you move, the whole plan goes to hell. Remember that."

"Couldn't you have just told me?"

"I thought you would remember better this way. Okay, your turn."

Jacob shook his head, still a little flustered. He gathered himself and tried to sound confident. "Looks easy enough."

"Good, now go and stand where I was standing."

Jacob stood ready. He was breathing heavily.

"Hey, take it easy," Sullivan called out.

Jacob took a few deep breaths. His pulse began to quiet down. "Go ahead, shoot."

Sullivan took aim and fired two rapid shots at Jacob. The art dealer tumbled to the hardwood floor.

"Good job, Jacob," said Sullivan. "There's a lot to work with here. Have you done this sort of thing before?"

"I've had practice this weekend."

"Make sure you don't use you hand to break the fall. Might break it. Fall on the part where you buttock meets your thigh, on the meaty part. That's the way to break the fall."

"Excuse me?"

"On your ass, Jacob," Sullivan barked. "Need me to show you again?"

"No, no, I think I know what you mean. Like this?" Jacob tumbled to the floor again.

"Much better. One last time. And this time, hold the position you're in for a few seconds. I'm going to come over there and check you. Got it?"

"Yes, sir."

"All right, here we go. Bang."

Jacob fell to the floor and he froze his position. Sullivan came over toward him. He kicked his foot and Jacob, trying to summon up all of the thespian skills acquired while appearing in *Ten Little Indians* at Dalton, did his best to have his body remain limp.

"Good, nice work not being rigid. Most people think they have to keep everything in place. All right, get up. I think you got it."

The FBI agent walked Jacob back to the elevator. "Just press the main button and you'll return to the lobby. Good luck and I'll see you at the museum in a bit," said Sullivan with a wink.

"Thank you, Sullivan."

When he returned to the suite it was already 11:30, and he noticed the light on the phone blinking. He pressed the code for his message. It was from Raquel. *I am fine darling,* she said. *How are you doing? I'm so sorry this has turned into a nightmare for all of us. I'll see you in a few hours at the luncheon for Señor Trumball. I have the painting with me, and I will bring it to the museum. I love you.*

CHAPTER THIRTY-FOUR

It was 1:30 and time to leave for the Trumball fête. Jacob carried the garment bag with the phony painting. The old man held his black hat in his hand. A porter followed with their luggage, as they waited for Ortiz to pull the Mercedes around. There was no sign of him, so Jacob tipped the attendant and grabbed the valises.

Just then, Jacob noticed crowds pouring out of the lobby and spilling out the doors to gawk at several television camera crews setting up. Moments later, CBS anchorman Dan Rather moved into place, drew his microphone close, and, with the cool aplomb of a surgeon, announced: "Several hundred army dissidents have staged a mutiny and have captured the Argentine Army headquarters."

Jacob heard the newscaster deliver this alarming news straight into the camera lens. He poked at Trumball.

"The cat's out of the bag. We're not getting out of here."

Trumball growled, "Meow, meow."

Jacob rolled his eyes.

Rather's voice turned grim: "Buenos Aires has become a battleground just as the U.S. president is about to arrive for an economic summit for the Americas. Air Force One was circling the civilian airport when fighting broke out, and the presidential plane is believed to have returned to a base in Uruguay."

"A nightmare. This entire weekend. For your fifteen minutes of glory," Jacob mumbled at Trumball.

After a few minutes, the camera crews packed up and dispersed, while the two started walking down the hotel's lengthy driveway, carrying their luggage, and looking for Ortiz.

"Quick, quick," an excited voice called to them.

"Where?" Trumball asked, disoriented. "Where are you?"

"Who the hell are you?" Jacob asked, more importantly. He looked around and saw nobody actually speaking directly to them.

"Pssst. Pssst. Señors." It was Ortiz, the driver, his head sticking out of the sunroof of the Mercedes, parked on a side lawn of the driveway entrance. He motioned to them frantically. They ran the few yards to the car, and Ortiz got out and took their bags to the trunk. Jacob pushed the old man through the open rear door and into the backseat. He slid in after him.

"Hey," scolded Trumball. "Just who do you think you're shoving ... the señorita?"

"Take it easy," Jacob said, adjusting himself in his seat, the extra weight of the vest disrupting his comfort.

"Where is she, anyway?" Trumball asked.

"She'll follow later," Jacob lied.

Ortiz quickly locked all doors and windows, and they sped off past a gathering of tanks and armored vehicles. Television trucks, equipped with mobile satellite dishes, sat like sculpture on the sides of the road.

"You're okay, aren't you?" Jacob asked Trumball.

"Yeah, but you don't have to break an old man's bones."

"Here, let me get you buckled up." Jacob pulled the seat belt around the squirming artist.

"Everything is fine. Don't worry," Ortiz said. "They drove at a steady speed to Avenida Sante Fe, heading toward the museum.

"Don't worry? This is World War Three," Trumball said, his voiced heavy with sarcasm.

"The dissidents have already surrendered," Ortiz asserted, as if he were passing on secret information.

"Surrendered?" Jacob asked.

"Sí, it is over. I heard a military officer tell your journalists, just before I found you."

"And you believe it?" Jacob asked in exasperation.

"What did I tell you?" Trumball interrupted. "They carry on this way, every day, just like this. They're lunatics."

Jacob ignored the artist and took out his cell phone. He pressed General De Solis' number as Ortiz sped through the streets, inching in and out of slow-moving lanes, much like a New York cab driver in rush-hour traffic. Jacob heard clicking sounds on the phone. The signal didn't go through. He tried several times more, but he received only a "no signal" display. Where the hell is Raquel?

"Will it take us hours to get to the museum?" Jacob asked.

"No, no, señor. We will be there in minutes."

They had no trouble moving around the city. There weren't even any roadblocks to obstruct them. Sure enough, they parked outside the museum in less than fifteen minutes. When they stepped out of the limousine, Jacob heard popping sounds from automatic weapons still reverberating in the air, a sign of victory, Ortiz assured. Jacob stared at a passing bus riddled with bullets. Two museum guards formed a cordon as the two New Yorkers hustled inside.

Inside the entrance to the grand hall, Mendoza embraced Trumball and then awkwardly hugged Jacob, who assumed this was some kind of victory gesture.

An aide ran toward Mendoza, handing him a note. "She's all right," the director said excitedly.

"She's all right. How do you know?" Jacob asked, looking straight at the director's face.

"General De Solis called to give you the message. Why didn't you tell me she's with the general."

Jacob shrugged his shoulders.

"Knowing what a skeptic you are, the general put her on the phone with my assistant. You are relieved to get this message, Jacob. Yes?" the director asked.

"He is, Señor Director," Trumball answered for Jacob. Quickly shifting topics, Trumball said, "Give the director the painting, Jacob. My art dealer insisted on handing it to you personally, Señor Mendoza." The director signaled to several guards, who gently lifted the canvas from Jacob's hands. They were to take it to the special booth at the top of the rotunda, where it would be lowered in that evening's special ceremony.

A curious smile spread over the director's face. "Why is the señorita with the general? I thought you and she are—"

"He's a friend from her early days in movies," Jacob said, cutting short Mendoza's comments.

"I see," said the museum director, who turned to take Trumball's arm and steer him into the crowd. Jacob grabbed a glass of champagne from a passing tray, and forced himself to smile at passersby. When he heard the orchestra tune up, he relaxed, beginning to believe that some measure of calm was beginning. He yearned to dance with Raquel, to swirl her across the floor as her dress billowed and they held one another close. Frankly, he had never so much as danced a waltz with her, and so he wondered if they would move around the floor easily together.

He looked around for Mendoza and asked if he could make a personal phone call from his office. Nobody showed any hint of distress over the danger outside, though four large, projection-screen televisions at opposite ends of the rotunda were tuned to the news on CNN.

"Tell the señorita to hurry," Mendoza said.

When Jacob pressed De Solis' telephone number again, a stream of electronic grunts and sputters came on the line. "Damn," he mumbled, certain that it had been his cell phone.

When he returned to the hall, the director called him over.

"Señor Rose, please meet Señora Marie Elena Ricci. She is our minister of culture, a friend to modern art the world over."

Ricci was wearing a pink tulle outfit and diamond earrings. Her hair was swept back in a bun, like Eva Perón. She appeared genuinely interested to meet Jacob in person, though they'd spoken by phone several times before as the plans for this Trumball salute were taking shape.

"We've e-mailed each other for more than a half year," he told Mendoza, as he gently took her hand and bestowed upon her a Continental kiss. They exchanged a few words before Trumball joined them in conversation. Jacob shifted uncomfortably. The artist pulled on Jacob's sleeve. "I imagined I'd get a tribute in a museum like this only after I'd been dead and long gone."

"Artists haven't been given the recognition they deserve," Señora Ricci said. "I hope you will feel differently this afternoon, Señor Trumball."

"Señor Trumball, our guests are looking for you," Mendoza said, returning to remind him of his social obligations.

"I have him," Señora Ricci said with a laugh.

"As I was saying, we artists don't often get this kind of tribute when we're living and breathing," Trumball said.

"No. I'm afraid the politicians take the spotlight, don't they?" the Señora replied. There was a pause. Above the commotion Jacob recognized the haunting rumba riffs of "Besame Mucho."

"Let them dance," Trumball said. "Let everybody dance." The singer's husky male voice rose above the music.

Fear flashed across the museum director's face as he looked at one of the television screens. "Tanks are in the streets of Palermo Chico," he said. "That's where the señorita is, yes?"

"Will you escort me to the television, Señor Mendoza?" Jacob asked, slowly shaking his head.

"Excuse us for a moment," Mendoza told the group. "Our friend is concerned with the latest news reports."

Mendoza led Jacob to the TV near the open bar, where several guests, many with their backs to the screen, chatted idly.

Jacob had to find a way to get to the villa safely. He remembered the ride to the museum. Bullets were flying, but everybody went about their regular business. Now more guests were filing into the great hall. What a frightening event, he thought as he stared vacantly at the huge television screen.

CHAPTER THIRTY-FIVE

In a drawing room in General de Solis' villa, an agitated Raquel sat, holding onto the armrests of the Chippendale wingback chair as if she were bracing herself for a terrible fall. She was well aware that she would be late meeting Jacob, who had already gone ahead to the museum luncheon. She also knew that he'd be in desperate straits after her absence of more than twenty-four hours and the e-mail she was certain he'd found when he'd checked his mail this morning. Moreover, the real *Lea with Two Love-Apples* was expected to return with her for the presentation to honor Laban Trumball.

Alfredo, her personal hairdresser, fussed vigorously with a styling comb, testing the buoyancy of her curls. Because she had expressly requested him to do her hair for the luncheon, he was granted permission to pass the protective blockade barrier at the entrance to De Solis' compound. Despite her earlier gratitude to the general for this indulgence, she was now extremely angry, forced, as she was, to await her release so close to her expected arrival at the museum.

"I do not like being detained," she said sharply to the two armed guards who stood at attention, watching protectively over the garment bag containing Trumball's expensive canvas as if it were some religious icon. "Particularly when my parents are expecting me," she said to the soldiers. She impatiently sipped a glass of red burgundy, mindful of Albert and Emma Gingold's desire to see their only child once again.

"Señorita," said one of the soldiers, a tall, handsome youth with baby-smooth skin, "we are doing what we have been ordered to do."

"I want my driver," she demanded, disrupting Alfredo's last-minute spray of hair control. "Alfredo, haven't you finished yet?" she asked her hairdresser. "Had I not warned you all with sufficient notice that I have a very important engagement?"

"Your hair es muy linda!" whispered Alfredo, who understood Raquel's urgency. He backed away, and she rose from the chair, grabbing the garment bag and her purse as if ready to depart.

"We understand, señorita. We will be driving you to the museum," said the youthful guard. His flaxen curls reminded her of a statue of Apollo that she'd seen in one of the numerous art books in Jacob's Manhattan loft. "But you cannot leave just yet. We are still awaiting our orders."

Defeated, she placed her things down on the sofa.

"My dear, you are just a little boy playing soldier," she said, patronizingly, to the handsome guard, as she cupped his smooth face in her hand. "Now be a good boy, and let mama go."

She planted a moist kiss on his cheek, and he turned vivid red.

"Please, señorita," interrupted the other soldier, a coarser-looking man with a stocky build and a severe five o'clock shadow, "we will have word from the general soon enough," he assured her. "He knows that you are expected at the museum."

"Well?" she threw her arms up, "Where the hell is Juan Domingo, and what is taking him so damn long to return?" she asked.

"We do not know," answered the handsome guard.

"What time is it, Alfredo?"

"Two thirty," he said, pointing to his watch. "You should have left a half hour ago," he continued in hushed tones before requesting that she twirl to see how her hair would move with the Ungaro, floral, silk halter-dress she'd chosen to take from the wardrobe the general had provided upstairs.

"I am more interested in the news than looking pretty," she said, requesting a television from the guards. Raquel suspected that De Solis might be staging some kind of revolution, to usurp control in the wake of the country's economic collapse, and that it probably accounted for his long absences from the compound. Still, given what she'd witnessed only hours before, she was in a hurry to get back to Jacob.

"General De Solis asked that we not turn on the news," replied the handsome soldier as he set up the portable TV. "Perhaps you wish to look at a movie?"

"Screw the general," Raquel hollered. "I have already seen my share of movies," she said, grabbing the remote control to click on the news channel. Earlier in the day as Alfredo worked on her hairstyle, she watched a video of Quentin Tarantino's *Pulp Fiction*.

Back inside the great hall of the Modern Art Museum of Buenos Aires, a sober but cheery voice blared from over a loudspeaker:

"Government forces have recaptured regimental headquarters in the Cordoba district."

"I think that's good news," Jacob said, gulping his vodka martini with relief, to Trumball who was uninterested in anything but his luncheon. He held a silver lamé balloon's string tightly and turned his attention to Señor Reuben Mendoza, the director, who was approaching with two guests eager for an audience with the artist. Jacob winced when he recognized Bertha Lavazzo, in a boisterous red caftan, on Mendoza's arm, walking exuberantly toward them. Alice, in a black pantsuit and starkly devoid of the makeup Bertha applied by the yard, trailed dutifully behind them, trying to keep up.

"Well, well, Señor Rose, I didn't expect to see you again," said Bertha, dispensing with a greeting. "You've gotten a taste today of what life in Buenos Aires has become." Alice nodded hello, breathless and bored.

Jacob screwed up his lips. "So I have."

Ignoring Jacob's remark, Bertha went on. "My dear, Laban." Trumball responded with a wet kiss. Mendoza, perplexed by the proceedings, smiled attentively. "Señor Mendoza," Bertha announced, "have I ever told you the story of how Señor Trumball and I had lunch with Imelda Marcos?" The museum director, curious and rapt, shook his head, as Bertha began to dominate the conversation.

"Raquel's got to return here," Jacob whispered to the old man. "You do understand that, don't you?" Trumball ignored him and took another swig of his Stolichnaya as he listened to Bertha tell the story. "Old man, they'll be dimming the lights for the presentation, and we won't be able to switch the paintings."

As Bertha prattled on, Jacob realized that there would be no need to switch the canvases: De Solis, after all, didn't honor his purchase, and the museum wasn't in a position to buy it either. Mendoza had merely asked that the painting be at the museum for the program. What difference would it make if a forgery descended in a darkened rotunda?

No one at Raquel's parents' home had spotted the fake, and all the lights were on.

With all that had happened this weekend, he was almost relieved that he no longer had to cope with this technicality, even if it meant going home without a check for $9 million. Everything else was in place with the plans he'd arranged with Sullivan, whom he had yet to spot among the mingling guests.

Now if only Raquel would arrive, Jacob thought.

Bertha, having finished with her anecdote, grabbed Alice and bade all a fare-thee-well as they strode away to look at the rest of the exhibit. Jacob said nothing as they departed. Trumball awaited the next set of guests to be brought before him as if he were a king receiving his countrymen. His next pair of admirers was Señor and Señora Hernandez d'Amontillado, wealthy benefactors of the museum, somewhere in their late seventies. The gentleman kindly asked Jacob if he would mind taking a picture of them with Trumball, Mendoza, and the minister of culture, who'd brought them over to meet the artist. Jacob took the camera, an old-fashioned Leica, and snapped two shots, then handed it back to the gentleman before turning his back briefly to try to reach Raquel again on his cell phone.

Still no connection.

Jacob wasn't about to leave Buenos Aires without that canvas. He had to contact Raquel somehow. Why wasn't there an answer from at De Solis' villa? He waited for the group's small talk to abate before he interrupted Mendoza and Señora Ricci, the Argentine minister of culture, to ask for a private line. The director offered his office without missing a beat of the conversation he was having with Trumball and the ardent patrons. Jacob nodded politely as he walked off to the office, suddenly trailed by two armed men, who lingered in the hallway outside the office while Jacob went inside to make the call.

"Señor Mendoza has allowed me to use his phone," he explained to them. They nodded, but never took their eyes off him while he pressed De Solis' number. Jacob stared back at them as he waited for a connection, inhaling Reuben Mendoza's particular aftershave, which permeated the receiver and every inch of his office.

"Raquel?" He couldn't believe he had reached her so easily, even after seven rings. After a slight struggle, she managed to grab the phone away from the attempts of the guard, who tried to intercept the call.

"Yes, darling?" she said flatly, glaring at the guard. "I'm afraid I'm still being detained." Her impatience overwhelmed her excitement at hearing Jacob's voice.

"Raquel, it's me, Jacob." He felt euphoric just at the sound of her voice.

"Of course, I know who you are." Her voice was spiritless, devoid of its usual lilt.

He paused for a second and told her he loved her.

"I'm coming to get you."

"I can manage to get there myself," she told him. "If I can ever get out of here!" She offered the latter response to the audience of guards who stood by the canvas.

"I want to bring you here." He had sensed some melancholy in her voice, some disillusionment. "Is something wrong, Raquel?"

"Yes."

"What is it? What's wrong?" She was silent. "I'm worried sick about you." He was staring wildly around the room, looking for a clock, as he noted the soldiers listening to his every word. Then he remembered to look at his watch. "Two forty-five," he said.

"Jacob, what are you mumbling?"

"The time. I'm sorry. Listen, I've got to get to you here right away."

"No, darling, please stay where you are."

"What are you saying?"

"I will be fine" she said. "I'll get there eventually. Don't worry about me."

He straightened up and cleared his throat. The two soldiers were watching his every move. He mopped his brow with his handkerchief and pushed his fingers through his hair.

"Are you safe?"

"Oh, yes, I am quite safe. I have soldiers here, protecting me," she said with sarcasm.

He thought about asking after the painting, but he hesitated.

"Stay cool, darling. I'm on my way."

"Jacob…"

He hung up, determined to free her despite what lay ahead at De Solis' compound, with the general now dead, and with Smith still likely on the rampage.

As he made his way back to the group surrounding Trumball, Mendoza stepped forward: "It is over, Señor Rose. Our government troops have seized all the mutinous army barracks from the rebel soldiers loyal to De Solis." Jacob was still unsure of what all this meant, but he had sensed that it had to have something to do with De Solis' death.

In the great hall, the wide-screen televisions had now become the focus of every guest's attention. Trumball seemed annoyed. "Do they have to show this crap now, during my gala?"

Jacob ignored the artist and moved toward one of the screens. He could see crowds of journalists clamoring and pushing outside the Libertador Building, the army headquarters opposite the presidential palace, thrusting microphones and cameras at a government spokesperson.

At first, the announcements over the loudspeakers in the museum's great hall were in Spanish, but as the guests started cheering and clapping loudly, the announcer translated the news of this event in a clipped British English accent:

"Mutinous forces have accepted the presidential demand for an unconditional surrender. This mutiny has been quashed, and the rebels have been defeated. Their leaders have been identified. The government is withholding until morning the names of all surviving officers involved in the attempted coup. No civilian casualties have been reported, but more than 100 military personnel have died, with several hundred more wounded. Among those killed by our government military forces is the former General Juan Domingo De Solis, who had personally directed his own special team of mercenaries to overthrow our government. The former general and his men were ambushed early this morning on a road to Cordoba. Further details will be announced within the hour."

CHAPTER THIRTY-SIX

Jacob rushed out to the waiting limousine. One thought raced through his mind as Ortiz drove off: to get Raquel out of the general's compound. He tried reaching her again on his cell. This time the phone rang. "Come on, come on. Please, baby, pick up." Finally, a voice on the other end of the line.

"*¿Hola?*" a shaken Raquel answered.

"Raquel?"

"Darling! There's nobody here but my hairdresser."

Of all the things to worry about at a time like this, he thought, biting his tongue. "We're on our way. Wait near the gate."

The Mercedes moved swiftly and freely through a series of blinking yellow and red stoplights. He figured the trip there and back to the museum would be under thirty minutes.

The roads outside the villa were eerily quiet. Jacob felt his muscles tense up, though it was a relief to be moments from the gate. Unknown to Jacob, twenty yards from the compound, a transponder blinked on the dashboard of a car hidden behind tall hedges. Ortiz turned right now, toward a sweeping expanse of green, bringing the tires to a screeching halt outside the villa as Raquel and her dresser stepped through the gate.

Jacob pushed the door open. "Get in, quick!"

"Darling, this is Alfredo, my dresser—"

"There is no time. Get in. Go, Ortiz."

Just as they were picking up speed, a man jumped out from behind a tall hedge, waving a white cloth, as if seeking asylum or surrender.

"*Dios mio,*" Ortiz jammed the brake violently, stopping the car just inches from the man.

Jacob's head smacked against the open windowpane of his door.

"Out of there, quickly. Get out!" the man shouted. Jacob had hardly gotten a good look at him, when the man seized the still disoriented art dealer in a headlock and pulled him from the limousine. In the struggle to free himself, Jacob punched his assailant, landing a blow squarely on the man's jaw over the flesh covering the man's lower molars. The assailant threw Jacob hard to the ground. Jacob looked up and saw Smith standing over him, blood shooting from his mouth. Smith wiped his mouth with a handkerchief and muttered a stream of expletives. He was dressed in black-tie, and his blood dripped onto his satin lapel.

"Smith!" Jacob stared at his attacker. "What do you want?"

"You pack a solid punch."

"I saw you murdered. With my own eyes. What's going on here?" he said, slowly getting up.

Smith didn't answer. He moved quietly toward Jacob and punched him twice in the abdomen, knocking the art dealer back to the ground.

"This is crap!" Jacob got up once more and staggered toward Smith. He held the man's lapels in a feeble grip. "What do you want from me? Why are you doing this?"

Smith kicked Jacob's ankle with the point of his boot. Jacob pulled back and took another swing at Smith, just grazing his cheek. Smith grabbed Jacob from behind, pinning his arms. "Listen up, buddy," Smith whispered into his ear. "I mean you no real harm."

"Bullshit!"

"No. This is the politics of persuasion."

"You're crazy," Jacob moaned.

"I have a matter of unfinished business with you. I want the code." Smith tightened his grip. "The code," Smith said from behind, jerking Jacob's arm even harder.

"You're talking shit." It suddenly dawned on Jacob that he could easily tell Smith that he'd provide the code if they returned to the museum

"What are you doing?" Raquel screamed, getting out of the car.

"Ma'am, please get back in the car. I'd hate to have to hurt you, as well," Smith warned.

"Who? You? JD's faithful aide?" she asked, mockingly, defiantly.

Smith pulled out his gun and shot the air out of the Mercedes limousine tires. Ortiz froze with fear behind the wheel, afraid he might be next. "There are six bullets left in this gun. That's two for each of you. Don't make me use them," Smith warned again, ignoring her ridicule.

"Raquel, shut up. You'll get hurt. The guy's crazy," Jacob pleaded.

Unexpectedly, the deserted road erupted with a rumble as a convoy of trucks appeared, carrying dozens of government soldiers yelling at the tops of their lungs.

"*Paren, paren.* Stop, stop," Raquel shouted. "Stop this man. He is a murderer!"

With an instinctive response, Smith knocked Jacob over and dragged him, like a fleeing panther with his prey, toward his Lincoln, hidden behind the hedges. Years of combat experience paid off yet again. Shoving Jacob in the backseat, Smith jumped in behind the wheel and sped off.

The military convoy was in the throes of their victory song, and Smith was already a faraway blur. "It's over, it's over," the soldiers whooped in Spanish, while some of them were singing the national anthem, hanging from the passing vehicles. Raquel quickly flagged down a flatbed truck. Panic crossed her face.

"The authorities are at the museum. There is nothing we can do now," she said, without addressing anyone in particular.

"We will escort the Señorita Raquel," whooped a soldier. Several of the men whistled, cheered, and hollered as a distraught Raquel, with Alfredo and Ortiz, were helped aboard the truck.

"Ten minutes," they assured her it would take them to reach her destination.

"For the famous actress, we arrive in whatever time you wish," added the driver of another truck.

Raquel grabbed her hairdresser's cell phone and pressed Jacob's number. No answer. Several clicks and still no answer. Her heart sank. Seconds later, she pressed the number again and a voice came on the other end. "Who's this?"

"Raquel. And who are you?"

"Jacob's okay. He's sleeping. He'll be with you shortly. I promise."

"Why are you doing this?" She recognized Smith's voice.

"It's personal. I'll bring him back in one piece. You have my word."

"I don't understand." Her voice became more anxious.

"He'll tell you later. Trust me. Don't talk to anyone. Keep your mouth shut and no one will get hurt. Trust me." The line went dead.

Raquel quietly sobbed. She kept her face down, speaking softly into the mouthpiece. "Please don't hurt him, Smith."

Minutes later the convoy reached the museum, where they drew a crowd of curious civilians and other soldiers, who milled around them, inspecting this unusual livery service. Ortiz jumped off first and helped the other two off the slow-moving truck, gently lifting each into his arms before planting them on the ground. The hairdresser dusted himself off, took a last glance at Raquel, and told her she was stunning.

CHAPTER THIRTY-SEVEN

Once he was aware he that wasn't being followed, Smith turned onto a dirt road, cutting across an open field. A purple sky hung overhead, with a rainbow arc of colors in the distant horizon. He stopped in the middle of the field and glanced back at Jacob, who had blacked out. Taking duct tape from the car's glove compartment, Smith tore off strips, swiftly taped Jacob's hands behind his back, and then taped his mouth. Smith slid back into the driver's seat. "Sorry, buddy. This is for your own good."

He drove over the field and onto the main road at the other end that led to the Palacio, the grimy bar that he'd frequented with Esau. Blaring from the speakers, his favorite Doors song came on yet again.

Love me two times, baby.

Love me twice today....

"Yeah, yeah," Smith shouted.

The music continued, and Smith repeated his chorus of "Yeah, yeah."

He raised the volume, causing reverb in the speakers and waking Jacob, who grunted from the backseat.

"Hold on, Jake. You're okay."

Jacob's head spun. He struggled to free his hands. He needed to get his bearings. Despite the torrent of questions racing through his thoughts, he knew only one thing mattered now—saving his life. Moments ago, he'd rushed from the museum to get Raquel at the general's villa. Now he was imprisoned in the backseat of a car, speeding off to who knows where, and scared stiff that something awful might happen to her. He remembered, though, the victorious soldiers passing in trucks. They got her to safety, he hoped.

"We're a few minutes away. That's all. A few more minutes."

As the car approached the Palacio, rain began to fall. They pulled into a rear parking lot, and Smith got out, dragging Jacob with him, a gun pressing on the art dealer's ribs. Moving across a small courtyard to the back door, the rain hit hard, soaking to the two men in their black tuxedos.

Jacob felt weary and ached. Bodily pain was the last thing he needed now. *Where is he dragging me? Would Smith kill me? Bury me alive in this hellhole of a joint?* He realized that if Smith wanted to kill him, he'd have done so already. *Yet Smith had seen military action and on top of that seemed the type to commit cold-blooded murder. And so did Esau!* He thought that the brother he'd known, his twin brother, seemed further from him than any stranger on the street. Time seemed to freeze for Jacob for a moment, then dissolved into a slow-motion dream as he saw his entire world fall apart. For a full second, he didn't breathe, but gasped for air. His cold, wet body trembled.

Smith led Jacob like someone escorting a blind man though the dark main room of the Palacio to an area behind red velvet drapes.

"Sit. Listen. Don't say a word."

"Let's make this quick, I have business to attend to."

"Don't try to be smart. I will shoot you."

"I need a drink."

"Hey, Pietro!"

"Sí, señor." A burly young man, with a bar towel tucked through his belt loops, looking every inch like the hard rock singer Meatloaf, approached.

"Two scotches. On the rocks. Pronto, pronto!" Smith yelled.

"Again, why am I here," Jacob demanded.

"You remember our drive from the airport? You wanted to ask me about Esau. We never had a chance to do that."

"Yes, I remember," Jacob said, wondering where the conversation was headed.

"I'm ready to talk."

Jacob leaned back. "You could've just asked to meet me at a café."

"I prefer this place."

"What does this hellhole have to do with Esau?"

"Look around this seedy bar."

"I don't need to."

"Go ahead. Get up and take a look around. Check this place out."

"I don't want to."

"You are here, buddy, because this is the place Esau and I used to hang out."

"I don't want to hear that my brother hung out in a bar like this."

"Yeah. This dark and seedy place. With lots of lowlifes. That bothers you, doesn't it?"

"Get to the point, Smith. Why did you bring me here?"

There was a long pause. Smith seemed to relish Jacob's impatience. "Esau was my lover."

"Your what?" Jacob stood up.

"Sit down. This is where we hung out. We could do our thing. We wore frumpy dresses and danced to cheesy jukebox songs. Yeah, buddy, Esau and I were lovers."

Jacob looked at him, eyes wide and angry. "So what?"

"We spent hours together here. In each other's arms."

Pietro pushed through the drapes and placed two tumblers of scotch and a dish of pretzels on the table. He left quickly, without looking at either one of them. Jacob could feel tears well up.

"You look at little green around the gills."

"I feel like I am going to be sick."

"That's not a nice thing to say."

"Why is everyone trying to disgrace Esau's memory? First Bertha, now you."

"Disgrace?"

"Telling me these bullshit stories. What are you trying to accomplish here?"

"I'm not lying. I'm telling you about us because I want you to know that I'm on your side. You hear me? I'm on your side."

"I can tell. I would do the same thing. I always kidnap people who are on my side."

Smith chuckled for a moment. "I had to make sure I got to talk to you, alone. There isn't time, so listen closely. Your brother was murdered."

Jacob felt the scotch warming his blood. He reached across the table, grabbed Smith's lapels, and screamed in his face: "You're bullshitting me. I am sick and tired of this. What are you trying to pull here?"

Smith maneuvered quickly, pressing Jacob's thumbs back, causing the art dealer great pain. Jacob slumped in his seat. "I need you to chill. I do not intend to hurt you. What I have to tell you might be painful, but pay attention. I'll get the son of bitch who killed Esau. I got rid of one piece of the puzzle. De Solis arranged the murder. He ordered the hit. I put a bullet in his head."

"I'm listening."

"I have a pretty good idea who the killer was, and he'll pay for this. Just watch me."

Smith reached inside his jacket, pulled out his Glock, and aimed at the wall at an imaginary target. "Pietro, another round for us. We're thirsty here." Smith cocked his pistol, waited, and shot at the wall, exploding the plaster. When the drapes parted, Pietro stood with a tray with two more drinks. "What the—" he blurted. He stopped short, his voice trailing off, as Smith swerved and aimed at the bartender. A security guard, built thick, with a ponytail, followed, bursting in like a bull in a ring. "Hey!" He stopped himself after seeing Smith. "Okay. I didn't know it was you." The two men left quickly.

Jacob squirmed in his seat but remained silent. He avoided Smith's eyes, staring instead at the wall, riveted to the bullet hole. Smith eyed him carefully and smiled, returning the gun to the holster.

"You want to tell *me* about you and Esau. *Your* lives together. You don't have to." Jacob leaned back now and looked up at the filth-encrusted ceiling.

"Hey, that's your brother I'm talking about."

"You want to explain something to me. I don't want to know."

"What are you afraid of?"

"Nothing."

"So listen."

"No. Certain habits of our loved ones and our own lives ought to be kept secret. I loved my brother. We did everything together."

"I know."

"He was the fun, energetic guy, and I was the stoic ... student. He had a way with people. And suddenly, he turned his back on me and our parents, and I hated him for that. If you want to tell me something about Esau, answer me this. Did he talk about his mom and pop? Did he ever say to you that he wanted to see them, speak to them, hug them, check how they're doing? They're getting older. Was he ever worried about their health? And what about me? Did he ever give a damn about me? Damn him. We were boys together. We were inseparable growing up. Joking, learning, roughhousing, all of that we did together, as brothers. And then, he simply abandoned us. Maybe I abandoned everyone, too, in my own way. I got caught up in the battle of life, the chase, the art of the deal, subterfuges, and putting one over on the next guy. And maybe I forget to love. Stop the world, Smith, I want to get on."

Smith laughed softly. "You know, you talk like Esau."

"I talk like him. That's all you can say?"

"All right, enough of this. Let me tell you why you're here."

"Tell me, don't tell me. I don't care any more. I just want to get home and away from this hellhole."

"You'll get home, soon. Back to the US of A. But now you have something that is mine."

"What?"

"The money. The eighty million that belonged to Esau and me. I think he cut a deal with you, and you know where that money is."

"You're out of your mind. I have nothing to do with this."

"You're twins."

"I'm not Esau."

"Then help me. Work with me to figure out where the money is."

"Why should I trust you?"

"Because I know who killed Esau. I believe you know him, too."

Jacob wrinkled up his forehead. "Yeah, who? Who will you invent as my brother's killer?"

Smith waited, his eyes fixed on Jacob. "Alfred Sullivan."

"You're nuts."

"He worked for De Solis in the '80s, before joining the bureau."

"So what? Maybe he was undercover. Maybe CIA. I don't now. You guys take on many roles. Don't you?"

"Didn't it seem strange to you that an FBI guy would tell you about a suicide? There was no toxicology report, the whole thing was railroaded, and they never did a complete investigation. Esau would not blow his brains out. There was no suicide note. He was ready to get out of this whole damn business. We were going to use that money to disappear together. Buddy, this was our retirement fund."

Jacob considered it. He remembered that he, too, questioned why Sullivan informed him about the suicide. Jacob recalled that he suspected forgeries. *Yet, Sullivan moved quickly in getting Esau's body returned to the family. Was that a sign that he cared, showed compassion, or that he wanted to distance himself quickly from this whole damn thing?* "But he saved my life at the racetrack."

"From getting hit with fake bullets."

"Assuming I would believe this story. What happens next?"

Smith glanced at his watch. "It's 3:15, and at 5:30 the presidential motorcade is scheduled to arrive at the hotel. Why am I telling you this? Remember how you were talking to Raquel about those soldiers with machine guns on the roofs?"

"How do you know about that?"

"We bugged your place. Hey, you certainly have enough stamina to keep up with her. Anyway, DeSolis instructed me to scout positions for him. He wanted an insurance policy in case the first attempt at the coup goes wrong. He intended to use the chaos of an assassination attempt on POTUS to gain control of the Argentine military. The only problem is I shot De Solis. He knew the code word for the stand-down order. Son of a bitch never let anyone in on anything."

"What does that mean?"

Smith nodded. "Who's to say they're going to miss? This is the deal. Give me the code for the money, and I'll take out the assassin."

"If I go along with this, what happens to Sullivan?"

"Is he going to be at the museum?"

Jacob quickly weighed his options. He was feeling a bit more secure. He had the passports and airline tickets in his pocket. "I'm supposed to meet him at Mendoza's office. At 3:45."

"Then we better get going."

When they got to they car, Smith pulled out his key chain, pushed the button to open the trunk, and pulled out a bag. He tossed it to Jacob.

"Put this on under you tuxedo shirt."

"What is it?"

"Kevlar vest. You never know."

"Does it stop fake bullets?" Jacob mocked.

"No, just the real ones."

CHAPTER THIRTY-EIGHT

At the Modern Art Museum's great hall, the strains of the Lopicito Orchestra played the tango for a dance floor crowd of some thirty couples. Each so well practiced in the dance's precise body gestures and synchronized turnabouts that it looked like a sequence choreographed from a late 1930s MGM spectacular. When Raquel walked in with her dresser, two guards rushed over to take her bag, to which she merely, but politely, shook her head as she strode by in search of her parents. A picture of regal composure, yet deep down Raquel felt hesitant about how to proceed. She began recounting to herself the events that afternoon on the road outside De Solis' villa.

A small crowd gathered, shaking her from her thoughts, among them, Señora Ricci, the minister of culture. A waiter quickly appeared, holding a tray with glasses of champagne. The señora, her beady black eyes holding Raquel's attention for the moment, told her how horrified she was to hear the news about Juan Domingo's death. "It was cruel. Those troops should have arrested him so that he could be brought to trial." Raquel nodded distractedly, but continued to look for her parents. The day so far had been exhausting. She, too, wanted the Trumball celebration to be over and done with. Everything seemed to change for her today.

An attendant arrived with a phone, interrupting her conversation with the minister. "A personal call, señorita." Raquel excused herself and moved to a corner of the hall.

"I'm just minutes away, babe," she heard Jacob say.

"Oh, thank God. You're all right."

"I'm fine. Really. We're around the corner from the museum. See you in seconds."

Raquel felt as if a heavy stone had been lifted from her shoulders. A few feet away, she noticed Emma talking to several happy guests and breathed another sigh of relief.

"Your dress is beautiful," Emma said quietly, and hugged her daughter. The guests asked her about her next film. As Raquel explained her production schedule to the eager listeners, many of whom she knew by name, Albert walked over to kiss his daughter. Soon Mendoza and Trumball joined the group, and the director gave Raquel a big hug.

"Come, Albert, I think we should take our seats now," Emma said. The group began to do the same and they scattered about in search of an usher to lead them to their tables.

The music faded. Mendoza guided Trumball to the dais, while an usher led Raquel to a table directly in front of the platform where Trumball would later stand and receive his painting.

As they waited for the ceremonies to begin, Raquel placed the garment bag beneath her chair, one foot pushing against the bag. She glanced at the empty chair next to her, waiting for Jacob to arrive.

Mendoza introduced the guests on the dais and asked that nobody applaud until the final introduction. Señora Ricci spoke next about the relationship of Trumball to contemporary art history. Several magnums of chilled champagne were placed around the center of each table near a bouquet of yellow and purple orchids floating in water.

As the waiters began to serve the first course of sliced melon, a beleaguered Jacob, with a cleaned-up face and combed hair, hurried to the table, checking his watch. Raquel smiled, hugging his shoulders as he sat. "I was so worried. What on earth was he doing with you? Where did he take you?"

"I can't talk about it now. Let's just get this over with and then go home."

"I was so worried; I thought I'd lost you ... forever. I can't bear the thought of losing you."

"Raquel, you won't lose me. I love you. I want to be with you."

Instinctively, he felt his breast pocket—tickets and passport were in place. He was almost home.

A representative for the United States president, a Clint Eastwood look-alike, gray-haired and tall, with a muscular frame, spoke after the minister of culture. He expressed his concern over, as he put it, "the disturbances in the streets" during the last couple of hours and thanked the artist for not canceling.

"The president of the United States will be arriving in Buenos Aires in a few moments. This is a great day for Argentine and U.S. affairs. We're proud to be a part of this celebration for Laban Trumball." He went on to express the government's gratitude during this time of cultural and economic cooperation. Both Raquel and Jacob joined in the applause.

Jacob glanced at the doors leading to the kitchen and noticed Smith leaning against the wall. Smith or Sullivan, whom should he believe? Was Sullivan the man Smith had depicted? He had no choice, he told himself, surprised at how little he believed Smith.

This weekend—no, this day, these last few hours, had changed everything for him. The things he'd learned about the way Esau had chosen to live his life, so different from Jacob's, made him wonder whether you ever truly know anyone—even your twin brother. He wondered what had turned Esau to deceit. What was it that his brother had seen in those jungles of Southeast Asia that had transformed him into the person he was? And why, of all people, would Esau choose to spend the rest of his life with Smith?

Sullivan brought him to safety at the racetrack; Sullivan had agreed to the plan to draw out and trap the remaining criminals, so that Jacob, Trumball, and Raquel would have safe passage. Jacob felt a sudden weariness. Smith faked his death to throw him to the wolves and killed De Solis by his own admission. He would think no more; he would do what he considered crucial to getting the hell out of Argentina, safely and alive.

The speeches dragged on, and Jacob was fidgety, eager to begin the charade. While the chilled cucumber soup was served, Raquel brushed his cheeks with her lips a couple of times and showed no sign of her earlier feelings of apprehension. Trumball was surprisingly alert throughout the speeches, resisting his usual succession of vodkas. The Maestro, as a few of the speakers affectionately referred to him, just stared into the mouths of the speakers, laughing at the occasional jokes and applauding vigorously.

Mendoza introduced the two remaining speakers while the main course, prime Argentine beefsteak on large, white platters with whipped potatoes and broccoli, was served. A man from the Argentine national tourism office spoke about cultural exchanges between the U.S. and Argentina. He went on for what seemed an eternity to Jacob. "Why is it that the less prestigious the post, the more people like to hear themselves talk?" he chortled to Raquel. Finally, a lady from the American Embassy, a former trustee of the Whitney Museum in New York, praised Trumball and his place in the history of American art, bringing tears to Trumball's eyes and an ovation from the guests. "He stands tall among our greatest: DeKooning, Lichtenstein, Pollack, Nevelson, and Warhol."

At last, the waiters brought out demitasse and sorbet, and it was Jacob's turn to ascend the dais. He told about first meeting Trumball, which was punctuated by a round of applause four times. "Honored guests," Jacob went on, "in a moment, the lights will go out, and Laban Trumball will recount the history of this cherished work of art. When he finishes his talk, a vast canvas will descend from the right, while various others, in this museum's permanent collection, will descend from the left. Finally, *Lea with Two Love-Apples* will be lowered into the hands of the artist."

The lights dimmed, Raquel placed the garment bag on her lap. Jacob led the old man to the middle of the rotunda and sat him on a chair on top of a round platform designed to rotate when the painting was lowered. He checked to make sure that the microphone was still pinned to Trumball's tuxedo lapel. Jacob rejoined Raquel.

The orchestra began searching for a new key, while the chorus assembled to sing in tribute. Violins and cellos were bowed and plucked, and the horns blared up and down the scale. Then they rendered that old chestnut, "Pomp and Circumstance."

In the darkened hall, illuminated only by a bright, pin spotlight pointed down on Trumball, the fake painting descended slowly from a booth at the top of the rotunda, and the audience rose in unison with resounding applause. Trumball clutched *Lea with Two Love-Apples* like Moses holding the Tablets of the Law. Jacob excused himself and told Raquel to safeguard the garment bag. "I'll be back in a few minutes," he whispered through the roar of the crowd. She smiled and kissed his cheek as he quietly and discretely stepped away.

The luncheon guests in the rotunda were silent as Trumball began his meandering narration of his life in art: "I sat with Chagall and Leger. Chaim Soutine was my mentor. And Pascin." He explained how Jules Pascin had committed suicide, less than a month after Trumball had arrived in Paris. Jacob knew this story well. The painter's voice droned on. "He first slashed his wrists, then wrote 'Adieu, Lucy' with his blood on the back of a door, and finally hanged himself. Soon after, we experienced the horror of the Nazi takeover of France. Was Jules' act a premonition?" the old man asked. The hall was eerily silent. "What a welcome to Paris for me. Europe's cataclysm was beginning," Trumball thundered. "The darkest hour of history for all humanity had lifted its grotesque head. We artists kept our heads in the sand."

Jacob, using the opportunity of darkness, whispered into Raquel's ear, then stole away.

"By 1940, we fled Paris, those of us lucky enough to get out. Dalí, Mondrian, Duchamp, Leger, Chagall, and I made it to the United States. Picasso remained in France. Jewish artists were arrested in Montparnasse, sent to deportation camps in Drancy and then to Auschwitz. My paintings offended the Nazis, and they burned seventeen pieces. The painting you're about to see, survived...."

CHAPTER THIRTY-NINE

Special Agent Alfred Sullivan was already in Mendoza's office, on the second floor of the atrium, setting up. He pressed the start button on the computer and hacked into the terminal on the opposite side of the atrium, where the conference room was. Sullivan picked up a signal through his earpiece: "POTUS motorcade in route." He had his work to do at the museum; the president was in the secure hands of the Secret Service boys.

As Sullivan worked with a blue-filtered flashlight in the darkened office, he pieced together the barrel of his sniper rifle, the silencer, tripod, and the night-vision, telescopic range finder to ensure an accurate hit. He rehearsed his aim with the rifle where Jacob would be standing.

Jacob and Smith reached the conference room level. Jacob was drenched in sweat as he told Smith: "Go over to that computer. Wait. Here's good luck." Jacob placed an American flag pin in the lapel of Smith's tuxedo. "Pull up the Internet, and I'll read off the numbers to you. After you press those numbers, you'll see the money. But…."

"But what?"

"There's eight, not eighty million."

"I'll worry about that," Smith replied as he attached the silencer to his gun. He sat down at the computer and instructed Jacob to remain inside the doorway. "Don't let him see you. And no tricks, we understand each other? I'll be watching through the corner of my eyes. I'm a fast shot, so don't test me."

"No tricks," Jacob assured.

Smith clicked his flashlight on and off three times, the signal Jacob had chosen to alert Sullivan. The only other lights were the illumination of exit signs.

Jacob rehearsed in his mind what he and Sullivan had planned. He would go to the computer in full sight, and in shooting range of Sullivan, as he logged on to Esau's account. Sullivan would fire the fake bullets, and Jacob would fall just as they'd rehearsed. Smith and De Solis' goons would quickly come forward and Sullivan's men would trap them. Emergency personnel were standing by to rush in, place Jacob on a stretcher, and carry him out to the waiting ambulance. The driver would then speed off to the airport, where Jacob, passport and tickets in hand, would reunite with Raquel and the old man and board the flight to New York.

Smith typed an address into the search engine. The screen opened on "First Bank of Cayman."

"Give me that user ID for the Swiss bank," Smith demanded.

"16216101112."

"Where the hell did you come up with that?"

"My secret."

Smith entered Jacob's user ID.

"You need the password," Jacob asked.

"No thanks, I got my own," Smith said as he typed in *180by19 South* and hit enter. The screen opened onto a page listing accounts and balances. The first line read *Suva here we come*, and the figure at the end of the line was $80,000,000. The capital of Fiji, the place where they'd retire. "Hell yeah," Smith exclaimed, pumping his fists into the air.

Across the atrium, Sullivan looked at his computer screen. "Eighty million, huh? So long, Jacob." He aimed and squeezed the trigger.

"Did it work?" Jacob asked just as Smith was thrown out of the chair by the force of Sullivan's bullet.

"Holy Shit," Jacob exclaimed, "that bullet was meant for me."

"Down and don't say another word," Smith ordered and lay down motionless.

Sullivan came flying through the door, running toward Smith's body. "You've been keeping secrets from me, Jacob. You never told me about the Caymans," Sullivan said as he turned over Smith's body.

"Don't worry, it will be warm where you're going." Smith shot a startled Sullivan in the face.

"What the hell are you doing?" Jacob asked.

"Something I should have done a long time ago," Smith said as he emptied his clip into Sullivan already dead body.

The silence in the room was thick at first. Jacob straightened up to look at Smith. "I didn't believe you until the moment that bullet hit you."

Smith bent down, removed Sullivan's radio and earpiece, then looked squarely at Jacob. "You have a plane to catch, and I have some business to attend to." He turned to the screen, clicked the back button, and copied down the user ID Jacob had given him. He turned to go.

"Hey, Smith. Thanks. You saved my life."

"I did it for your brother," Smith said as he disappeared into the darkened hallway.

Jacob's stared at the spot where his brother's lover had been standing. In a parallel universe, Smith would be a hero, not a thug, right now.

Jacob ran out the front doors. As planned, an ambulance was waiting, with Agent Dumont at its wheel. Jacob stopped and shook his head. "No way, Dumont. Plans have changed."

Ortiz swerved quickly into the museum driveway.

"To the airport," Jacob yelled, and Ortiz sped off.

CHAPTER FOURTY

Smith sped through local streets to arrive at the far end of Plaza San Martin, past the black marble monument to Argentine soldiers killed in the Falkland/Malvinas war. "I got the money, Esau. You should be here with me," he hollered.

He had the code. He didn't concern himself how Jacob managed to figure it out. Jacob did, however, and that's all that mattered, though Smith wondered where 16216101112 came from. Smith kept the final password, a login code that he and Esau established for emergency uses. He held that piece of the puzzle, a tiny fraction of the whole that he knew nobody, not even Jacob would ever discover.

The Lincoln swerved past the fortress-like Casa Rosada and its sweeping balconies where Perón and Evita had spoken to masses of people. A setting sun waited to sink beneath the distant horizon, expecting the arrival of a gray dusk. Smith grinned as he thought of Sullivan—the one-armed cowboy who betrayed him and murdered Esau. He had his revenge. Sullivan was dead. "Let him rot in hell." Now Smith had the money. "Eighty mill, baby," he sang out. Still, he made a bargain that he would keep, if only for Esau. He had no time to stir up old feuds.

The presidential motorcade moved swiftly along Nueve de Julio on their way to the Sheraton. Through his earpiece, Smith heard, "POTUS' approach imminent. Countdown: T minus sixty and counting. T minus fifty-nine and counting. T minus fifty-eight and counting." Smith spun the Lincoln into a no-parking zone at the Retiro train station, exited the vehicle, checked his bulletproof vest, and mixed in with sightseers queuing on the streets leading to the hotel for a glimpse of the presidential motorcade. He felt a familiar surge of rage as his eyes absorbed the ornate stone and red brick building with the huge clock tower that looked onto the Sheraton. Smith checked his watch; it flashed 5: 21. He picked out the silhouette of the gunman among the three soldiers in place on a terrace beneath the giant clock hands.

"T minus 30 and counting," he heard as he rushed into the building. Two soldiers aimed Uzis at him. "Stop. We'll shoot." Smith slid to the floor and fired at their ankles, then quickly knocked the firearms out of their hands as they struggled in pain. He ran up the stairway to the clock tower, with a soldier on his heels. He doubled back and drop-kicked the youth, knocking him out.

"T minus ten and counting. T minus nine and counting. T minus eight and counting." Two heavily armed men in grey suits emerged at the top of the stairs. Smith quickly grabbed the first man, who was still going for his weapon, threw him at the second one, and knocked them both out with a deft jujitsu move. Five more paces, he told himself, as he leaped over them and pushed a door wide open, startling the three soldiers with machine guns in place. They swerved and fired. Smith went down. He felt a searing heat as blood exploded fiercely from his face. He could still hear: "T minus four and counting. T minus three and counting. T minus...." The voice seemed to trail off to a whisper. Gasping for breath, he called out, "I'm still alive." He felt a surge of adrenaline. Writhing in agony, he pulled every ounce of strength he had left in him for the last second of his life. The gunman locked his sight on the driveway of the hotel across the way. Smith could see the trigger finger firmly in position. "T minus one and counting. Smith steadied his hand, blasting the gunman. Screams from the crowd below filled the area as the assassin plunged to the street, landing with a loud thud on the roof of a parked sedan. The last declaration Smith heard over his earpiece brought a chilling smirk to his lips:

"Arrival achieved. POTUS secure and inside hotel."

CHAPTER FOURTY-ONE

During the twenty-five-minute ride, Jacob thought of Raquel—how he would hug and kiss her. They had been through so much these last four days. He knew he could love again, something he'd never thought possible. Jacob rolled down the window to let the evening air cool his face. He decided he would ask her to move in with him.

His thoughts drifted toward Esau. What had been his real intent in all of this? He wouldn't accept that his brother had wished only to put him in harm's way and reward him with eight million dollars of blood money. That letter had saved his ass, Jacob concluded. "And the son-of-a-bitch Smith," he said, placing the palm of his hand against his forehead. He had been his brother's lover. Had they lived together? Did I really matter whom Esau chose to love? No. They'd had to hide their lifestyle. "At least they found love."

Ortiz stopped the limousine at the entrance to the international terminal. He jumped out and held the door open for Jacob.

"Señor, it has been my pleasure to serve you."

Jacob thrust five one-hundred-dollar bills in his hand. "There are no words to thank you enough."

Jacob walked briskly inside the terminal, savoring his return flight, grateful that he was finally leaving. Sometimes it takes the risk of nearly losing your life to awaken you to the things you love, he mused. When he reached the entrance to the gate, he saw Trumball in a wheelchair, asleep, flanked by two airline attendants. Raquel waited with her dresser.

"Four days of hell," he said, wrapping his arms tightly around Raquel.

"I love you, Jacob."

He pulled back from her and smiled. "I love you, too." A weird chill went through his body. They looked at the old man snoring and both laughed.

"He's a beautiful person, isn't he darling?"

"I think that you're more beautiful." He held her to his chest tightly. "Were you frightened when Agent Reinhart drove you here?" he asked.

"Not frightened, no. I remembered her from our meeting at the embassy. Trumball was cursing everybody. Of course, he didn't want to leave the site of his glory. Finally, Agent Reinhart pulled out a syringe and slipped Maestro's jacket off to roll up his shirtsleeve. You should have seen the Maestro. I wouldn't have thought there was that much strength left in the old man. It didn't take long for the tranquilizer to take effect. As soon as we were put in the FBI van, he fell asleep."

"I'm glad this stinking affair is over."

"I would have thought your new friend Agent Sullivan would have been here to see us off."

"That's a whole other story. Over and gone," he said. Jacob lifted her up off her feet. "Over and gone, darling."

"Nothing truly is ever over."

"We'll be getting on that plane and saying good-bye to all of these bizarre incidents. We went through one hell of an adventure, didn't we? Well, you can thank Esau for that."

"Jacob, don't say that, please."

"How I come to terms with my brother's life ... that's my problem."

"Time will heal."

"Does it really? Or leave a hole in our hearts?"

"I'm not sure."

"Raquel, I love you very much."

"I know that. Believe me, too, when I tell you that I love you."

He shook his head in agreement.

"Jacob, I must confess something to you," she whispered.

"What is it? The old man won't hear a thing," Jacob laughed.

"I can't leave Argentina now."

Jacob was stunned. He covered his face for a moment. "You must be joking."

"You must go back to New York, with the Maestro, without me."

"I put my life on the line here in Argentina."

"Please don't be angry. Let me finish."

"Don't be angry? We're safe now and we're alive. And we've got one another."

"And Juan Domingo is dead."

"I can't believe I'm hearing this. So he's dead. I don't give a damn. Killed on the battlefield for a phony coup. He was a killer. He killed my brother. Wake up! I can't believe you're telling me this. Now?"

"No, Jacob, please listen to me. I am not staying here because of him. I must stay and sort this out." She stood motionless and silent for a moment. "I thought I knew him but I didn't. He betrayed me and he betrayed Argentina. Please understand," Raquel pleaded.

"I understand that you're dumping me for some political nonsense."

"Darling, I am not staying here for 'some political nonsense.' I can't leave now. My parents live here. I cannot leave them alone at a time like this."

He felt his face flush. She held out her hand to him, and he squeezed it firmly. An attendant wheeled the old man through the door leading to their flight. Jacob grabbed Raquel. They kissed and held each other closely.

"So you must stay here," Jacob asked, his voice trailing off.

"I'm afraid so, darling."

"We both know ... that we belong ... with each other," he said with some difficulty.

"Of course, we do."

"So this is good-bye?"

"Jacob, we'll always have the time spent in New York. Always, darling. Those memories will never fade. This is something I need to do now."

Raquel pulled away. She handed him the garment bag. Tears streamed down her face. She turned and began walking slowly to the exit. Jacob watched her leave, hoping that she might turn around one last time. He felt a knot in his stomach, a painful mixture of pain and regret. She kept walking until she reached the door to the outside of the terminal, where she stood for a moment, smiled, and waved good-bye.

Jacob waved back and kept waving until he couldn't see her anymore.

He replayed this last moment with her in his mind—a kind of mantra that looped through his thoughts on the twelve-hour flight back to New York.

THE END

ABOUT THE AUTHOR

Gerald Rothberg is the editor-in-chief of *Circus Magazine,* the rock and roll publication. He lives in New York City and is the author of *The Golem Code,* a thriller.

Printed in the United States
29577LVS00003B/25-45

9 781418 486617